REIKO

A Japanese Ghost Story

James Avonleigh

To my children…

MEMORY OF A JOURNEY

'Japanese ghosts are different. Your ghosts would not feel at home here.'

I remember little else Professor Atami said that day, but these words stayed with me. They nagged at me through the first sunlit hours and on into the days that followed, challenging me to understand them, until at last I did.

I had come to Japan as a 23 year-old, armed with the arrogance of youth and an unshakeable belief in my own destiny. I was immortal. I was blessed. Nothing and no one could touch me.

How soon the order of things changes. How quickly the shadows creep up and fear finds a foothold. How helplessly I watched as that youthful arrogance crumbled and all hope of some great destiny vanished.

Now I'm afraid of everything.

I'm afraid of the ticking of clocks, static on a television, the ringing of a telephone in a quiet house. I'm afraid of the distant sound of sirens, footsteps that pass in the street outside, muffled voices heard through walls.

I'm afraid of mirrors, afraid of what I might see standing at my shoulder or emerging into the room behind me.

And there is nothing I can do.

People know me as easy-going and sociable. They invite me to parties, introduce me to friends, seek me out for advice in times of need. I enjoy outdoor and recreational activities, swimming after work, football at the weekends, camping in the holidays. I cling to life as a drowning man clings to the listing hull of his boat.

Everyone has secrets. Things they keep close to their chests. Things they don't talk about at dinner parties. I have more than most. No one would guess from my outward demeanour that I am haunted. No one sees the sudden shortness of breath, the trembling of hands, the terrible conviction that although no one is with me, I am not alone.

Some nights, between the hours of two and three, I will wake with a start. I will hear a door opening in the depths of the house, a light footfall on the stair, the sound of breathing in the hallway. And I will close my eyes and wait.

My name is James and I am still alive. Against the odds, I am still alive.

THE ARRIVAL

The sun was setting as my plane touched down at Kansai International Airport. I'd noticed it first on the descent – a blood-red orb, like the national flag being ceremoniously lowered into the hills around Osaka. There was a pleasing irony in arriving in the Land of the Rising Sun just as the sun was setting. As my guidebook repeated with monotonous regularity, Japan was a country of contradictions, and here was my first taste of that thesis.

I wished there were someone with whom I could share this thought, but my first interaction on Japanese soil was with a standard-issue immigration official and he didn't seem the chatty type. He studied my visa with suspicion, long enough to convince me he'd spotted some administrative irregularity. For a few tense moments I had a vision of airport security leading me away for immediate deportation, my new life cut short in its infancy. Then, showing no sign that he was satisfied, he seized his stamp and validated my passport with a practiced flourish. I was in.

I stood in the arrivals lobby, watching through the cathedral-like windows as the sun disappeared behind the hills. All the roads of my life led to this juncture and an overwhelming sense of well-being came over me.

I boarded the shuttle for Central Osaka and settled back in the cool air-conditioned carriage for the adventure to begin. The train set off so soundlessly that it took a moment for me to realize we were moving. A helium-voiced announcer accompanied us as we slid gracefully out of the airport complex and across the Sky Gate Bridge and the Bay of Osaka. I had hoped to see signs of the old Japan – paddy fields and pine-clad hills – but the moment we hit dry land we plunged into the heart of a concrete metropolis.

Here were all the contradictions my guidebook had spoken about. As the shuttle slid silently along its metal rails, the city unfolded before me. A group of schoolgirls in pristine white sailor uniforms, with blue collars and red ribbons, loitered at a crossing waiting for the train to pass. Next to them stood a hunched old lady in the overalls of another era, silhouetted against the bright neon sign of a *pachinko* parlour. Businessmen in regulation white shirts streamed from their offices in search of after-hours refreshment. Overhead a giant LCD screen broadcast an advertisement for Suntory whisky.

Then there was the dizzying mishmash of old and new: ramshackle hundred year-old houses nestling amidst hi-tech office blocks, Shinto shrines squeezed between vending machines and newspaper kiosks. And everywhere power lines, crisscrossing the sky above.

These images registered as they do in dreams, with comprehension trailing in their wake. It was too much for my weary brain to process and I sat back in the comfortable seat and closed my eyes.

At Namba Station my feet finally touched down on Japanese soil and I followed the signs through a maze of bright, clean corridors. It was a far cry from the dingy London Tube stations I was accustomed to. I found myself enjoying being swept along by the busy commuter surge – in a strange country even rush hour can be a beautiful thing.

I found a taxi rank, where a courteous driver wearing spotless white gloves ushered me into his cab. On a backseat covered with a white sheet I settled down for the last leg of my exhilarating journey.

After a while we left the city behind and journeyed into the suburbs of Osaka, past manicured gardens and the well-to-do dwellings of the sprawling middle-class.

Then, as the suburbs thinned out and the hills loomed large in front of me, I caught sight of the imposing iron archway I remembered from the brochure.

Faithful to its name, the Osaka University for Foreign Studies specialized in languages and culture. Whilst not in the Japanese Ivy League bracket, it was well enough respected in its area of expertise. According to the promotional material I had read so exhaustively in the preceding weeks, it was founded in the late 19th century to spread the light of foreign civilization to a country just emerging from centuries of feudalism. It also accepted a large number of foreign research students each year, which was where I fitted in.

The foreigners' dormitory stood at the far edge of the campus, effectively where the campus ended and the hills began. Seven floors high, it was officially the university's tallest building and the literature they'd sent me affectionately referred to it as '*the Tower*'.

To the front was a gravel football pitch and running track, whilst to the back the pine-clad hills rose up steeply. Seen from a distance the Tower seemed to merge into the hills behind and it stood oddly separate from the rest of the campus. A cynic might say it was positioned to keep the foreigners a safe distance from the rest of the university. Certainly its architect hadn't lingered over the design, delivering a functional seven-storey box with windows. But it could have been built of wattle and daub for all I cared. I hadn't come to Japan to study aesthetics or architecture.

My cases set down inside the foyer, I took in my surroundings. I stood in a spacious area with an impressive row of drink vending machines down one wall and a series of notice boards down the other.

I poked my head round the door of the concierge's office and a wiry old man in a smart blue uniform jumped up and greeted me warmly. Though many decades my senior, he wrestled the heaviest bag from my grasp and marched it to the lift. I was still protesting as the lift opened on the fifth floor and he started off down the corridor. I followed him meekly, our footsteps echoing on the hard floor, to the door of my room. He turned the key in the lock, pushed the door open and ushered me inside. After twenty hours on the move, I had reached my destination.

I didn't move for several minutes after the concierge had gone, letting the enormity of the experience sink in. It had started in my bedroom on the other side of the world, packing my bags, bidding my parents farewell. From the plane I had watched the sun set on Europe, then appear again over the icy wastes of Siberia, and finally rise to its zenith over the Japan Sea. Then to this place, this room, and a balmy evening in the suburbs of Osaka.

I groped for the chair and sat down, overwhelmed. The room was small and functional, dominated by a window which spanned the full width of the room. A narrow bed ran the length of one wall, while a desk and chair occupied the other. The only other features were a cupboard and small basin by the door. It was compact and comfortable and sufficient for my needs.

For most of that first evening I sat in the dark gazing out over the gravel football pitch at the long shadows cast by the occasional passer-by. The official academic year had ended a few days earlier and it looked as if most people had already packed up and left.

I'd come early partly to acclimatize and partly because there was nothing for me back in England. I had taken a course in Japanese for the past year as part of my degree and spent most of that year looking for funding for postgraduate study in Japan. Success came at the eleventh hour with a bizarre proposal to an even more bizarre foundation. I would be coming to Japan to study differences in perceptions of supernatural phenomena between the Eastern Buddhist tradition and the Western Christian tradition. In layman's terms my remit was to find out if ghosts were different in Japan. It would be an understatement to say I'd never given the subject much thought, but my tutor had been tipped off that the Ayukawa foundation would be receptive to such a proposal and I wasn't going to let the subject matter deter me.

Initially my only motivation had been to live in Japan, but to my surprise I'd found interest in my chosen subject start to grow. I was assigned to Professor Atami, a former lecturer in Social Anthropology at a prominent American university and a leading authority on Japanese folklore. He'd also taught the man in whose footsteps I was following, a brilliant scholar of Japanese called Charlie Whitehurst.

And sitting there in that dark dormitory room, my mind turned to Charlie, my ill-fated predecessor. He too had come to the university on an Ayukawa scholarship and he too had come to study differences in perceptions of supernatural phenomena. An Oxford graduate, he had impressed everyone with his application and enthusiasm. It was six months into his research when he travelled north to the village of Izumi in Fukushima Prefecture, an infamous haunting spot. No one knew whether it was the nature of his research or an increasing sense of isolation that unbalanced him. But he cut his visit to Izumi short, made the long journey back to the dormitory and hung himself from the window frame with the cord of his dressing-gown.

Professor Atami

'Japanese ghosts are different. Your ghosts would not feel at home here.'

Professor Atami's English was precise and elegant, with the faintest hint of an American accent. He sat huddled behind his desk, every bit the eccentric academic: tweed jacket, unkempt beard, ever so slight facial tic.

'In fact, the usual translation for ghost is *yurei*, but this refers to a very specific concept.'

He trailed off, seeming to lose the train of his thoughts. There was a monastic quality to the room, with the small window in the corner and the walls packed floor to ceiling with learned books. If he owned a computer or any other gadgetry, they were safely hidden from view. It was somehow comforting to see that in a country of technological marvel, here was a man time had left behind.

'Your ghosts come in all shapes and sizes. Some are male, some are female, some are animals. They can be young or old, full of purpose or confused. They dress as they dressed in life or they wear their funeral garments. They can appear at any time of the day or night and have any number of motivations. Maybe they're revisiting their loved ones. Maybe they're reliving some scene from their lives. Or maybe they're lost and need help. Anyway, Japanese ghosts are different.'

I leaned forward, eager to pick up the thread. 'That's what I'm interested in. The differences. The differences between ghosts in Japan and ghosts in the West. My thesis is very straightforward: that supernatural manifestations are culture-specific. They're inseparable from the belief systems and folklore traditions of a particular country. Every account of the supernatural is informed by cultural references. I don't believe in ghosts and I've never had a supernatural experience, but if there really was something out there, there'd be a uniform standard. There isn't. As you said, ghosts in Japan are different.'

Professor Atami digested this in silence. It was a relief to get some of these things off my chest. I'd been pondering the subject for months, without ever having an audience. It wasn't something you discussed over a drink with friends. This was an occasion when an eccentric academic came in handy.

'I see.' He looked up at the ceiling and scratched his beard.

For a moment nothing was said. Then Professor Atami furrowed his brow and fixed me with a stern expression.

'You're not the first English student to come to me with this subject. Maybe you know that.'

'I did hear something.'

'Charlie. Charlie Whitehurst. He was here three years ago. He was a strong student, serious about his studies and eager to learn all about Japanese language and culture. I was very impressed...' He broke off and shook his head slowly.

'So he had the same thesis as me?'

'No,' he said softly. 'No. In fact, he had precisely the opposite thesis. From what you've told me, you're interested in the differences between cultural perceptions. Charlie was different. Charlie wanted to emphasize the similarities. Charlie believed very strongly in the existence of a spirit world.'

Professor Atami looked at me intently as he told me this. In a way it was a comfort. It provided a clue as to why Charlie might have lost his grip. He was clearly far too wrapped up in his research.

'He saw visions.' Professor Atami continued to stare at me, watching for a reaction, and it occurred to me that he might be looking for signs of instability on my part. This made sense. He didn't want a second paranormal researcher dying on him.

'Did he see ghosts?' I asked, a little clumsily.

'I don't know what he saw. He never told me.'

Professor Atami looked away and I wondered if I'd passed the test. He got up from his chair and stepped over to a large filing cabinet in the corner. He opened the door then crouched down and began scrabbling around in the bottom. With a satisfied grunt he pulled out a smart black file and brought it back to the desk.

'This belonged to Charlie. It contains some of his research and notes. After he died his parents came to collect his belongings, but they didn't want this. I suppose I should have thrown it away, but I couldn't bring myself to do it. Maybe it could be helpful to you.'

I looked at the file sitting in front of me with a sense of unease. It wasn't really surprising that his

and later executed, but with no obvious motive, many commentators suggested he was a scapegoat. In addition, he could not be connected to the subsequent deaths.

I could understand Charlie's interest in this unsolved mystery. It made for fascinating reading. I wanted to find out more about it, even if I would be going to Izumi for more serious research.

'Go to Izumi if you must. If you have to go, best do it now. But I guarantee you'll come back disappointed.'

I nodded. Besides the research aspect, I figured it would also be a chance to see a part of Japan few visitors got to see.

Professor Atami looked at his watch, as though anxious to end the meeting. 'I've arranged for Josh to come. He's another of my foreign students. He's meant to be doing a thesis on ancient Japanese history, but I think he's more interested in studying the nightlife of Osaka. I thought he could show you round.'

I thanked him for this gesture. I realized he didn't approve of the proposed Izumi trip, but I could understand him being sensitive after what had happened with Charlie.

As he got up from his desk to show me to the door he asked if I had any more questions.

'You were saying before about Japanese *yurei*, about how they're different to Western ghosts...'

He smiled. 'Ah yes, *yurei*. Traditionally, *yurei* are spirits of the dead, who remain on earth. This is a very Buddhist concept. You see, when a person dies they need some time to repose themselves. They need peace so that they have the spiritual calm to attain Buddhahood. But if a person dies unexpectedly or violently, they do not have that calm. They will feel only confusion and hatred in their last moments. And they are forced to wander the earth as spirits, trying to fulfil some purpose and find the spiritual calm necessary to achieve Nirvana.'

'That doesn't sound so different to our ghosts in the West. They usually have some kind of issue with the living.'

Professor Atami considered this and nodded his head slowly. 'You may be right. That is exactly what Charlie used to tell me. But over the years the popular image of the ghost in Japan has become very narrow and, as you said, culture-specific. They are almost always young and female with long hair. They appear in the dead of night between the hours of two and three. But in this particular point they are true to the definition of *yurei*. They have only one purpose here on earth. Revenge.'

JOSH

'Japan is fucking amazing. I love it here.'

I was sitting with Josh on a bench at the far end of the gravel pitch, looking across at the dormitory and the green hills beyond. He gestured towards the Tower with a broad sweep of the arm.

'This is home. This is where I want to be and I don't ever want to leave.'

At six foot one I was considered tall, but Josh was a six foot five American Football playing giant of a man. He would have turned heads on an English street, but in Japan he appeared almost superhuman and the fact wasn't lost on him.

'I'd never been special until I came here. Never been anyone. Here, I feel like a rock star.'

'Sounds like you have the perfect lifestyle.'

Josh laughed. 'Oh, you have no idea. I never knew what a lifestyle was until I came here. Look around you. Look at the sky.'

We tilted our heads back to look at the clear blue sky. Just forty-eight hours earlier I had left London shrouded in grey cloud and light drizzle. Now here I was on the other side of the world in short sleeves, feeling a warm tropical breeze on my skin.

'And the girls!'

Josh switched his attention from the sky to a couple of passing Japanese girls, impeccably groomed, with long raven-black hair. One of them caught us looking in her direction and smiled. Josh beamed with satisfaction and waved flirtatiously.

'God, they're beautiful,' he said, his eyes following them. 'There's no woman on this earth more exquisite than the Japanese female. That's a fact.'

'You have a girlfriend?'

Josh gave me a mischievous look. 'Don't go there. Don't get me started on that.'

We sat in silence for a while, basking in the sun, and I felt my body start to relax. I was still dazed and jet-lagged, but Josh was mellow and made for easy company.

'I'm going in. You coming?' Josh got to his feet and stretched his arms.

I got up and we began to walk slowly round the edge of the pitch.

'So you're studying Japanese ghosts or something? Atami told me about it.'

'More like perceptions of supernatural phenomena in the Buddhist tradition. But, yeah, basically ghosts.'

'You interested in that kind of thing?'

I shrugged. I knew I'd have to face a lot of questions like this and I needed a stock response. It didn't have to be true, but I needed something to say.

Josh sensed my hesitation. 'To be honest, I didn't come here for the academic stuff. I wanted to live in Japan and this was the easiest route for me. Half the time, I can't even remember what I'm studying.'

It was nice that Josh was on my wavelength. 'Yeah, it's the same for me. I just did whatever I could get the funding for. Turned out to be ghosts, which is fine.'

Josh also seemed pleased to have found a partner in crime. 'Don't worry. Atami doesn't care. We just get assigned to him. Considering the last guy doing your thing killed himself, I don't think he's going to be too harsh on you.'

'You know about that?'

'Everyone knows about that. I guess it's a cautionary tale. I even know where his room was.'

We had rounded the corner of the pitch and were on the approach to the Tower. Josh pointed up. 'Third floor down, second window from the right.'

I stopped in my tracks as I realized it was my floor. A sudden fear gripped me, but counting across, it was clear it couldn't possibly be my room. I might be carrying the dead guy's file in my bag, but I didn't want to be sleeping in his bed.

Josh continued, warming to the subject. 'Actually, this place is a popular suicide spot, probably the number one suicide spot in the area. It's a tall building, you have easy access to the roof and panoramic views for your last look at the world.'

'People have jumped, then?'

'Regularly. Usually one a year, sometimes two. It's a problem. There was one just after I arrived. Some guy stepped off the roof while we were having lunch in the canteen. We all heard it and went over to the window and there he was.' Josh stopped in front of the building and pointed to a spot near the entrance. 'I never saw anything like that before. The twisted body, the blood, people screaming.'

'Who was he? A student?'

Josh nodded. 'They say it happens a lot in Japan. Social pressure, academic pressure, that kind of thing. But it's even worse here. This university specializes in foreign languages and the kind of Japanese people attracted to foreign things are often the social misfits. I've heard this from a lot of people. They don't fit in, so they're looking for escape. But the sense of national identity is so strong that there is no escape. It's what I've heard, anyway.'

'That's pretty horrible.'

Josh caught my expression and laughed. 'Hey, lighten up. It's something that happens, is all. You try to make light of it. If you didn't laugh about it, you'd cry. Now every time we hear a thud, we say "hey, there goes another one". It's our way of dealing with it.'

We parted company outside the lifts with an arrangement to go into Osaka later that night, and I returned to my room feeling tired and disjointed. The afternoon was drawing on and my jet-lag was kicking in. It had been nice sitting outside with Josh, but the conversation about suicides had left me depressed. Given the nature of my thesis, I couldn't avoid people telling me grim stories, but it was just a bit too much too soon. Not only was I carrying around a dead man's research notes, but I was also living in the university's most desirable suicide location.

I took Charlie's file out of my bag and laid it on the desk. I debated whether or not to take a peek, but somehow it didn't seem right. With a heavy sigh, I opened a drawer and shoved it in. I didn't want it looking at me. Stepping over my suitcase, still only half-unpacked, I lay down on the bed for a rest.

I fell asleep the moment my head hit the pillow.

OSAKA BY NIGHT

I woke from a dreamless sleep to the sound of knocking at the door.

'James. Are you there?'

The evening had drawn in and the room was deep in shadow. I sat up and peered through the gloom, trying to get my bearings.

'Just a minute,' I called. I realized I must have missed my rendezvous with Josh in the foyer.

His voice rang out in the corridor. 'Sorry to wake you. I'll be waiting downstairs, okay.'

I struggled to my feet and groped for the light switch. Stooping in front of the basin to splash my face, I was shocked to see my reflection. I looked pale and haggard and in need of sleep. But Josh had offered to take me out on the town and it was too late to back down. I took a deep breath and resolved to make the most of it.

We caught a bus from the campus gates, which took us on a meandering tour through the same peaceful suburbs I had seen on my way in. By the light of the street lamps it was different: quieter and eerier. We passed elegant houses, with topiarized hedges, miniature stone pagodas and dense clusters of bamboo in inner courtyards. I watched in silence as the suburbs gave way to the city and the Zen tranquility became a blast of noise and neon. Of course, I had seen images of Asian cityscapes, but the reality was so much more vibrant and breathtaking in the flesh. Everything pulsed with life and light and energy. This was the Japan I had come to see, burning itself on to the retina like the beating heart of the world.

We got off the bus and travelled a few stops by metro to Namba, the heart of nightlife in Osaka. The place was bustling with the youth of Japan, sporting an astonishing array of weird and wonderful fashions. Every street was nothing less than a public catwalk. The girls, heavily spray-tanned, wearing thigh-length boots or platform shoes and blonde highlights, stood around in groups. The young men wore grungy T-shirts and peered moodily from underneath floppy hats. I walked with a sense of shame, hopelessly underdressed in a pair of bland beige chinos and white polo shirt.

Josh was in search of his favourite *kaiten-zushi*, which he translated as 'revolving sushi'. We turned down a busy street of bars and restaurants, where a sea of neon signs jostled for attention. We passed a giant, mechanical crab with moving claws suspended over a restaurant, and a cheery street vendor hawking *yakitori* chicken skewers. With a cry of recognition, Josh darted down a few steps to a well-concealed door and I stepped into the revolving sushi bar.

We were greeted by the shrill welcoming cries of *irasshaimase*, which I'd read was the standard welcome on arriving in any shop or restaurant. The room was

'I'm interested to hear what Japanese people think of Izumi and about ghosts in general. I want to know how it fits in with the culture. It's part of my research to find out these things.'

Shinichi sighed heavily. 'In Japan, it's bad luck to talk about ghosts. I don't know why. I'm not a superstitious person, but I really don't like talking about ghosts. They say that if you talk about ghosts or dead people, they will hear.'

I laughed. 'Are you serious?'

Shinichi nodded. 'Ghosts will hear you. It's bad luck.'

I wasn't sure how to take this. Here was Shinichi, a floppy-haired Bohemian wanting to live like Baudelaire, telling me that we shouldn't talk about ghosts in case they overheard. I wanted to ask what would happen if they did overhear. What would they do? Would they take it as an opportunity to haunt us?

Josh started to say something about moving on to somewhere livelier, but was interrupted by Etsuko, who had been looking at me intensely throughout the whole conversation.

'When I was a schoolgirl, I heard a story about Izumi. Hundreds of years ago, in the Tokugawa period, there was a Buddhist priest who was famous for his visions. While he was travelling around Japan, he stayed one night in a temple at Izumi. While he was asleep, he dreamed that a demon visited him. The demon said he had something to show the priest and led him to a house where the local feudal lord lived. He stopped in front of a sliding screen at the back of the house. The screen was very beautiful, decorated with peaceful scenes of nature, and the priest asked the demon why he was being shown this screen. The demon laughed and said that this was a unique screen. He said that Izumi village in Fukushima Prefecture had a very unique secret and it could be found behind this screen. The priest asked why the screen was unique and what was behind it. The demon told him that hidden behind the screen was the entrance to hell.'

THE BLACK FILE

'They're not normally like that. Sorry.'

It was gone one o'clock as Josh and I made our way back to the Tower. The campus was deserted and we cut solitary figures as we skirted the edge of the gravel football pitch, casting long shadows.

'They're normally pretty chilled out,' he continued. 'That's why I introduced you. I don't know why they had a problem with this haunted village.'

'It's okay. What they said was interesting. The part about the entrance to hell was news to me. Kind of makes me even more determined to check this place out.'

'I didn't even know Buddhists had a hell. I thought hell was just a Christian thing.'

I had a mental image of sliding back a screen door to find the raging fires of hell and it made me laugh. 'I'll just have to be extra careful with those sliding screens.'

'Yeah, you might be looking for the bathroom, you open the wrong door and, oops, you've opened the door to hell.'

It had been a long evening and I was glad to end it on a light note. I hadn't expected Shinichi and Etsuko to be so sensitive about Izumi and I was troubled that they didn't want to talk about ghosts for fear of being overheard. I'd been hoping to do fieldwork as part of my research, asking ordinary Japanese people about their perceptions of the supernatural, but if I couldn't get those two to talk, what hope did I have with anyone else.

On entering the foyer we found an 'out of order' sign standing in front of the lifts, a regular event according to Josh. We trudged up the narrow and dingy emergency steps in silence until we reached my floor. Josh's room was on the floor above, so I said 'goodnight' and turned to leave.

He called after me. 'You're all right in the head, aren't you?'

I would have laughed, but there was no flippancy in his tone. 'I think so. What a weird question.'

'Maybe it's what happened to the other guy. I've just got a bad feeling about something. I don't know what it is.'

'I'm different to the other guy. Sounds like he had a whole lot of other problems.'

Josh looked at me doubtfully, then turned and shook his head. 'I'm sorry. That was not a cool thing to ask. I'm a little tired.'

'Yeah, me too.'

I watched Josh as he made his way up the steps and I couldn't help feeling taken aback by his question. I may have only known him half a day, but it seemed out of character. He'd been so completely carefree earlier on, filled with stories about his hedonistic lifestyle and amorous adventures and here he was worrying about my mental health.

Back in my room, I put the conversation behind me and got on with my preparations for bed. I'd seen and heard enough for one day and I needed my sleep. I gave my face a quick wash, tore off my smoky clothes, flicked off the light switch and crashed out on the mattress.

I tried to sleep. God knows I tried, but jet-lag can play strange games. For over an hour I tried everything in the book. I cleared my mind of thought, I counted sheep, I imagined sinking slowly into a bed of soft feathers. I turned from side to side, on to my back, back on to my front again, kicked off the sheets, pulled the pillow over my head. In mounting frustration I shouted out loud, telling myself I'd only slept a few hours in days and, dammit, I should be tired. But to no avail. I gave up and opened my eyes.

The bright moon didn't help. Through a thin veil of curtain it cast a silvery pall over the sparse furnishings. But there was something else. It had started as a nagging voice at the back of my mind, but in my weakened state the voice had become too loud to ignore. And now, at five to three in the morning, I finally yielded. By banishing the file from my sight I thought I'd forget it was there. I was wrong.

I got out of bed and switched on the desk lamp. Then I opened the drawer, hauled out the file and laid it down in front of me. There it was. The work of a dead scholar. The work of a man who had hung himself by the neck just a few doors down from where I stood. I still had a sense that it was wrong to be looking at it without his permission, no matter what Professor

Atami might have said. But I also knew that I wouldn't get another ounce of sleep if I didn't take a look.

I sat down on the chair and, with a deep breath, opened it up. My first impression was that for a man supposedly losing his sanity it was a remarkably neat and well-ordered file. Certainly, I had never approached that level of organization in any work I'd done. On the opening page there was a glossary of subjects and, looking across, I noticed that each section had been clearly marked with a coloured divider.

I opened the first section entitled '*Japanese Spirits: an Overview*' and was immediately floored by Charlie's handwriting. It was astonishing to behold – a beautiful copperplate style, straight from the time of Queen Victoria, full of loops and flourishes and exquisite artistry. Even more remarkable was that nowhere on this first page, or any of the pages immediately following, could I see a word crossed out or a smudge or even an untidy line-break. Either Charlie had liked to make a neat copy of his work or he simply didn't make mistakes. There was something unnerving about it.

I looked at some of the descriptions in his overview. *Oni* he had translated as 'a demon, a horned beast, often portrayed in ancient art or theatre'. *Yokai* was described as 'a bewitching presence, appearing in the hours of dusk or dawn'. Further down, *yurei* was down as 'a spirit of the dead, who remains among the living for a specific purpose, usually vengeance'. I turned the page, the novelty of Charlie's handwriting beginning to wear thin.

There were individual sections on *yokai* and *yurei* and some of the other supernatural apparitions, but my eye had already been caught by the bulging entry for Izumi.

I flipped forward and recoiled in disbelief. It couldn't be the same person. Gone was the copperplate handwriting and seamless presentation, replaced by an incoherent jumble of messy scrawls, corrections and random doodles. If I'd had no insight into Charlie's state of mind before, I did have now. At some point during his research, and certainly by the time he got to Izumi, Charlie had gone mad.

I turned the pages slowly, taking in the disjointed fragments, unfinished sentences and Japanese characters written over and over again. I didn't have an adequate grasp of written Japanese to know what they meant, but there was enough English scrawled in the margins to give an alarming taste of a man on the edge. Phrases like *'help me'*, *'I'm lost'* and biblical snippets like *'why hast thou forsaken me?'* were all testimony to Charlie's failing mental health. At one point he had even written *'dig me a shallow grave'* and drawn a coffin-shaped box round the words.

Seeing the palpable nature of his descent into madness I felt angry with Professor Atami for giving me the file. Had he actually looked at it before making the decision to keep it? Surely any decent human being would have respected the wishes of Charlie's parents and destroyed it. I had a sudden impulse to light a match and burn the thing there and then, and if I'd had a match to hand I think I might have done just that. But it was too late. I needed to see more.

I continued turning the pages until I came to a plastic envelope containing a series of six by four inch photo portraits of high school students, possibly taken for a school yearbook. I knew instantly who they were. I had read about the Izumi tragedy, I knew the names of the students involved and I knew the manner of their deaths. Yet I couldn't explain why my fingers trembled as I removed the pictures and laid them out in front of me.

The first photo was of a boy with a strong, handsome face and friendly smile. He was wearing the standard-issue school uniform, a plain black button-up jacket, modelled on the dress worn in German military academies of the nineteenth century. Turning the picture over, I found the name, Hideki Sano, written in Charlie's immaculate copperplate.

The next photo was of a girl in a navy sailor uniform, with three white stripes and a crimson ribbon tied in the middle. She wore her hair in a ponytail and smiled at the camera. This was Saori Kumano.

There were photos of two other students whose names I recognized: Jun Takada and his girlfriend Kanae Kubota.

Those were the four students whose bodies were recovered. But the most famous case of all was that of Reiko Shimura, the first of the students to disappear and the only one whose body was never recovered. I had seen a blurred photograph on the web, but now, looking at a proper portrait for the first time, I felt a shiver run the length of my body. The other four had looked little different to any other seventeen year-olds, with relaxed expressions and confident smiles. Reiko was different. For a start she was strikingly beautiful, with high cheekbones, almond-shaped brown eyes, sculpted nose and delicate lips. But her expression hinted at something much darker underneath, as though she had some premonition of her terrible fate. Like a Leonardo virgin, she seemed to look straight through me and into the dark places of my soul. Maybe it was her arresting beauty and the knowledge of her tragic fate that led me to look for hidden depths. Maybe she was just an ordinary schoolgirl, bored at the prospect of having to sit for a photograph.

I don't know how long I sat there staring at the portrait, studying the contours of her face, trying to fathom its mysteries. But I could understand now why her case held such a powerful fascination.

The sound of footsteps outside in the corridor finally broke the spell. I hastily stuffed the pictures back into the envelope and snapped the file shut. As the footsteps approached the door, I was convinced it was my door they were heading towards. I braced myself for a heavy knock or even the turning of the door handle – perhaps the ghost of Charlie returned to reclaim his file – but the footsteps passed by and continued down the corridor. They stopped a little way down and I listened with relief as a door was unlocked and then closed with a bang. Just a late night reveller returning home. I felt strangely comforted by this evidence of life somewhere else on the floor. With term ended and the dormitory near-deserted, the silence had been oppressive.

I sighed heavily and got to my feet. My curiosity sated, perhaps now my mind would give me some respite. But I had also seen Reiko. And having looked into her eyes and caught a glimpse of that unquiet soul, I knew instinctively that I had opened a Pandora's Box. I didn't know what had happened in Izumi, or what had led Charlie to lose his mind, but I couldn't shake the fear that he and I shared some common destiny.

YOSHI

I awoke to a glorious spring day at the window. For a while I lay there without moving, enjoying the sensation of sun-bathing in bed, feeling a deep sense of relaxation for the first time in days. I had expected restless dreams in the wake of my nocturnal researches, but as far as I could remember my sleep had been undisturbed. Finally rousing myself enough to sit up, I peered through the curtains at the cloudless sky.

I met Josh in the foyer, leaning against the vending machines, chatting to a couple of students. Judging by the number of suitcases standing around, I guessed they must be leaving the dorm.

'Hey there. Just get up?' Josh patted me on the shoulder.

To avoid any further doubts about my mental health, I told him I'd slept like a baby. He then introduced me to Jan and Piet, who were Dutch students at the end of two-year research scholarships and heading back to Amsterdam. When I mentioned my name, there was a flash of recognition and they glanced at Josh for confirmation.

'You're the guy studying the paranormal?' Jan asked.

I nodded my head, not certain whether to take this recognition as a compliment.

There was an awkward silence which Josh hurried to dispel. 'We're going to be pretty much on our own for the next couple of weeks. We were just trying to figure out how many people were left in this place.'

'How many people normally live here?' I asked.

'About sixty,' said Piet, with a heavy Dutch accent. 'Most of the students are on one-year government scholarships issued by *Mombusho*, which is the Japanese Ministry of Education. They're all here to study the Japanese language, but their visas run out pretty quickly. That's why they leave so soon.'

'Which leaves researchers like us.' Josh gave me a conspiratorial wink. 'There are about fifteen or twenty of us coming back for next term. In theory you could spend your whole time here, but most people want to use the holidays to travel.'

'So how many are still here?'

'That's what we're trying to figure. Two Indonesians down on the second. No one knows what their plans are. Then there's Anne, the Australian, on the fourth. And a French girl on the sixth, just down from me.'

'And we're leaving today,' added Piet.

Josh put his hand on my shoulder. 'And then you're off to your haunted village, so eventually it could be me all on my ownsome.'

'So why aren't you travelling?'

Josh shook his head ruefully. 'I haven't been the best student this year. I'm embarrassed every time I see

Atami, so I promised him I'd use this time to catch up. And anyway, I'm not really the travelling type.'

I was about to make my excuses and go look for some late breakfast, when I remembered something.

'There's someone else on the fifth floor.'

Josh looked at Jan and Piet for help, but they shook their heads. 'Are you sure about that?'

'Yeah, he came back in the night. Or she, it could've been a she.'

Josh wasn't convinced. 'They were all language students on your floor. They all left before you got here.'

I tried to convince him, but he remained adamant that I must have misheard. He told me I'd been dreaming or that someone had wandered in from outside and got lost up there. I explained I'd heard the door being unlocked, opened and closed, but to no effect. All the while, Jan and Piet were watching me carefully, their suspicions about the ghost-hunter confirmed.

I tried to act unconcerned, but I was irritated with Josh. I knew what I'd heard and I wasn't about to be labelled a lunatic because Josh didn't have his facts right. How the hell did he know who was in the building anyway? Just because people had left, it didn't mean that others like me hadn't arrived. And even if he was convinced I was screwy, he could have bitten his tongue and humoured me in front of the Dutch lads. He'd already questioned my sanity the night before, and here he was doing it again. I didn't want to be tarred with the same brush as Charlie just because I was doing the same research subject.

Over the next few days I began to settle into my new life. The sun continued to shine, the clouds kept their distance and I got out and explored my new surroundings. The warm weather had brought on an early show of cherry blossoms and I was able to see the spring revellers lay out their mats beneath the trees and get merrily wasted on *sake*.

The campus was pretty empty, which provided a good opportunity to check out the facilities at my leisure – the library, the swimming pool, the cafeteria. Josh accompanied me on most of my wanderings, eager for distractions from his research. By day we explored some of the outlying hills, wading through lush vegetation and watching the wild monkeys roam free. In the evenings we hit some of the *gaijin* foreigner bars, where Josh demonstrated his techniques for picking up Japanese girls. There was the wink, the cheesy smile and the introductory, *'hey, what's your name?'* and that seemed to get him the result he wanted. He freely admitted that the Japanese girls turning up to *gaijin* bars were generally looking to be picked up and tended not to offer much of a challenge. Despite this, Josh seemed to get genuinely upset that some of the Western men picking up Japanese girls weren't up to standard. Most of them, he insisted, clearly couldn't get girlfriends back home.

On each of our *gaijin* bar forays, he would encourage me to follow his lead, delivering persuasive sales pitches on the enduring qualities of the Japanese female. I kept resisting, maintaining that I'd just ended a messy relationship and wasn't about to step into another. What I didn't tell him was that the relationship in question had ended over two years before and I was still struggling to come to terms with it. I thought admitting as much would confirm all his suspicions about my mental health.

I also ventured into Osaka on my own one day to make arrangements for my Izumi trip. I found a sympathetic travel agent, who either understood my phrasebook Japanese or was very good at guessing. I would take the Tokkaido bullet train to Tokyo, then take the Tohoku bullet train to Shirakawa in Fukushima Prefecture. From there I would take a local train to the station at Izumi. In all, I could expect the journey to take up to six hours, but the route would take in a long stretch of Central Japan, including Mount Fuji, where the winter snow still covered its peak. I would also get to see Tokyo, if only to change trains. As for accommodation, the agent gave me a list of guest houses and Japanese style *ryokan* inns in the area, where I could either book ahead or turn up unannounced. The only awkward moment came when I first mentioned that it was Izumi I was travelling to. The agent stiffened and asked what the purpose of my visit was, as though he were duty-bound to clear my motives prior to issuing me a ticket. Though tempted to look up the words for '*none of your business*', I flicked through my phrasebook to find the word for tourist: *kankyaku*. He regarded me critically for a second, then got on with his job.

As well as Josh, I got to hang out with Shinichi and Etsuko, who seemed to have come to terms with the subject of my thesis. They accompanied me on a visit to Osaka castle, an impregnable fortress, which could well have stood for a thousand years. I felt a certain disillusionment when they told me it was a concrete replica built in the twenties, after centuries of feudal warfare had laid waste to the original. There are very few old buildings in Japan, they said. Even the most beautiful temples had often been torn down and rebuilt over the years. They told me there was a deep sense of impermanence in the Japanese psyche. Throughout its history, Japan had been persistently ravaged by war and natural disaster. Why build something to last a thousand years, when an earthquake could level it tomorrow?

They said it was this sensibility which explained the symbolic importance of the cherry blossom to Japanese poets and artists through the ages. The cherry blossom, with its brief and spectacular flowering, most accurately summed up the beauty and brevity of life.

As for my study, I succeeded in putting it on the back-burner for a while. For several nights, Charlie's black file remained in the drawer and I'd felt no inclination to take it out. Laid low by jet-lag and exhaustion, I'd let the whole issue of Charlie get me down for the first couple of days. Now that I was rested and beginning to enjoy life in Osaka, I was also coming to terms with what had happened to him. Although he'd done the same kind of research, I'd seen the state of his file and knew that he'd had some deep-seated personal problems. I convinced myself there was no possible comparison.

It was the night before I was due to go to Izumi that I met a young man named Yoshi.

I had returned to my room after an evening at 'Sakura', a low-key local bar. After several late nights on the trot, neither Josh nor I had been in the mood for a big evening, so we sat in the deserted bar and talked about our futures, what we'd do when our time came to join the workforce. We both had little enough to say on the subject, so decided to call it a night after a couple of beers and go our separate ways. Besides, I had some packing to do.

For a while I pondered writing a letter to my parents, giving them a taste of the sort of life I was now leading. I would paint a vivid picture of the beautiful weather, the lush greenery and the heady nightlife. I even got as far as writing *'Dear Mum and Dad'* at the top of the page, then decided it was too much effort. An e-mail would do the trick.

I considered taking Charlie's file out and swotting up on Izumi, but I was feeling too mellow to be drawn back into Charlie's world. So I decided upon a walk down to the vending machines.

I opened my door and stepped out into the corridor, pausing to listen for any signs of life. I still hadn't discovered the identity of my elusive neighbour and every time I stepped out I hoped to meet him or her, if only to prove Josh wrong. I'd tried knocking on all the doors, to no avail. I'd even resolved to question the concierge, but every time I saw him I was with Josh and didn't want to make it into an issue.

I put it out of my mind and made my way to the lift, which was still waiting at the fifth floor where I'd left it.

Predictably the foyer was deserted and the only sound was the monotonous buzz of the vending machines and the flapping of moths around the overhead lights. There were five machines in all, arranged in an orderly row, three of them selling soft drinks, one hot drinks and one chocolate and snacks. I studied the selection of soft drinks, which ranged from the familiar Coca Cola and Fanta to weird Japanese isotonic drinks with even weirder names: *Calpis* and *Pocari Sweat*.

I settled on a chilled Jasmine tea and dug around in my pocket for change. A handful of ten yen coins didn't add up to the required amount, so I fished a one thousand yen note from my wallet. I inserted this into the slot, but it came straight back out again. I flattened it out and tried again, with the same result. I turned it over, turned it back again, flattened it once more, but each time the result was the same.

I was about to give up and return to my room empty-handed when a young man appeared at the main doors. He was a Japanese student, dressed in beige chinos and a white T-shirt. He acknowledged my presence with a brief nod of the head and I decided he might have some insight into the correct handling of Japanese banknotes.

'Excuse me. Would you be able to help?'

He looked surprised at the question, but he had a friendly face.

'I'm sorry. Do you speak English?'

'A little.' He held up thumb and forefinger to indicate the amount.

I showed him my note. 'Sorry, I can't get this thing in. I wondered if there was a trick.'

He took it from me and started rubbing it vigorously between the palms of his hands in an effort to straighten it. Satisfied, he carefully slid it into the slot. This time the machine accepted it.

'Wow. How did you do that?'

He smiled modestly, with a slight bow of the head.

I selected my Jasmine tea and the can dropped into the tray with a thud. I stuck out my hand. 'I'm James, by the way.'

He took it after a hesitation. 'I'm Yoshi.'

'Yoshi. Nice to meet you. Are you a student here?'

He nodded.

'What are you majoring in?'

'French language and literature.'

We moved over to the lift and stepped in. I pushed the button for the fifth floor. 'Do you know a guy called Shinichi? He's doing French too.'

Yoshi shook his head shyly.

The lift doors closed and we travelled up in silence. Yoshi kept his eyes on the floor and only raised them when the lift doors opened on the fifth.

I suddenly realized he must be friends with Francoise, the French research student a few doors down from Josh. 'You know Francoise?'

Yoshi was in a world of his own, but he nodded his head with a faint smile as I exited the lift.

'Maybe see you around,' I said. I was eager to meet as many Japanese students as possible and Yoshi seemed like a nice enough guy.

'Goodbye,' he said, as the lift doors closed.

Francoise was the sort of person who had time for everyone and I considered following Yoshi up there for a moment. From what Josh had said, she was something of a night owl, so no doubt she wouldn't mind the extra company. But it was late and I had an early morning start, so I thought better of it. I needed to make sure I was packed and well rested for my journey.

Back in my room, I pulled out my rucksack from under the bed and propped it up against the wall. Time to start the packing. I was planning to stay a week in Izumi, so with this in mind I began to make little piles of clothes on the bed. First I needed T-shirts, which were all I'd been wearing for the past few days. But Etsuko had told me that the climate was different in Fukushima Prefecture so I'd have to take something warmer. I took out a couple of sweatshirts from the cupboard and laid them alongside the T-shirts. Trousers were easy – I only had two pairs of jeans which were endlessly recycled. Socks and underwear – one pair per day…

Then something happened.

It happened so suddenly and so violently that for a while it didn't register. But life is like that. There I was, standing in the middle of the room holding an odd sock, wondering what I'd done with its pair. I glanced casually in the direction of the window, and that was it.

Just a flash of white crossing my field of vision, there and gone in the blink of an eye. And then a sickening thud.

I was momentarily confused. I'd seen so much over the past week that possibly my senses were dulled. After the event I tried to remember what I'd thought, but the truth is, I'd thought nothing. I'd just stood there holding the sock, staring out of the window, feeling numb. I knew what I'd seen and I knew who it was – after all, I'd just spoken to the lad – but I couldn't make sense of it. I couldn't accept that the person I'd just been speaking to, who had helped me buy the drink that now stood half-drunk on my desk, whose name I knew, was lying dead on the ground outside. So I just stood rooted to the spot for a long time, until I heard the sound of someone screaming.

Strangely, my first real emotion was not concern for Yoshi, or even horror at what I'd seen, but homesickness. I thought of home, of my parents sitting at the kitchen table thinking of me in this far away place. I thought of the room I'd grown up in, the shelves of familiar things, the childish posters on the wall. I wanted to be surrounded by comfort and love and an assurance that all would be well in the end.

We stood by the entrance to the Tower and watched the paramedics and police go about their work. I wondered how often they had to deal with things like this and how they learned to cope. Did they ever think about the person lying motionless beneath the white sheet, consider the circumstances that had led them there, feel any pain or sorrow or pity?

Josh stood next to me huddled in a dressing gown several sizes too small for him. Francoise, whose friend I'd assumed Yoshi to be, leaned against the wall sobbing quietly. The two Indonesian men spoke in hushed tones to one another. In some ways it was a mercy it had happened out of term. It was not something anyone should have to witness.

Josh seemed to have taken it particularly hard, it being his second experience. He kept shaking his head and cursing under his breath. I didn't want to tell him that I'd spoken to the man just minutes before his fall. I wondered if I would ever come to terms with it, or whether that brief exchange by the drink machines would haunt me for the rest of my days.

Josh sighed loudly. 'How could this happen? How could this happen twice. It's not normal.'

'Like you told me, this is where they come.'

Josh shook his head. 'I don't understand it.'

I stared at the flashing beacons on the police cars and reflected that just an hour before, the building's forecourt had been quiet and deserted. 'Neither do I.'

'Poor fucker. I wonder who he was.'

'Yoshi,' I said.

Josh looked up in surprise.

'Yoshi. His name was Yoshi.'

I turned from the scene of his death and went back through the door, past the drink machines where Yoshi had performed his last act of kindness and straight into the lift which I'd shared with him on his final journey. I didn't know what to do or what to think, except that somehow I had to put it behind me and move on.

THE JOURNEY

Osaka was still shrouded in early morning mist as the bullet-train pulled soundlessly out of the station. I sat back in my window seat, determined to enjoy the journey. It was a new carriage, spotlessly clean, and the seats had the kind of leg-room unthinkable on an English train.

It was a relief to be on the move and as the train picked up pace I felt I was putting behind me the traumatic events of the previous evening. At one point in the night I'd even decided I was too upset to travel and it would be better to postpone the trip. But in the end there didn't seem much point. Yoshi was dead and there was nothing I could do to change that. I hadn't known him and it had been pure chance that I'd interrupted him on his way to the roof. I'd lain awake wondering if there was anything I could possibly have said to change his mind. What if I'd offered him a drink for his trouble? Or made a bit more effort at conversation? Would that have restored his balance and distracted him from his plan? Surely there must have been some sign I could have picked up on. But, apart from seeming a bit distracted, he hadn't had the air of someone at the end of their tether. He'd been calm and composed, just an ordinary guy on his way to visit a friend.

It was the coincidence factor that bothered me the most. First, he had chosen to walk into the building at the exact moment I was grappling with the drinks machine. Then he had chosen to jump at the exact moment I turned to look out of the window, on a flight path that took him right past me. A suicide while I was in the building would have been bad enough, but having to meet him and then see him fall was downright unfair. I felt like the victim of some cosmic practical joke. After all, I was still struggling to come to terms with my connection to Charlie Whitehurst.

The only consoling thought, as the train glided through the dizzying urban sprawl, was that whatever awaited me in Izumi could not be any worse. I even smiled at the irony of travelling to Japan's most haunted village as a way of recovering my emotional balance. Maybe I should have been getting off at the next stop, Kyoto, as Professor Atami had suggested, and spending a pleasant week visiting Zen temples and gardens.

For my choice of depressing literature to occupy me on my journey, I had packed Charlie's file. Despite my unease, his notes on Izumi's history were extensive and as long as I stuck to the more lucid passages, I thought he might provide some decent background.

Outside, the city gradually thinned out, but I had been forewarned that the line between Osaka and Tokyo was probably the most built-up stretch of railway track in the world; that in four hours on a high-speed train, you never truly saw the countryside. So I took the opportunity to take Charlie's file out and read.

He began with a whole ream of facts and figures, most of them ridiculously obscure, such as the names of post-war mayors or a breakdown of rice production by village sector. Charlie was nothing if not thorough. I learned that Izumi was originally a small farming community of a few hundred people which grew rapidly, with the post-war economic prosperity and the relocation of industries from the Tokyo area, to its present population of just over ten thousand. It had two elementary schools, two junior highs and a high school.

There were several pages dedicated to the village's ancient history. Apparently its reputation as a haunting hot-spot could be traced to the concentration of *kofun* within its boundaries. *Kofun* were huge earthen mounds erected as burial tombs from about the third century. There was no obvious explanation why Izumi was so rich in *kofun*, but some of them measured several hundred feet in diameter. With the arrival of Buddhism in the seventh century, the tombs were no longer built and, over the centuries, were gradually levelled to make way for agriculture and buildings. Charlie's thesis seem-ed to be that Izumi's long history of violence and hauntings could be traced to angry spirits from these disturbed tombs.

I had to smile at this theory. It was a hell of a long time to remain pissed off about some disturbed earth. You'd be hard-pushed to find a well-tended third century grave anywhere in the world.

By the eleventh century the region was still a farming backwater, but the village did get a mention in the diary of a courtier dispatched to the provinces from the capital Kyoto to patch up some local dispute. He referred to it as a devilish place, home to an angry spirit who liked nothing more than to impale a passing traveller or behead an unfortunate peasant as he tilled the land.

Charlie rattled through a number of gruesome stories about murderous local lords and masterless samurai with itchy blades. Most of the stories ended with mutilated peasants and rivers of blood, with some of the peasants coming back to wreak more havoc and avenge themselves on the innocent.

It was enough. I snapped the file shut and turned my attention to the passing scenery. There was something oppressive about being in Charlie's world, beyond the gloomy subject matter. It was his obsessive attention to detail, his ability to string out a simple point into a paragraph-long treatise, his long lists of pointless statistics. Then there was the last section, presumably just before his suicide, when his discipline had abandoned him. I was determined not to look at those pages out of respect – in fact, I had fastened them with a paperclip – the same way I had decided not to look at the photographs of the high school victims, even though the fascination remained. Even now, watching towns and houses flit past the window, I could feel Reiko Shimura's eyes watching me from some dark place in my soul.

Mount Fuji was beautiful. It was everything I had imagined and more. I knew it had come into view from the collective excitement of my fellow passengers. At first I couldn't see anything, until I realized that I needed to look further upwards. And there it was, high up in the clouds, its perfect cone capped in snow. Of course I'd seen it a thousand times, reproduced in photos and woodblock prints, but nothing had prepared me for its size and splendour. The only blot on the perfect view was a bank of cloud making its way from the east and starting to obscure the peak.

I sat back in my seat and sighed. This was a scene I'd imagined for a long time – casually looking out at Mount Fuji from the window of a passing bullet train as I journeyed across Japan.

By the time the train pulled into Tokyo Station, the weather had changed: the sky was dark and brooding, a downpour imminent. I stepped onto the platform, dazed after what I'd seen over the last half hour: the mother of all metropolises. I realized Osaka was a minnow by comparison and, making my way through the labyrinthine station, I felt as though I'd stepped into another dimension. I caught the subway to Ueno Station, then made my way through more space-age tunnels to the Tohoku bullet-train terminal.

The rain had begun to fall as the train pulled out of Ueno Station and, after a week of glaring sunshine, it gave a different complexion to the cityscape. I was also looking forward to seeing some real Japanese country-side after the monotonous urban sprawl stretching between Osaka and Tokyo. The trolley came past and I bought a green tea from an impeccably dressed server who bowed gracefully at each stage of the transaction. Then, drink in hand, I settled back in my seat to wait for the city to thin out and the countryside to begin.

Maybe it was the sleepless night I'd had or the ample chicken *yakitori* lunchbox making me drowsy, but I found my eyes nodding to the gentle rhythm of the train.

Before long I fell asleep and while I slept I had a dream.

I dreamt we were gliding through the same urban landscape and I was watching the same parade of non-descript apartment blocks and office buildings. The carriage was quiet as before and I sat back in my seat sipping green tea.

The train slowed to a crawl as we approached a signal outside a large block of flats. I looked out at the flats – the clothes hanging on the lines, the pictures on the walls, the cosy little family units – enjoying this insight into all these lives.

Then the train came to a complete stop with the block of flats no more than twenty metres from the track. I started wondering what it must be like to live so close to a mainline bullet-train route, what kind of discount you got on your rent, or whether people just grew accustomed to the constant noise. Then something caught my eye. I looked upwards and my heart sank. Standing on the roof of the building, on the uppermost ledge, in his beige chinos and white T-shirt, was Yoshi. He was staring straight at me, a half-smile on his face.

He raised his hand in greeting and I exclaimed loudly, making the old lady sitting next to me jump. My cup of tea fell to the floor and I slammed the palm of my hand on the window. Desperate, I waved my arms vigorously at him, trying to tell him, 'no'. He smiled and shook his head, unfazed.

I continued to slam my fist on the window, shouting 'no, no, no', so that everyone in the carriage look rounded at me. I jabbed my finger against the glass, pointing at Yoshi, screaming 'he's going to kill himself, he's going to kill himself'. No one seemed to see what I saw, just stared in alarm at the mad foreigner.

Yoshi watched me calmly as I became hysterical. I banged my fist on the glass and shouted for help, looking around for an emergency cord or button. Around me the other passengers were getting agitated and speaking animatedly.

Still I banged on the glass, crying in anger and frustration: 'please help, somebody help'. I realized I needed to take matters into my own hands and I left my seat, clambering over the cowering lady and into the aisle. I needed to get to the door, to alert the guard, to alert someone. Two young men grabbed hold of me in an attempt to restrain me. 'Please, I need to go, I need to get help,' I shouted, but they held on to me and shouted something in Japanese which I couldn't understand.

The train started to move off and I wrenched myself free and forced my way to the window. Yoshi was waving at me as the train moved off, waving at me with a smile on his face. I watched, my face pressed up against the glass, sobbing loudly as we pulled away. I watched helplessly as Yoshi took a short step forward and plunged to his death.

I woke with a start.

For a moment I didn't know where I was or what had happened. Then I saw that people were peering round at me with concern. By the agitated look of the lady sitting next to me, I realized I must have said something or cried out in my sleep. Not only that, but my knees were sopping wet from where I'd dropped my green tea. As far as I could remember I'd never done anything like that in public before. But the dream had been horribly vivid and I was still shaking with emotion. Yoshi's features had been so clear, his wave so genuine. I wanted to tell the other passengers what I'd been through the night before, so that they'd understand. I didn't want them to think of me as some random foreign fruitcake. If I could just explain myself to the lady next to me in my broken Japanese, maybe she'd be able to pass on the message.

I looked at her for a moment, weighing up my options, but she looked as though she might turn tail and run if I even opened my mouth. Better not to embark on some cross-cultural damage limitation exercise. Just shut up and pray for my stop.

But I couldn't put the image of Yoshi out of my mind. I kept returning to the last moment of the dream: my face pressed up against the window, tears running down my cheeks, watching him silhouetted against the grey sky, taking that last step. It was the one view I hadn't had the previous evening, the full wide-angle, no-holds-barred money-shot. If I hadn't been haunted by that particular image before, then I certainly was now.

I turned back to the window and began to think of home.

SARAH

Seeing Izumi for the first time, it was hard to imagine that somewhere so picturesque and tranquil could have seen a history so violent. The rickety local train rattled slowly towards the station and I saw a level plain of farms and houses, surrounded by hills which rose up with alarming abruptness. The station platform had seen better days, with weeds growing through the cracks in the paving and a weatherworn sign in English reading '*Welcome to Izumi*'. The village elders were not taking advantage of the village's cult status among supernatural tourists.

The deadpan conductor announced the station and the train creaked to a juddering halt. As I opened the door and stepped off, I saw a young Western woman sitting on the bench, huddled under an umbrella. Professor Atami had kindly rung the village and got me the contact details of the local language teacher, an English girl called Sarah Mayhew. But I hadn't expected her to be waiting for me at the station. She smiled and got to her feet.

'Hi, I expect you're James. I'm Sarah.'

'It's nice of you to meet me. I wasn't expecting anything.'

She laughed. 'As you can probably guess, there's not a lot to do around here.'

It was a relief to see a friendly face and hear a familiar accent after the mild trauma of the journey. 'So, this is where you call home now?'

'Yep, this is home. At least, this is where they placed me. What about you? I understand you're a ghost-hunter.'

I smiled at the label. 'Yeah, but I'm not as weird as I sound.'

Sarah pointed towards the station exit and we began walking towards it. She lifted the umbrella, inviting me under. 'You've just arrived here, haven't you? So you may still think you're pretty normal. A lot of people even continue thinking they're pretty normal. But the one thing I've learnt about the foreigners here – and I include myself – is that we're all weird. By definition. It's the nature of this place, the lifestyle, the way it affects you. So if you weren't already weird when you got off the plane, you soon will be.'

We emerged from the station and Sarah pointed to a white Toyota parked by the side of the road. 'My courtesy car. Without it, I'd have lost my mind already.'

I looked round at the station forecourt and was surprised to see it was completely deserted. No one else had got on the train, no one else had got off and no one else had been waiting. There were a few decrepit houses dotted around, but besides Sarah, there was no sign of human habitation. Izumi could have been a ghost town and Sarah an emissary from the netherworld sent to welcome me.

'Have you made any arrangements for accommodation?'

I pulled myself together and showed her my list of guesthouses. 'Do you know any of these?'

She glanced at them and wrinkled her nose. 'I wouldn't bother with all that. Crash at mine. I've got more space than I know what to do with.'

Given she'd only met me two minutes ago and all she knew about me was that I hunted ghosts, I was a little surprised by the offer. I certainly wouldn't have offered a place on my floor to someone with my credentials. 'Are you sure about that?'

She started to laugh. 'I told you this place does things to your mind. I'll be honest with you, I've been here for nine months and you're the first visitor I've had. I know I don't exactly know you, but I'll take my chances.'

It was nice to get into the car and out of the rain and not have to worry about accommodation. And sitting alongside this down-to-earth English girl, I felt the previous night's stress start to ease. The thing that had worried me most about leaving Osaka and travelling to Izumi was the thought of being alone and not having Josh or anyone else to hang out with. The feeling had grown as the train neared Izumi and I'd started to think about having to find accommodation in some Spartan inn. My dream about Yoshi had been a symptom of that mounting anxiety. Truthfully I hadn't expected much of the resident English teacher. Given all I'd heard about Izumi I was rather expecting a twitching neurotic wreck and not an answer to a prayer.

Driving through the village, I looked out at the rain-sodden houses and ramshackle shops and was struck by how different everything looked. I'd never seen the Japanese countryside before, but the contrast with the city was remarkable. Professor Atami had told me that the Japanese view of the countryside was unlike that of the English. In England, city dwellers dream of living in the countryside, surrounded by nature and tranquillity. In Japan, the countryside is an undesirable backwater, just a place for farmers and yokels. In Japan everyone would live in Tokyo given the choice.

'Do you like it here?'

Sarah shrugged. 'It's okay. I didn't really have a choice about my posting. When I signed up to teach in Japan, this isn't exactly what I imagined. I wanted to be in a city, somewhere with a bit of life. As you can see, there isn't much of that around here.'

Looking out I saw a couple of old women in smocks hobbling along the sidepath and, further on, a group of young children on bikes.

'There aren't any young people, put it that way. Everyone's very nice, they invite you into their houses, they shower you with attention, but there's no one of my age. When people reach eighteen, the first thing they do is head to the city, go to college, get out of here. No one wants to be left behind with a bunch of school kids and geriatrics. So you get a kind of eighteen to eighty vacuum.' She started to laugh. 'Sorry, you've just got off a train and I'm already giving you a sob story. It's not too late to change your mind and go to one of those guesthouses.'

'That's okay. You can hear some of my sob stories later.' I turned back to the window, wondering what she'd think if I told her I'd seen a man die the previous night. Would she still want me to stay with her?

'The only things that keep me sane are candles and Gregorian chant.'

After arriving at her flat and taking the tour, I'd been overcome by tiredness. Sarah had encouraged me to rest, laying out a futon for me in the spare room. There I'd enjoyed a deep dreamless sleep until seven, when she had woken me for dinner. She'd cooked a tasty meal of yakisoba noodles which we ate cross-legged around the low table in the centre of the room. She even gave me an elementary lesson in the use and misuse of chopsticks, all the while extolling the virtues of Japanese food, insisting the Japanese had the healthiest diet in the world. I wasn't a gourmet, but the food was excellent and I ate with relish.

And now I was sitting in a room surrounded by candles.

'I know it must seem a bit gloomy, but I had a religious upbringing. I'm not religious now, but for some reason this bit stuck. I find it relaxing.'

Except in a church I'd never seen so many candles in such a small space. There were candles on the book-case, candles on the window ledge, candles on upturned tins and boxes placed round the edges of the traditional *tatami* mat floor. I could barely move for fear of setting fire to myself, while the Gregorian chant made for a slightly sombre atmosphere.

'So why did you come here?' I asked.

She sighed and looked around the room, considering the question. 'Same reason everyone else did. To find something new. Maybe to escape.'

'Escape?'

'Yeah. Everyone has something to escape from. And I don't mean the obvious things, like a doomed romance or credit card debts. People come here to

escape their upbringing, expectations, the fear of failure. Most people don't even know what they're trying
to escape from.'

'It's a long way to come to escape.'

'Of course, no one would actually say they've come
to escape. Most people don't even think it. They say
they've always been interested in foreign culture or
exotic travel. They say they want life experiences or
something. But I've met a lot of the foreign teachers
out here and they've all got secrets. They've all got
things lurking beneath the surface, things they're afraid
to talk about. The bottom line is, most of us here were
social misfits at home. So we think if we travel halfway
across the globe, we might find acceptance.'

'You really think that?'

She smiled, perking up a little. 'Sorry, I've gone all
gloomy again. I admit I do have problems. Maybe it
was my parents. They wanted me to be something
special and I wasn't up to the challenge. Maybe that's
what I'm escaping from.'

In a way, it was a relief to hear Sarah talking so
openly. It helped to dissipate the shadow of Yoshi
hanging over me. 'Well, it's better to be honest about
it.'

'Some place to escape to, isn't it.' She started to
laugh. 'So, what about you? I've said my piece. What
brought you to the other side of the world looking for
ghosts? I've been wondering about that.'

It was strange, but I felt I hadn't really talked about
myself to anyone in years. Most of my friends were
men and we didn't tend to speak about what went on
inside our heads. What Sarah had said about escape
actually made a lot of sense. I had absolutely come to
escape. 'I don't know. Before I came, people kept

asking me why I was going to Japan and why I was studying ghosts. The last question is easy. That's what I got funding to do. The first question is more difficult.'

She topped up my beer glass as encouragement.

'I didn't have a very happy upbringing. My parents were too caught up in their own issues, so I kind of disappeared into my shell. I comforted myself with dreams of going places and being important and doing remarkable things. I grew up in a small town, where everyone knew everyone else and nothing ever happened, so I guess I wanted to rise above my roots. I went to university, which was a kind of escape and I did okay. But then I fell in love and that took over my life. It was the first and only time and I didn't handle it too well. I thought she was the answer to everything, but I always had this feeling she was too good for me and that sooner or later she'd realize it and leave. So I ended up being possessive and neurotic. I saw every other guy she knew or spoke to as a threat which just drove her mad, so she left me. She said I loved her more than she loved me, that I was jealous, that I was dependent on her, that I needed to grow up. And the worst thing was, she was absolutely right on every point. It's easy to hate someone if you know they're being unfair. But she wasn't and I've never really recovered from that.'

I'd said a lot more than I'd meant. It all seemed to come gushing out and I was unable to stem the tide. It was my life story in abridged form and something I could only really have given to someone I didn't know very well.

Sarah didn't say anything for a while, then yawned, stretched her arms and pulled herself to her feet. 'Well, it's all out in the open now. No more unhealthy skeletons in the closet, no more secrets. There's a small bar just down the road, so I say we sod our insecurities and go out and raise a glass. What do you think?'

'What are we raising a glass to?'

'No idea. We'll think of something on the way. Come on.'

'Count me in.' She was a godsend. As far as I was concerned, she'd already booked her place in heaven.

Sarah assured me it was a pretty decent turnout for a Tuesday night: the two of us, a maudlin man in his fifties propped against the bar supping on whisky, and the stony-faced proprietor. I looked round at the small dark room: a handful of tables and stools, a few shabby shelves behind the bar lined with bottles and a couple of framed photographs on the wall. The place was in dire need of an interior design overhaul.

'It's not jolly, but it's damn convenient. If any friends visit, which isn't likely, at least I know I can bring them here for a taste of Izumi nightlife.'

We were seated at a table in the corner and every now and then the proprietor lifted his gaze and regarded us quizzically, as though incredulous that anyone would want to patronize his bar. I wanted to ask him how he managed to keep the place open.

'It's cosy,' I said, looking for positives.

'I don't know if 'cosy' is the word, but I appreciate your tact.'

I pointed at the photographs on the wall, which seemed to be of local landscapes. 'I guess those are old photos of Izumi.'

'From the last century by the looks of it, before the bulldozers moved in. It used to be quite picturesque.'

I got up and, under the watchful eye of the proprietor, inspected the photographs. They were badly faded, but I could make out the hills and fields and, in the corner of one of them, giant earthen mounds. I jabbed at the picture with my finger. 'That's them. The burial mounds. Look.'

She came over and squinted with me. 'Oh, those little hillocks. There are a few of them around.'

'Apparently the village used to be covered in them. That's where its reputation comes from.'

She went back to her seat. 'So that's what you want to see then? Burial mounds?'

I shrugged. 'I guess I just wanted to see somewhere different, maybe talk to people here about all the stories. It's a famous haunting spot.'

'I know. Japan's most haunted village. It's funny, I remember waiting for weeks to hear where I was going to be placed. The letter comes, I do a quick search on Izumi and what do I get? Japan's most haunted fucking village.' She checked herself with a smile. 'Sorry, I know that's the whole reason you've come here. But then you can spend a week and go back to Osaka. I have to live here.'

'Do you hear any stories? I mean, that's if you don't mind talking about it. Back in Osaka I tried asking a couple of Japanese students and they completely freaked. They were broad-minded, educated, chilled-out, but still had these superstitious hang-ups. They said that the dead can hear you talk about them.'

Sarah sat back and finished her beer. 'That's pretty weird. I've never really paid much attention to the stories and I've not asked anyone specifically. I know a few people round the village and of course the teachers at the schools, but they're not generally from around here. I guess I've heard the high school students talk about ghosts. That's probably the age you're most interested in that stuff.'

'What do they say?'

'Well, there's the thing that happened a few years back. I don't know if you know about it. Five of the students at the school died within a short space of time.' She glanced round at the other two people in the bar, as though aware she was broaching a taboo subject.

'Are there hauntings?'

She leaned forward. 'A couple of the girls claim to have seen the ghosts of two of the students. These two were seeing one another without their parents' consent, so they used to meet in the school grounds late at night and sneak into the school. They didn't return home one night and were found dead the next morning, just as all the students were arriving for school.'

She was thoughtful for a moment, clearly affected by the story of these young lovers.

'Does anyone have any theories?'

'It was two weeks after the first girl disappeared. Reiko, I think her name was…'

'Reiko Shimura.'

She looked at me in surprise. 'So you know all about it?'

'I've read some stuff.'

'You probably know more than me then. Anyway, some people seemed to think it was a suicide pact, that they'd had enough of their parents' disapproval and were unbalanced after the disappearance of their friend Reiko. But that doesn't make sense. The body of the girl was found at the bottom of a steep flight of steps leading to the classrooms, which suggests she'd fallen or been pushed. But if you were going to kill yourself, would you throw yourself down a set of steps on the off-chance you sustain a head injury serious enough to kill you? I certainly wouldn't. Now, the boy's case is even stranger. He fell or was thrown from the third floor classroom window, straight through the glass. But a lot of the chairs and desks in the classroom were scattered about, so it looks like there was a pursuit of some kind.' Sarah broke off and, seeing her glass was finished, took a sip from mine. 'And how many suicide lovers decide to die in different places?'

I wasn't surprised Sarah knew all about the affair, given she was teaching in the school where it had happened. But hearing her talking about it and recalling Charlie's copious notes on the subject, I felt myself getting drawn into the unsolved mystery. I thought about the portraits of the two students, Jun Takada and Kanae Kubota, and it was clear to me that their deaths weren't self-inflicted. They may have been grieving for their friend, but I could tell they were happy, confident students, and they had surely come to the school that night for no other purpose than to meet one another.

'There was something strange about every one of those deaths,' Sarah said solemnly.

'What about the ghosts? What have the students seen?'

'They've seen the two lovers at the window of their classroom looking out. They've seen them walking past the classroom during lessons. And they've seen bloodstains appear on the ground where the girl fell. Of course, it's not something you're meant to talk about. It's a small community so everyone knows someone connected to the victims. And a lot of the teachers at the school actually taught the students.'

'None of the teachers have said anything then?'

'Actually, I'm on pretty good terms with a couple of the English teachers. They've talked a bit about it, but only outside school. I think they'd feel uncomfortable talking at school.'

'Because of the ghosts?'

'I don't think it's that. I think it's because no one knows what really happened. Five students die in the space of a month, but no one knows how or why. Some vagrant is convicted for the murder of the first girl, on the basis of finding something of hers on him. But that doesn't explain what happened to the others. He denies it, but he doesn't have a defence and gets the death penalty. Lethal injection. Which is all very well, you have yourself a scapegoat for one student – but what about the other four?'

'What did happen to the others? Could they have been suicides too?'

'Who knows? One boy either threw himself or was pushed into the path of a lorry in the middle of the night. And the other girl was impaled on broken glass in her bedroom. No one knows what happened. If there had been an explanation people could forget about it and move on. And of course Reiko was never found and that's probably the worst part of the whole thing.' Sarah shook her head and sipped slowly from my drink, caught up in the story of the five tragic students.

I had originally only wanted to ask about the sightings of ghosts, but it seemed like a trivial question now. I sat there wondering what else I could ask.

She sighed heavily. 'Actually, apart from the teachers, my host family when I arrived might be able to tell you a thing or two. I'll introduce you.'

She looked at her watch and yawned. It was time to go.

As we headed back down the quiet country road, I was struck by how dark it was. There was no light from the moon, no street lamps, not even the headlights of a car to alleviate the darkness. With an effort I could just discern the outline of the hills against the sky. A sprinkling of houselights offered the only sign of human habitation.

Sarah was quiet as we walked, still wrapped up in the fate of the high school students. Suddenly she turned and spoke, a little hesitantly. 'There was someone else, wasn't there?'

'What do you mean?'

'There was another supernatural researcher from your university.'

'You heard about him?

'People told me about him. He came here and talked to a lot of people, asked a lot of questions. They know what happened to him. And when your professor rang me up to tell me you were coming, he mentioned it too.'

I didn't know what to say about Charlie. I only knew that I had to distance myself from him. 'I know about it.'

'Doesn't it freak you out, coming here after what happened to him?'

'It doesn't bother me. I've actually read his research notes and I can tell you he was a sick man when he came here.'

We turned into Sarah's apartment block and up the stairs to the second floor. She stopped at the door. 'There's something about this place. I'm the third teacher to come here in as many years. Neither of the last two saw out their contracts. In fact, both of them left suddenly, without a moment's notice. I think people are expecting the same of me.'

I was glad that my bed was already prepared and waiting as sleep couldn't come soon enough. I lay down with a sigh of relief and turned out the light. Sarah was on the other side of the sliding screen partition and I could see the light through the crack in the door. I realized how much I'd needed her company after arriving in Izumi. If I'd been stuck in some fleapit guesthouse I would have sat in all night agonizing over Yoshi's death and planning a quick return to Osaka. Even if we'd spent the evening talking about dark subjects, at least that was what I'd come to Izumi to do. And I really did enjoy her company.

I burrowed under the duvet and felt my lids grow heavy. Sleep came swiftly and for the second time that day, I had unquiet dreams.

In my dream I awoke in the night to the sound of hushed voices from Sarah's room and light coming from the crack between the sliding screen doors.

I glanced at the clock and saw it was half past two. It seemed strange to be receiving visitors at this time, so I crawled over to the door and peered through the crack. It was too narrow to see anything much, so very carefully I pulled back the screen to reveal a room filled with candles.

Sarah sat at the table, talking to a young man with fair hair and a roll-neck jumper. They were deep in discussion, but my arrival prompted them to look up.

'Hello, sleepy head,' Sarah said with a smile.

'Sorry, to disturb you,' I said, squinting in the light from the candles.

'Would you like to join us?' she asked. 'Have some green tea.'

As I stepped towards the table, I saw that the fair-haired man was looking at me with interest. I looked down at the table and froze. Charlie's file lay on the table in front of him, open at the photograph of Reiko Shimura. And at that moment, I realized who he was.

I looked at Sarah in horror, but she simply beckoned me to join them. 'Sit down.'

Then the man spoke to me, his voice hollow like one unused to speech. 'Sit down. I've got something to show you.'

I shook my head.

He patted the floor next to him. 'Come on, there's so much you don't know. I can help you. I can be your mentor.'

I looked to Sarah for help, but there was none forthcoming.

The man spoke again, his tone firmer, and I took a step backwards. 'James, you'd do well to listen to me. If you sit down, I can explain.'

I recoiled from him. 'I know who you are. I know everything about you. I've read your file.'

'Not all of it.'

'I've read all I want.' I turned to leave.

I saw that Sarah had lost her friendly air and was staring at me with icy detachment.

The young man continued. 'Don't turn your back. I'm the only one who can save you, James. I'm the only one who knows what to do.'

I stepped back into the shadows. 'I'm sorry. I don't mean to be rude, but I don't need your help.' I fumbled for the sliding screen to pull it across.

The young man laughed. 'You don't know, James. You have no idea. You'll make exactly the same mistake I did. And, just like me, you'll die.'

He raised his hands and slowly began to peel away the jumper from his neck. My heart turned to ice at the sight of his blue and bloody neck, the lacerations from the rope as fresh as on the night he hung himself.

'Do you want to die, James? Do you want to die?'

I pulled the screen door across with a crash.

IZUMI HIGH

I awoke to the sound of Gregorian chant from the room next door. I opened my eyes and looked about the small *tatami* mat room, at the bare walls, the sliding screen door and the small paper lantern above my head. My travel bag was propped in the corner, but otherwise the room was empty.

I could hear Sarah pottering about in the kitchen and the memory of my dream returned to me. I had been wondering what Charlie looked like and now my mind had concocted a photo-fit. What did the dream mean? Was it my subconscious encouraging me to make better use of his file? Glancing over at my bag, I could see it poking out provocatively. No, I would leave it for the time-being. I would form my own impressions of Izumi, draw my own conclusions. I wouldn't rely on the scribblings of a dead scholar. And in Sarah I had the best possible guide and mentor.

'What would you like to do today?'

We were sitting on the balcony in the sun, looking out over the apartment block car park and to the hills beyond. Sarah had prepared some fresh coffee and toast.

'I don't have a particular plan. I was just going to wander about. Do you have any suggestions?'

'I could give you a guided tour. Not that it'll last very long.'

'You sure about that? You don't have stuff you want to do?'

She grinned at me over her mug. 'You should know me better by now. I have absolutely nothing to do. It's a lovely place as you can see, but it's the holidays and I'm bored shitless. So if you don't mind I'll show you around.'

'Are you planning to do much travelling in Japan?'

She put her mug down on the rail with a sigh. 'I came here with a bit of debt. I haven't always been a very sensible girl so now I'm saving all I can. Basically I'm stuck here.'

I'd hoped that Sarah would accompany me, but I hadn't wanted to be presumptuous. With the memory of Yoshi still fresh in my mind I was grateful for the company.

'I'll take you to the school. It's out of term time, but the teachers come in anyway. I can introduce you to some of the English teachers.' She stopped, then seemed to have an afterthought. 'And later on I'll introduce you to someone who might be able to give you some real insight.'

She stood up, stretched, and disappeared into the flat. The more time I spent with her, the more I admired her. She had a freshness and honesty about her and didn't try to play it cool and pretend she had her life sorted. I, who had always strained to hide my deficiencies, had a lot to learn from her.

Izumi in the sun was a whole new prospect. It sparkled on the paddy fields, glinted on the tiled roofs of houses and brought people out into the fresh air. The village children were out in force, hailing the car as it passed with loud cries of '*Seeraa-sensei*'. Even the younger children, who Sarah didn't teach, seemed to know her name. One of the perks of being the only foreigner in a rural Japanese village, she told me, was instant celebrity status. It wasn't just the kids either. The old men and women, shuffling along by the sides of the roads, bowed cordially in our direction, all gold teeth and wizened faces. During a week in Osaka I couldn't recall a single stare or wave or look of surprise. Here, I suddenly felt like a foreigner. I felt different.

'So now you know what it's like to be a star,' I said.

'Yeah, and it definitely isn't all it's cracked up to be.' Sarah broke off and pointed to a building up ahead. 'That's it. That's the school.'

Izumi High was built according to the Ministry of Education standard-issue model. Impressive steel gates led to a large, well-tended forecourt enclosed on three sides by the school buildings. The main entrance was straight ahead, but the eyes were drawn upwards to an improbably large clock and the name of the school in ornate Japanese characters which Sarah spelled out for me: *Izumi Koutou Gakkou*. To either side of the forecourt were faceless grey blocks of classrooms. The whole thing was ugly and functional in equal measures.

I approached the building with a sense of trepidation, knowing that terrible things had happened within its walls and aware that unquiet spirits might walk its corridors.

Sarah showed me in and pointed to a series of pigeon holes where visitors' slippers were kept. I watched her remove her shoes and slip into a pink fluffy pair, a revolt against the grey standard-issue number I was trying to squeeze my feet into.

'Do all the pupils have to wear these things?'

'Absolutely. You don't bring your outdoor shoes into the school.'

I followed her into the main foyer, tripping on my slippers as I went. It was the first time I'd stepped inside a school building since leaving my own school many years before and, as the click-clack of my slippers echoed round the Spartan corridor, memories of my own unhappy schooldays besieged me. There had been some effort at prettifying the grey breeze-block walls with pictures and student project work, but not enough to expunge the oppressive feeling of melancholy.

'What do you think?' she asked, sensing my unease.

'I feel the same way about schools as I do about hospitals.'

'And how's that?'

'Petrified.'

She laughed and started down the corridor. I began to follow then stopped abruptly. A flight of steps rose steeply to my left and I looked up with a faint feeling of nausea. Was this really the place?

Sarah stopped and looked round. 'What?'

'Are these the steps?'

She came and stood beside me, following my gaze upwards. 'I think they probably are.'

I wasn't sure how to feel, standing in the exact spot where Kanae Kubota had fallen to her death. Perhaps the memory of Yoshi's twisted corpse was still too fresh in my mind.

'Come on.' Sarah pulled on my arm and we continued down the corridor.

The staffroom was more like a corporate office than the one I remembered from my own school days. The desks were ranged in orderly rows and piled high with files and paper, while grey filing cabinets lined the walls. Most of the teachers seemed to be present and correct, hunched over their desks or sat in a communal area chatting. A few raised their heads at our entrance and greeted Sarah with polite bows of the head. Following her lead, I returned as many bows as I could.

'My sanctuary,' she said, pointing to the only desk not weighed under with piles of paper. A row of soft toys and a stack of novels indicated an absence of any administrative responsibility. She drew up a chair and invited me to sit.

'What do you do when you're in here?' I asked.

She shrugged. 'Not much. Chat to the teachers, read books, write e-mails.'

'Do they all talk to you?'

'I've chatted to them all at one time or another, but I have most to do with the English teachers. There's Aya over there. With Numata-san.' Sarah pointed to a young female teacher by the window chatting to a severe-looking older man in a dapper green suit. 'Aya is probably my best friend here. Similar age, similar out-look, doesn't have the hang-ups the older generation have.'

Aya looked over and noticed us sitting there. Making her excuses to Numata-san, she threaded her way across the room with a broad smile.

'Hello,' she said, more to me than to Sarah. 'Sarah told me she had a visitor.'

'This is James. The ghost-hunter.'

Aya held her hand over her mouth and giggled and I flashed Sarah a look of disapproval. It was obviously a joke they'd enjoyed earlier.

'It's not as bad as it sounds,' I said earnestly. 'I'm actually researching differences in Eastern and Western attitudes towards the supernatural.' I knew I had to whittle my self-introduction down to something more manageable, but I just hadn't had the time. Maybe I would have to resign myself to being a 'ghost-hunter'.

'I'm Aya. I'm an English teacher.' Her pronunciation was excellent and I guessed she'd studied abroad at some point.

'I'm going to give James the tour now,' Sarah said. 'Do you want to come along?'

'I'm sorry, I have to meet the Headmaster now. But I can see you after that.'

Standing next to Aya I could feel myself blushing. She had a natural grace and elegance and, within sixty seconds, had won me over completely.

'What do you think of her?' Sarah asked, as we made her way back down the corridor.

'Seems very nice.'

'She is. She's the staffroom heartthrob actually. Between lessons, the men form an orderly queue to speak to her. A queue you jumped by the way so if you see any of them giving you looks, that's the reason.'

Once again we passed the fateful spot at the bottom of the steps and I found myself giving it a wide berth.

Sarah spotted this. 'I thought you told me you weren't superstitious.'

'I didn't think I was. But there's something about this thing...'

She laughed. 'Conquer your fears. We're going up.'

I followed her, our footsteps echoing round the walls, up to the first floor where a long gloomy corridor stretched out in front of us.

'Come on. I'll show you.'

The corridor was cold and devoid of features and seemed more suited to a prison camp than a school. To my right were windows which faced on to gravel playing fields behind the school. To my left were the classrooms, large and plain, with the chairs stacked up on the desks for the holidays.

'These are the first years' classrooms,' Sarah said, pushing back the sliding door of the first and stepping inside. The sign on the door announced it as classroom 1A. 'I've had some fun times in here.'

We stood at the back and I counted about forty desks, spaced apart in neat rows. I had imagined that in a country famed for its group mentality, the desks might also be in groups, but here each student was on their own. The window looked out on the forecourt and the hills beyond, so I pulled back a seat and sat down to admire the view. For a moment I was transported back to my own schooldays, sitting in a classroom on a warm June afternoon, dreaming of summer, of adventure, of escape from the endless monotony of hours and lessons.

'Did you enjoy school?' Like me, Sarah was staring out of the window.

'No. I suppose I didn't.'

'That's what I always think when I'm teaching. I'm thinking: I hated school, I hated my teachers, I counted down the days until the torture ended. And here I am standing in front of this lot inflicting the same ordeal on them. I shouldn't be doing this.'

'Someone has to do it.'

She turned away from the window. 'I suppose you're right. Someone does have to do it. Listen, do you want to see any more classrooms?'

'Those ghosts your students saw, where did they see them?'

She beamed. 'All right then, Mr Ghost-hunter, let's do the tour.'

'Isn't there a lift or something?' I was completely out of breath as we arrived at the third floor. It was hardly a mammoth climb and Sarah mocked me by offering a helping arm.

'Come on, old man, we're here.'

I got to the top of the steps and stared down at an exact replica of the last two floors: a long gloomy corridor, windows on one side, classrooms on the other. As soon as the echo of our footsteps died down an eerie silence took hold, like the silence of an empty chapel. I had the same feeling I used to have in the old country churches my parents used to drag me to in the summer holidays: the feeling that I was not alone, that unseen eyes were observing me from the shadows. Though I resolutely refused to believe in ghosts, the idea that the passing generations somehow left their mark was a compelling one.

'These are the third grade classrooms.'

'This is where the ghosts appear?'

Sarah nodded. 'One girl told me she saw a figure of a boy disappear into 3C. It was after school and there were only a few of them left doing club activities. She thought it was one of her friends, so she went to see and found the room empty. She told one of the teachers about this and they said that the dead students' classroom was 3C.'

'What about the one who jumped? Where did he jump from?'

'Classroom 3C. And there are other stories about that room. Strange figures walking towards it. Screams of pain, laughter, whispering, all sorts of things. Basically, the students are scared of this corridor, and at the end of the day there's a scramble to get out. No one wants to be the last one left in the evening. Just in case.'

'What about you? Do you get the creeps?'

'Listen, there's no way in hell I'd come up here on my own. No way in hell.'

We started to walk down the corridor, pausing to look in at the first classroom, 3A, an identikit version of 1A on the first floor.

'What about the current 3C crop? Does it bother them that their classroom is haunted?'

'There is no 3C. The classroom's still there, but there aren't enough third years to have more than two classes. After what happened there was a sharp drop-off in the number of enrolments. Parents would rather send their kids to private schools in Shirakawa. The school was built to accommodate five classes per year, so whoever designed it was being wildly optimistic.'

As we walked slowly past 3A and 3B, I noticed the extent of the school's disrepair. There were loose fittings on the lights, graffiti on the classroom doors, cracks on the dingy walls. And with dwindling numbers of students, who was going to stump up the money for a new paint job? Could a school ever recover from such a tragedy?

'3C will probably be empty,' she said as we approached the door. 'I don't know what they use it for.'

Maybe it was a culmination of all the things I had seen and heard over the past few days, but I had a strange sense of foreboding as Sarah ushered me towards the open door of room 3C: a sense that my destiny was bound up with this room, that it had always been there waiting for me to arrive.

I think it was this knot of tension that made me recoil in terror on entering the room. An old man with white hair and a scruffy blazer sat on a solitary chair in the middle of the room, staring down at the floor. He didn't move for several seconds, time enough for a cold chill to creep slowly up my spine. He was so oblivious to our presence that I started to believe this really was an apparition.

'Hello,' Sarah said quietly.

The man started violently and stood up, very much in the land of the living.

'Ah, hello,' he stuttered, trying to compose himself. I saw from his terrified expression that we'd startled him more than he'd startled us.

'I was giving a tour of the school to my friend,' Sarah said in slow, deliberate English.

The man nodded and bowed in my direction and I suddenly felt bad about the unwanted intrusion and suspecting him of being a ghost. It wasn't a nice thing to suspect of someone.

'It's Shirakami-san, one of the teachers,' Sarah whispered to me. 'I don't think he hears very well.'

'Nice to meet you,' I said, trying to muster a smile. Looking at the man I guessed he was about sixty, but prematurely aged. He was certainly close to retirement age.

'Shall we?' Sarah tugged at my shirt and I backed out of the room after her, returning the man's polite bow as I went. She shut the door and started to walk down the corridor, clearly disturbed by the encounter.

'Who is he?'

She ignored the question. 'That was weird. What was he doing there?'

'Maybe he was getting some peace and quiet.' I didn't know why I was making excuses, but for some reason I felt sorry for him. He'd simply looked old and vulnerable.

'There are a hundred empty classrooms in this place. Why does he choose that one?'

I shrugged my shoulders.

'He's a weird guy. He's never been friendly to me. Kind of keeps himself to himself. Sorry, but that just freaked me out. To go out of your way to sit in the haunted classroom, the classroom that everyone else tries to avoid.'

We reached the stairs and started down, Sarah hurrying on ahead of me. I didn't know the man, but there didn't seem anything threatening about him. And I recognized the urge to seek out the very places no one else wanted to go. In this case the one place he knew he wouldn't be disturbed.

'I think he's a very unhappy man.' Aya shook her head slowly, then breathed in heavily.

We'd managed to smuggle her away from her fan club in the staffroom and she'd joined us on a walk around the gravel playing pitches.

'He was just sitting there, looking at the floor,' Sarah said.

'He always looks at the floor, also when he talks to you.' Aya illustrated this with an exaggerated stare at the ground. 'I think he's had an unhappy life. He never got married and he's lived alone all his life. I think it's very hard to be so alone.'

'Does he always sit in that room?'

'I don't know. But I've heard that he goes there sometimes.'

'Is it anything to do with what happened?' Sarah asked.

We had got to the far side of the grounds and Aya stopped and looked across at the school, weighing up her response. Sarah had told me that if any of the teachers could talk about what happened then it was Aya. But having drawn a blank from Shinichi and Etsuko in Osaka, I wasn't holding my breath.

'I've heard some things about that. Shirakami-san was the homeroom teacher to those five students when they were in their first year. He was a very popular teacher and was always joking with the students. I think he was very close to Reiko Shimura, before she disappeared.'

'I can't imagine him joking,' Sarah exclaimed.

'Ah yes, it's the same for me. I only knew him after it happened, so I've never seen him laughing. He was a different man after those students died. He didn't make jokes and he didn't laugh anymore.'

Sarah seemed dissatisfied. 'If it was so bad, why didn't he leave?'

Aya shook her head. 'I don't know. In the past some of the teachers discussed the change in his personality, but not anymore. Like me, many of the teachers are new so they didn't know him before.'

'Do any of the old teachers ever talk about what happened? Or is it a taboo subject?' I felt presumptuous asking the question, but I knew Aya was my best hope in Izumi of learning something.

She started to walk again, her brow furrowed. 'We don't talk about it openly. Never. But some of us – the new teachers – talk about it privately. When I arrived I was very nervous. I didn't apply for a job in this school and I didn't want to come. I was placed here by the regional Board of Education. I could have refused, but I wouldn't have found another job. All the other new teachers had the same feeling.'

'Why didn't you want to come here? Were you afraid?'

'It was a very famous news story in Japan, so everyone knows Izumi high school. But it's not for a positive reason. When I meet people I don't like to say the name of my school, because I know how they'll react. I want to be a normal teacher so every year I apply to be placed in another school.'

For a while we walked in silence, a gloom descending over the conversation. I felt bad that I was responsible for the gloom. It was starting to hit home what an awful gloomy subject I'd chosen and what an awful gloomy decision it had been to come to Izumi. Here was Aya, the cheeriest person I'd met in Japan and within minutes I'd made her depressed. And Sarah, who'd welcomed me so kindly, was probably counting the days until I left. Was it really worth it?

'The mystery was never solved,' Aya said with a sudden resolve. 'No one knows what happened to Reiko Shimura. Perhaps she was murdered. Perhaps she is still alive. Nobody knows. And how did the other four students die? Nobody knows.' She shook her head in anguish, biting her lip.

'They charged someone with the murder of Reiko,' I said.

'Nobody believes it. Nobody. There is no proof. We often talk about this. The other four students all died after the man was charged and nobody knows why.' Aya lowered her voice. 'So, for certain, the killer is still around.'

'What do they say?' Sarah asked. 'Is there anyone they suspect? One of the teachers?'

This was a question too far and Aya shook her head abruptly, clearly uncomfortable. But she had said enough to reveal that the debate was still alive and well. And how could it not be, with five probable murders and no one to answer for them.

As Sarah and I were walking back to the car, I looked up at the school, at the dark windows of the classrooms, and I found my gaze drawn like a magnet to the top floor. I counted across to what I thought was room 3C and for a fleeting moment I saw, outlined in the window, the figure of an old man looking down at us, then quickly withdrawing into the shadows. And not for the first time since arriving in Japan, I felt afraid.

Mrs Azuma

I had come a long way in ten days.

I'd seen and heard things I wouldn't have believed when I'd boarded the plane in Heathrow. That seemed like a whole different life, certainly a less complicated one. Ever since leaving home at eighteen, I'd led a closeted student existence, preoccupied only with the minutiae of student life: sleeping in, trekking to the library, last-minute essay crises, late-night conversations setting the world to rights. All that time, I'd existed in a cosy cocoon, my only real concern being where my next funding would come from. My studies had always been a side-issue and the last thing I'd expected, embarking on my Japanese adventure, was that my thesis would start to exact a psychological toll. I had never aspired to have an intimate insight into the dark heart of humanity.

Lying on Sarah's *tatami* mat floor in the late afternoon I could see a hazy sun hovering above the hills to the west of Izumi. She was taking a shower and I lay back listening to the splash of water and trying to compose my thoughts.

I'd come to Japan to study differences in the way Eastern and Western cultures perceive supernatural phenomena. It was supposed to be a sociological and scientific study based on observation and reason. So what was I doing in Izumi? What was I there to achieve? Did I actually have a sound reason? I'd originally conceived of the trip as a way of crystallizing my ideas for my thesis and the direction I was going to take. It was meant to be part field-trip, part sightseeing trip. Most of all, it was meant to give me time to think.

But far from becoming clearer, my thoughts about my thesis were in complete disarray. Maybe Professor Atami had been right to dissuade me from coming to Izumi. Perhaps that had been his intention all along when he handed me Charlie's file to read. If he'd glimpsed the complete mental breakdown Charlie had experienced in Izumi, he may have kept the evidence as a cautionary tale. If so, he'd been unsuccessful. Not only had I carried out my threat to go to Izumi, but I'd also brought the file with me, its grim fascination getting the better of me. And it was grim fascination that was drawing me further into the story of the five tragic high school students, however much I'd promised myself not to bring sensationalist stories into my thesis.

I knew I'd gone too far to ignore it now. I'd seen their photographs, heard their stories and I'd wanted to find out more. And so I'd come to Izumi, seen their school and their classroom, met their teachers, stood on the exact spot where Kanae Kubota had plunged to her death. The mystery was too compelling to pass up. Perhaps if I declared it as my case study, it could be a handy point of reference for the serious analysis that was to follow.

Only my better nature told me that what I did was folly. Only a small persistent voice warned that I had no business here, that Izumi held secrets that were best left alone, that I should pack my bags and catch the first train out. All my life I had lived vicariously, learning about life from books, with nothing to threaten my safe little world. But within a short space of time I'd come into contact with the brutal spectres of madness, suicide and cold-blooded murder.

The splashing of water stopped and Sarah emerged from the bathroom, wrapped in a towel and rubbing her wet hair. I looked away quickly so as not to appear immodest.

'It's all right. It's tightly fastened.'

She was smiling at me, tickled by my embarrassment.

'Well, that feels better.' She came over and knelt down on the mat beside me with a satisfied sigh. She had come back from our visit to the school still creeped out about meeting Shirakami-san in room 3C. This hadn't been helped by Aya's speculating that a killer might still be at large, might even be connected to the school. I felt I'd at least done well not to mention that Shirakami-san had been watching us from the classroom window as we left. In fact, I'd tried to steer the conversation on to lighter topics, such as her flower arranging classes and things she missed about England.

'Should be a good evening,' she said, combing out her hair. 'I think you'll like Mrs Azuma. She's a bit of a gossip, so that probably suits you just fine.'

'What about her English?'

'Very good. She lived abroad for a couple of years. Her husband's a manager at a local factory and they spent some time in the States, then in Indonesia with his company. She's apparently got a good degree from a good university. And that stuff's important to her.'

'What stuff?'

Sarah looked thoughtful. 'Education. She's very big on education. She'll want to know all about where you studied, what you studied. And make sure to ask her about her children, where they're studying, what they're studying. One of her sons went to Meiji University, one of the top places in the country, so he's a bit of a local celebrity. The other only managed some small regional college, but she's still pretty proud. Yeah, that stuff means a lot to her.'

It was hard for me not to watch Sarah, sitting there wearing nothing but a towel, the hazy afternoon sun lighting her pale skin and alluring hair. My last relationship had ended a long time ago and I was unused to this kind of intimacy. I couldn't help feeling touched at how comfortable she was in my presence.

She continued, speaking enthusiastically about the woman I was going to meet. 'She's been a real godsend. When I arrived, she sorted everything out for me. I didn't even have to ask. She's had foreigners stay with her before, so she's used to dealing with us. I must've stayed there about two weeks before I got to move into my apartment. It helped me acclimatize to life here.'

'Do you think she'll be willing to talk about ghost-hunting?'

'I reckon she'll be cool about it. She's cool about most things. Just likes to talk mainly. I think one of her children was in the same year as the students who died, maybe even in the same class. So she may have some insight into all that. The other thing is, she met your predecessor.'

I sat up. 'She met Charlie?'

'I heard she invited him over for dinner.'

This was an unexpected piece of information. I'd been wondering where Charlie had stayed when he came to Izumi, who he'd talked to, what he'd done. I'd wondered whether he'd visited the high school, looked into the classrooms, met the teachers just like me. And maybe now I was about to find out.

Knowing he'd seen Sarah's host mum in the last week of his life, I was fuelled with a need to know more. The change in tone and appearance of his notes had happened with alarming suddenness, as though a particular event had ripped the ground from underneath him. What that was I didn't know. Out of respect or possibly fear, I had resisted reading the garbled notes of his final days. But what would Mrs Azuma have to say about his behaviour on the night he came to dinner?

We arrived at the Azuma residence right on time – Sarah told me this was the kind of thing Mrs Azuma appreciated. It was a large modern house on a typically quiet street at the foot of the hills. With its impressive gates and manicured traditional gardens, it stood out from the other houses. Sarah explained that Mr Azuma was rumoured to be raking it in as factory manager and Mrs Azuma had been born into one of Izumi's richest families, so by Izumi's standards they were royalty.

As we stood on the porch I was amazed to see a plaque on the door embossed with a floral pattern and bearing the legend '*Home Sweet Home*' in English. Sarah noticed my reaction and laughed.

The door swung open and Mrs Azuma appeared with a show of theatrical surprise. She was a small wiry woman with cropped hair, over-sized glasses and an irrepressible energy.

She dragged us off the porch, took our jackets and generally buzzed around like an excited child.

'Welcome, welcome,' she cried, patting me on the arm. 'You must be James.'

'Pleased to meet you. Thank you for inviting me tonight.'

Mrs Azuma clasped my hand with a powerful grip, then started pushing me towards the sitting room area. 'Come. Sit down. You must be very hungry.'

Entering the spacious sitting room the décor caught me by surprise, a weird blend of Eastern and Western furniture and artefacts. A small ancestral shrine with candles and burning incense was a feature along one wall, and this was flanked on either side by a collection of hideous porcelain dolls in glass cases. Against another wall was a kitsch red leather armchair and sofa set, beneath a beautiful classical Japanese wall-hanging. A low table in the centre of the room had been meticulously set for dinner and it was to this that Mrs Azuma led us.

'Sit,' she said, pointing the way.

Sarah nudged me in the back, enjoying the theatre of Mrs Azuma. 'Where shall we sit?'

'You sit together,' Mrs Azuma said with a twinkle in her eye, in no doubt that we were already more than just friends. Then, satisfied we were doing what she wanted, she darted out of the room.

'Wow,' I said to Sarah, 'that's one wired-up bunny.'

'It's no joke. You just have to batten down the hatches and go with the flow. Don't worry, she's pretty manic at the start of the evening, but she usually mellows out.'

'Nice display.' I pointed to the porcelain dolls, staring at us from their glass cases.

'Yeah, I know it's hard, but do say something nice about them. She got them in France and they're her pride and joy. They cost about three grand each as well.'

We sat in silence for a few moments while Mrs Azuma clattered about in the kitchen and I had a chance to take in the surroundings. It would definitely have been a lovely room, were it not for the Western tat. There were some beautiful traditional Japanese scrolls on the wall, a well-tended *bonsai* tree on the cabinet, while all the table settings were exquisite, with hand-painted lacquer bowls, carved wooden chopsticks and a bowl of floating orchid flowers as a centrepiece.

'Oh and if you could comment on those frames she'll love you forever.' Sarah gestured to a row of framed certificates on the wall. 'They're all to do with stuff her sons have done.'

'Are you ready to eat?' Mrs Azuma appeared at the door, then withdrew before we'd had a chance to answer.

'There's something else you should bear in mind. She'll feed you till you're blue in the face, so pace yourself. She's famous here for her hosting exploits.'

As soon as Sarah said this Mrs Azuma materialized in front of us and deposited an armful of plates onto the table. It was all weird and wonderful stuff and I recalled Josh joking that in Japan you never really knew what you were eating, that it was the culinary version of Russian roulette.

She plonked herself down beside us, sitting with her legs tucked underneath her in the traditional style of Japanese women, then began pointing to the different

91

dishes, explaining their contents and exhorting us to eat to our hearts' content. She also told us to bear in mind that this was only the first course, so to spare some room in our stomachs for several more. I replied by saying there was enough food in front of me to feed a small army. Getting caught up in this witty repartee, she then said her husband would be along soon and his appetite was roughly equivalent to that of a small army.

For a time, we tucked into the food and I got my first taste of seaweed salad, fried bean-curd parcels, octopus dumplings and a few things we couldn't find a translation for, including a plate of fermented soy beans which smelled rank and tasted even worse, but would apparently do our digestive systems a world of good. Mrs Azuma was an expert host, jumping up every two minutes to fetch something else, plying us with Japanese beer and offering us lessons in the correct use of chopsticks.

As we neared the end of the appetizers Mr Azuma came in from work, a quiet serious man who greeted us cordially but with no real enthusiasm. Either he'd never had any of his wife's sparkle or he'd long ago given up competing with her. Still, the poor guy had just walked in from work and the last thing he needed was to find two foreigners chowing down at his dinner table.

Having exhausted conversation about the food and how lovely it was, I decided to follow Sarah's suggestion and comment on the dolls. This succeeded in sending Mrs Azuma into overdrive as she bombarded us with details about them. And seeing her in such good spirits, I hazarded another change of conversation.

'Sarah told me that you met my predecessor, Charlie Whitehurst.'

Mrs Azuma put her cup down gravely and shook her head. 'Ah, that was very sad. He came here to do research. Like you.'

'I know. My professor told me.'

'I don't know why he came to Izumi. I don't know what he wanted to learn. I remember he asked me many difficult questions.'

Whatever Charlie's questions had been, Mrs Azuma clearly hadn't approved of them and I got the impression that, underneath her cheerful exterior, she was quick to disapprove. But I knew what a valuable source of local information she was and I was keen to take advantage. 'What kind of questions did he ask?'

She furrowed her brow and bowed her head in thought. Across the table Mr Azuma lit a cigarette and puffed on it languidly.

'He didn't ask me about the history of Izumi, about the many interesting events that have happened over the last two thousand years. He asked only about an incident that happened the year before. About Reiko, about Jun and Kanae, Hideki and Saori. My son was in the same class as those students. I knew some of them. I also knew their parents. It was difficult for me to talk about it then.'

I nodded my head sympathetically, keenly aware that I had just killed the atmosphere dead. Then I thought of Charlie in the last days of his short life, probably seated at the exact same table, trying to pick a reluctant Mrs Azuma's brain. I could understand what a delicate topic it was, but I also wondered if the lapse of time might have made it easier for Mrs Azuma to talk about it.

She continued to bow her head, as though paying her respects. 'It was such a tragedy. My eldest son is now an exchange student in America, so as a mother I know how it feels to be parted from your son.'

It seemed a good time to notch up some brownie points, so I asked about the certificates on the wall. This perked her up immediately – she sprang to her feet, went over and started pointing to each in its turn, providing a detailed commentary on the exploits of her two boys. The eldest – a genius and local celebrity – had various certificates for excellence in mathematics, judo and English conversation. His little brother – less able, but nonetheless brilliant – had mainly won plaudits for his chess-playing exploits. As I sipped my beer and listened attentively, I weighed up exactly what I could and couldn't ask, so as not to cause offence. While I was happy to hear about Izumi's ancient history, I desperately wanted to get some perspective on the high school incident from someone like Mrs Azuma, who had known all the main protagonists.

'Are you all right?' Sarah asked, when Mrs Azuma had gone to fetch the plates for the second course. 'You've gone quiet.'

'I was wondering whether I could ask the same things Charlie asked about. I don't want to piss her off.'

'You won't cause offence. She's not that easily offended. And anyway, when the other guy came it had only just happened, so the wounds were probably just a bit too fresh.'

I downed my glass of beer, thinking that if I slurred my words a little I could blame any transgressions on inebriation. I figured I'd already scored some valuable points by praising the dolls and showing an interest in the certificates.

Mrs Azuma returned shortly with another sumptuous array of dishes which must have cost a small fortune and taken the best part of a day to prepare. I exchanged a look with Sarah, embarrassed by this extravagant show of hospitality, considering I was only a passing tourist. Mrs Azuma talked us through the new arrivals, including both raw and cooked fish dishes with a selection of seasonings and dipping sauces. These were accompanied by what she referred to as the best food of all, a bowl of pure white glutinous rice.

We tucked in for a second time under our host's watchful eye, making the appropriate sounds of surprise and delight. I told Mrs Azuma that if I'd been dubious about Japanese food before, she now had a complete convert, while Sarah claimed it was the best meal she'd ever served up. Even Mr Azuma seemed to join in the general round of compliments and appreciation. Only once did I commit a social faux pas – having let my chopsticks roll off my plate for the third or fourth time, I decide to solve the problem by sticking them into my rice. This drew sharp cries of complaint from both my hosts, and Mrs Azuma patiently explained that this was something traditionally done at funerals and thus associated with death. To do it at any other time was extremely bad luck.

It was just as Mr Azuma was introducing me to the delights of Japanese *sake* that I felt bold enough to bring up the subject of ghosts at the school. I carefully laid down my chopsticks, let out a sigh of satisfaction at the succulent raw sea bream, then turned to Mrs Azuma.

'We went to visit the high school today.'

She sounded genuinely pleased for me. 'Did you meet some of the teachers?'

I could see Sarah looking at me from the corner of her eye, maybe wondering if I was going to bring up the subject of Shirakami-san. 'I met one or two. Do you know Aya, one of the English teachers?'

Mrs Azuma clapped her hands enthusiastically. 'Aya is a very nice girl. She is a good friend of Sarah's. But she is a new teacher, so I don't know her teaching style. She wasn't there when my youngest son was at the school.'

She lent forward and topped up my beer glass, which I took as a sign she might be amenable to the direction I was taking.

'I also heard some of the ghost stories,' I continued, making a point of downing my beer quickly. 'I know it might be difficult for you to talk about that subject, but it's something I'm interested in. It would be helpful for my research if you could tell me anything.'

A silence fell on the room as Mrs Azuma considered the question. After the effort she'd made in preparing the feast I knew I was taking a liberty, but I had both Sarah's assurances and a growing sense that Mrs Azuma actually wanted to talk despite her stated reluctance. Across the table, Mr Azuma dragged on his cigarette and watched his wife. Beside me, Sarah quietly took another piece of *sashimi* raw fish, dipped it in seasoning and popped it in her mouth. And from across the room the dolls watched me with beady eyes from their glass coffins.

At last Mrs Azuma lifted her head and, to my relief, gave me a pleasant smile. 'You can ask me any questions. It's okay. It happened many years ago now.'

This was what I wanted to hear. Sarah had been absolutely right about her.

'But first let's eat some more.'

More food was the last thing on my mind, but more there certainly was. No sooner had the fish plates been whisked from under our noses, than a round of succulent meat dishes appeared – fried meat, boiled meat and even, to my amazement, raw meat. Mrs Azuma had not held back and she proudly pointed to each in turn and explained what it was and how it was prepared. I could see Sarah looking horrified at the prospect of more food and Mr Azuma gave his first hearty laugh, as though to say 'look, she's gone and done it again'. But I rubbed my stomach and let her know there was ample room for whatever she had to throw at me. I only prayed there wasn't a cake tray to follow.

'How about this?' she said, pointing a little mischievously to the raw meat. 'You like raw meat?'

'I like raw fish. I didn't know you also ate raw meat.'

'This is special beef,' she said, pointing to a beautiful arrangement of blood-red pieces. 'And this is horse meat.'

'Horse meat,' Sarah exclaimed. 'You can't eat that.'

'It's very good,' Mr Azuma cried, virtually his first contribution of the evening.

'I'm certainly not touching it,' Sarah said, taking the easy option of some fried chicken.

'I'll try,' I said and, taking a piece, dipped it into my bowl of soy and put it in my mouth, eliciting a round of applause from my hosts. It didn't taste too bad, just like a very rare steak without the seared bit. I even decided to further endear myself by ducking in for more. I had read the rules of guest etiquette in my guidebook and these included being a good sport and trying everything your host offers you.

'I think you're mad,' Sarah said, making her disapproval known and causing further hilarity for the hosts.

With a belly full of raw horse meat and full pitcher of beer before me, I settled down to hear Mrs Azuma's take on the darkest period in the history of Izumi high school. I'd thought I might have to work hard for small titbits, but in the end she spoke willingly and at length. She told me that the school and village had been alive with rumour in the week after Reiko disappeared. She had been a very beautiful girl, the object of many boys' desires and the most popular theory had her eloping with an older man. However, she was also secretive and none of her friends knew of any liaisons. According to Mrs Azuma's son, Kenji, many boys were in love with her, but Reiko didn't appear to be interested in anyone. Kenji also said – and I was surprised that Mrs Azuma told me this – that some of the teachers were in love with her. One of them was even taken in for questioning by the police. Then an itinerant man, who occasionally passed through the village, was found in possession of Reiko's bloodstained scarf. He protested his innocence, claiming he didn't know how it came to be in his bag, but with a list of prior convictions to his name and no one to come to his defence, he was tried, found guilty and handed the death sentence. Mrs Azuma then said that she, like almost everyone else in the village, had serious doubts as to his guilt. He protested his innocence to the end and offered no clues as to what he'd done with the body.

He had been taken into custody seven days after Reiko's disappearance. Another seven days later Jun Takada and Kanae Kubota, two of Reiko's closest friends, were found dead at the school. According to Kenji, they often met up at school after hours and would leave a window open so they could sneak in and see one another. Both their parents disapproved of the liaison, so it was the only way they could meet. No one, including the police, knew whether it was a murder investigation or a lovers' suicide pact. However, they were found in separate places, one at the bottom of the steps by the main entrance, one on the forecourt after a plunge from the third floor. According to Kenji, they had not been themselves for a while after Reiko's death, so a popular theory in class had them arguing, with Jun pushing Kanae down the steps and accidentally killing her. Then, wracked by guilt and grief, he had returned to his classroom and leapt to his death.

Mrs Azuma was well into her stride, speaking gravely but animatedly, filling me in on plenty of incidental detail just as Sarah had predicted. She stopped only to offer everyone more beer before continuing with her tragic tale.

The police eventually settled on the suicide explanation, but most people believed that this was more for convenience's sake, seeing that their man was already behind bars. But then less than a week later another of Reiko's friends, Hideki Sano, was killed on the expressway. Kenji said that he'd been extremely depressed after the deaths of his friends, though he insisted to everyone that Jun and Kanae had not committed suicide. And few people could believe that he, out of all of them, would kill himself. The accident happened at nine o'clock at night, on the expressway, just outside the village. The driver of the truck claimed that one minute the road was clear, the next minute he had hit someone full on. He couldn't say if Hideki had jumped or been pushed, although a potential assassin would have had an easy escape route into the hills. He'd apparently told his parents that he was going for a walk, although, intriguingly, they had sworn that they'd heard voices in his room just prior to that. Most people who knew Hideki refused to believe that he could have jumped.

Just under a week later, the fourth in this grim sequence of deaths occurred. Saori Kumano had been Reiko's closest friend and confidante and she was found dead in her bedroom with the window broken and the skin on her arms ripped to shreds by the broken glass. It was certainly a violent death, but once again there was no firm proof that she had been helped along. The widespread belief was that she had been trying to escape from somebody and had tried to use the window as an escape route. But she had been alone in the house at the time and no one had heard her cry out. The official verdict was suicide.

After her death, school was suspended for several weeks and many families moved away, fearing further calamities. The village had never really returned to normal, Mrs Azuma added plaintively. She sighed and poured herself a glass of *sake*.

'What about your son? How did he cope?' I asked after a pause.

She brightened a little. 'He was fine. He was a very confident boy. He tried to cheer the other students up. It was very difficult for everyone and it was very disruptive for Kenji's education. Maybe if it hadn't been for that incident, he might have done better in his exams and gone to a better university.'

I hazarded another question. 'Did he ever mention seeing ghosts in the school?'

Mrs Azuma shook her head. 'No ghosts. Now the students at the school can make up stories about ghosts. It is four years since the incident happened. Most of them didn't know the students involved.'

'So you haven't heard any stories?'

'I'm a scientist. I have no interest in such things.'

Mrs Azuma had given me more insight than I'd expected into the grim details of the students' deaths, but would not be drawn on the subject of ghosts. I wondered if this reluctance was down to the same superstitious fears that had prevented Shinichi and Etsuko being drawn on the subject, the fear that there were ghostly listeners in the shadows waiting to catch her unawares. Somehow I couldn't quite believe it of Mrs Azuma.

I decided I should lay my cards firmly on the table. 'The main reason I came to Japan was to investigate Japanese attitudes to the paranormal. So far people have been reluctant to talk about these things.'

Mrs Azuma flashed me a conciliatory smile, as though to assure me she understood my dilemma. 'I'm sorry. It's a difficult subject for many Japanese.'

I nodded, resolving to leave the matter there. I still wasn't sure if I was being insensitive or not. I got the impression she wanted to talk, but first needed to go through the motions of appearing reluctant. Once she'd started on the story of the tragedy at the school, she'd talked for twenty minutes straight without the slightest inhibition.

She began to gather up the plates, asking us if we still had room for dessert and generally returning to her cheerful self. We explained that we were fit to burst and she took this as a compliment.

Then, as she was about to leave the room with an armful of plates, she turned and said 'There's something I remember about your friend.'

I assumed by 'my friend' she was referring to Charlie. 'Yes?'

She furrowed her brow, her voice solemn. 'He told me he'd seen a ghost in Izumi. He sat there where you're sitting and told me he saw the ghost of Reiko Shimura walking towards him along the road.'

'How are you feeling?'

We were standing in Sarah's kitchen, watching the kettle boil. 'Bloody full,' I said.

'I did warn you, she doesn't do restraint.'

'I felt a bit like an animal, eating all that meat dripping with blood.'

'How did you eat that raw horse meat? I bet you only did it to butter her up.'

'She's your host mum. What choice did I have?'

Sarah laughed. 'I don't remember anything in the etiquette books about being offered horse meat. I think it's one of those things they wheel out to frighten foreigners.'

I took the kettle off the hob and poured it into a pot with green tea leaves. I fancied the stuff as a night cap, even though Sarah assured me it contained almost as much caffeine as black tea and was guaranteed to keep me awake. 'I can't work out if she's frightened to talk about ghosts or if it's something else.'

'I don't think the woman's frightened of anything, so it's probably something else. Remember, it's not a normal thing to go around asking people about ghosts. Not everyone's comfortable with that kind of thing. And if you asked me now for a ghost story I knew, I couldn't tell you one off the top of my head. I'd at least have to go away and think about it. It's a weird subject.'

Sarah was right. Maybe I was expecting too much of Mrs Azuma. She'd spent the day slaving over a stove to create a sumptuous dinner for me and I was trying to pick her brains about the ghosts of her son's friends. Time to take a rain check.

'Don't worry. Tomorrow, I'll show you a few more sights.' She retreated to her room with a cup of camomile tea and I retreated to mine, even though there was only a flimsy sliding screen separating us.

For a while I lay there completely still, listening to her movements and her breathing. I saw her light go off and heard the rustle of her bedclothes and I couldn't repress the first pangs of desire, the reawakening of emotions I'd buried deep inside me. I knew she was just a naturally friendly person and it'd be wrong to confuse her hospitality with anything deeper. I'd spent most of my life misinterpreting signals and I was determined not to go down that road again.

But sleep didn't come easily. I felt the food churning in my stomach, a colourful cocktail of dark green seaweed, white sea bream and blood-red horse meat. And everything Mrs Azuma had described came back to visit me: visions of Jun and Kanae making their last fateful tryst, of Hideki seeing the lights of a truck bearing down on him and of Saori cutting her wrists on the broken window pane. The only thing I could not see was whether they died alone or whether they had company. Then other figures appeared, gatecrashing my rest. Yoshi, showing me how to insert a banknote into a drinks machine; Charlie, fresh laceration marks around his neck, bent over his file, scribbling furiously; Professor Atami, waggling his finger at me, giving me a stern rebuke for embarking on this journey against his advice; and Shirakami-san, sitting alone in a dark classroom, brooding on the deaths of his students.

No, sleep didn't come easily that night.

Izumi High Revisited

In a dream, I found myself standing at night in the deserted forecourt of Izumi high school. The bright moon cast a silvery pall over the scene. In front of the school building a line of cherry trees were shedding their snow-white blossom. I didn't know what had brought me there, but I looked up instinctively to the windows of the third-floor classrooms. There in the third window along I saw the figure of a schoolgirl, clear in the light of the moon. She was dressed in a sailor uniform and her ghostly pale face looked out at me. Then she turned from the window and was gone.

My feet took me forward, towards the main entrance where I paused to look up at the clock. It was two o'clock. I pushed open the door and went through to the main hall, then stopped in front of the flight of steps to my left. I didn't know what I was doing or where I was going, but something pulled me towards those steps. Looking down I saw I was standing in a pool of liquid, reflecting the silvery moonlight. I didn't stop to check, but I knew very well that it was blood.

I made my way up slowly, leaving a trail of bloody footprints in my wake. At the top of the steps a sudden sound stopped me in my tracks. I strained to hear and there, unmistakably, was the sound of a girl laughing close by. A gentle, teasing laugh, drawing me on.

I peered down the first floor corridor, saw that it was in darkness, then turned to face the second flight of steps. As I did so I saw, for the briefest of moments, a flash of sailor uniform at the top of the steps, appear and disappear into the shadows. I didn't know who it was, but I knew I had to follow.

I continued on up to the second floor, where I heard the same sound of laughter, only this time it was followed by the sound of a boy laughing. The girl was not alone. I glanced behind me and saw that my bloodstained footprints were still clear on the steps, reflecting the moonlight.

I didn't stop at the second floor corridor, but continued on upwards. I knew where I was going now. As I neared the third floor, the sound of laughter was closer and more distinct and, looking up, I saw, framed in the window at the top of steps, a boy and a girl in uniform. They stood there for an instant, their faces in shadow, watching me, then turned tail and ran, as though playing a game of catch with me.

I reached the third floor and looked down the corridor to see a single shaft of moonlight from an open doorway piercing the darkness further down. I knew already which door was open and, as I started down the corridor, I heard the sound of excited laughter. I assumed they had hidden themselves in the classroom and were waiting to be found.

As I neared the classroom, the laughter stopped and I had a sinking feeling in my gut. I picked up my pace.

The room was empty. No desks, no chairs, no signs of life. Only a few shards of glass lying on the floor by the window, where one of the window panes had been shattered. I hurried over, my feet crunching on the broken glass, my stomach turning somersaults. I leaned out and saw below, on the forecourt, two lifeless bodies, a young girl and a young boy. I felt the tears welling up inside me, tears of anger and sorrow for these two lives *cut down in their prime. Cherry blossoms, catching the moonlight, fluttered about their broken bodies, gracing them with a poetic valediction.*

I turned and slumped to the floor, clenching my fists and sobbing loudly. Then another feeling took hold: the feeling that I was not alone, that someone was observing me from the doorway. I looked up quickly, but the figure retreated into the shadows before I could properly see it. But my heart was too heavy to go in pursuit. I just sat there, amidst the scattered shards of glass, alone and full of sorrow.

AYA

The sorrow was still with me when I awoke.

The morning sun streamed into the room through the blind, promising another beautiful day. In spite of this I didn't feel well. I had a splitting headache and my stomach was still heavy after the evening's indulgence. Then there was the dream. Perhaps it was made vivid by the rich food I'd eaten. Or perhaps it was the lurid tale Mrs Azuma had told me. But I could still see my bloodstained steps in the moonlight, hear the sound of laughter, taste the salty tears I'd cried. The image of the two doomed lovers lying lifeless on the school fore-court beneath a flurry of cherry blossoms was one I couldn't dispel.

I stirred myself and resolved to concentrate my efforts on my task in hand: documenting attitudes to supernatural phenomena. I had to make more effort to keep an emotional distance from those tragic events at the high school.

Sarah was sitting cross-legged on the floor of her room, listening to Allegri's *Miserere* with a burning incense stick and a cup of coffee. She wore a beautiful white silk dressing gown and smiled when I appeared at the door.

'Hungover?'

'Is it that obvious?'

'Yeah, pretty much. Who cares, you're on holiday.'

I lowered myself onto the floor and breathed out heavily, trying to steady myself.

'Are you sure you're all right?'

I definitely wasn't sure. I took a few deep breaths, drinking in the fresh air from the open window. 'Have you got any aspirin?'

'I'll just get you some.' She got up to go to the kitchen then stopped at the door. 'You were pretty noisy in the night.'

'Noisy?'

She went into the kitchen and started rummaging about. 'Yeah, you were moaning,' she called.

'Moaning?' I felt I could only muster one word at a time.

She reappeared at the door with the aspirin. 'Yeah. I remember sharing a room once with this girl who did the same thing. I asked her what it was and she told me she was wrestling with the devil in her sleep. Said she did it all the time.'

I smiled. 'I wasn't wrestling with the devil. At least, I don't think I was.' I decided against telling Sarah about my dream for the time being.

'Well, that's a relief.' She handed me the aspirin and stretched her arms. 'What you need is some clean, fresh air. There's no hangover cure like it.'

She was right. But there was more in my head than just a headache. Something darker and more pernicious had taken root and I was powerless to fight it.

When Sarah told me she'd arranged for Aya to join us to do a little sightseeing, I was unable to suppress a broad smile. Sarah accused me of being no different to her other legion of panting admirers, then let me off because I was hungover.

'She's a pretty girl. If I were a man, I'd fancy her,' she said as we drove towards our meeting place, the local Seven-Eleven convenience store.

'Maybe outside of school, she'll be able to talk more freely. When we were in the grounds yesterday, she kept looking across at the building, as though it were keeping tabs on her.'

'You're probably right. She's always a bit more chatty outside school. Even likes to slag off the other teachers.'

We drove into the Seven-Eleven forecourt, where a row of bikes were neatly parked outside the shop front.

'This is where the local kids like to hang out,' Sarah said. 'It's kind of the focal point of village social life, sad as that sounds.'

We got out of the car and made our way into the shop, where a gaggle of schoolgirls descended upon us, giggling excitedly and pulling at Sarah's sleeve. There were five of them, maybe fifteen or sixteen years old, dolled up for the occasion, a blur of sparkly make-up and handbags. They all spoke at once with a mixture of Japanese and pidgin English and the only thing I recognized with any certainty was the long drawn-out cry of '*Seeera-sensei*'.

'These are some of my first years,' Sarah said above the din. 'I think they want to be introduced to you.'

The next thing I knew I was shaking their hands, saying my name and having it repeated back to me with an enthusiasm I was unaccustomed to. The next word that stood out amidst the chattering was '*boyfriend*', to which Sarah shook her head emphatically. Undeterred, they turned their attention to me, asking in a harmony of perfect *Japlish*, whether I had designs on their teacher, to which I answered 'no', though if I'd had the time and a less impatient audience, I might have qualified this slightly. No matter, they didn't seem to believe either of us and, after a little more harmless banter, left the store, giggling furiously as they went.

'Sorry about that,' Sarah said, as the dust settled. 'They're good girls. Just a little excitable.'

'They're not the ones who told you about the ghosts?'

She shook her head. 'I think that lot are more interested in boys than ghosts. Or English lessons for that matter.'

The door swung open and Aya appeared, a vision in blue jeans and white T-shirt, her face lit up with a smile.

'They're all talking about you outside,' she said.

Through the window I could see them standing around their bikes, looking towards us and gossiping excitedly. 'They think I'm Sarah's boyfriend.'

'Yes, they say you're very handsome.'

Sarah playfully locked her arm through mine. 'So they think I've done well then?'

Aya giggled. 'They say you make a beautiful couple.'

That was too much for me, and I felt my cheeks burn. God knows I tried to fight it, but blushing had always been a problem for me.

Aya insisted on driving us. As a Japanese person, she said she felt responsible for showing her foreign friends around. 'We're all ambassadors for our country,' she added, motioning out of the window with a theatrical sweep of the arm.

As we started out, I asked what had brought her to Izumi. She told me she was originally from Yokohama, but had come to study at Tohoku University, Fukushima Prefecture's most prestigious seat of learning. It had always been her intention to get back to the Greater Tokyo area, but somehow she had got stuck in a backwater. It reminded me of what Sarah had told me of the Japanese attitude towards the countryside. When she referred to it as 'a backwater', she really meant it. There was no point me harping on about clean air and birds singing in the hedgerows. This was no place for a young Japanese woman. 'I'm not getting any younger,' she said matter-of-factly as the car headed towards the hills.

Now that we had left houses and factories behind, the profusion of blossom suddenly struck me. If anything was going to cure my hangover and dodgy stomach, then it was the experience of passing beneath an avenue of cherry blossom trees. But these weren't just cherry trees we were passing. Soon Aya was reeling off names with the practiced nonchalance of an expert. Plum blossom, apple blossom, pear blossom, almond blossom. 'It's the kind of thing we had to learn at school,' she said. 'The names of trees, the names of flowers. There's always been an emphasis on nature vocabulary in Japanese schools.'

I may not have known the names of the trees in blossom, but I could certainly appreciate their beauty. And they seemed to grow in profusion as we reached our destination, Izumi *Jinja*, the village's main Shinto shrine, hidden deep in the hills. It was a peaceful site, removed from village life and, according to Aya, largely unvisited. She readily confessed that it had never occurred to her to visit it before.

We parked the car on the quiet path leading to the shrine and made our way towards a steep set of steps, overgrown with weeds and moss. At the foot of the steps two stone foxes stood like sentries one on either side, guarding the shrine. On the way up Aya explained to us that Shinto was the native religion of Japan and that, unlike Buddhism, which was a foreign import, had no scripture or dogma. She described it as a nature religion incorporating a profusion of gods and used mainly for ceremonial occasions. I asked what religion people adhered to and she replied that Shinto and Buddhism co-existed quite happily. There was no contradiction in taking on aspects of both religions, but people just weren't religious in the sense we understood in the West.

We got to the top of the steps and I was faced with a kind of giant stone wishing well, covered over with a wooden pagoda. The whole structure was old and dilapidated, but this somehow added to the atmosphere of the place. Aya went over to the water and, clapping her hands together, offered up a prayer.

'When do people come here?'

Aya shook her head. 'I don't know. Maybe if they want to make a wish or offer a prayer for the dead.'

Looking round there was little sign that the place was ever visited. Standing there with Aya and Sarah and only the sound of the wind for company, we could have been the only people in the world. For some reason I thought of Rip van Winkle going into the woods and emerging a hundred years later. I looked over at Sarah and Aya, who both seemed lost in their own thoughts.

'There is a ghost story about this place,' Aya said suddenly, turning to me.

We crouched down in the shadow of the pagoda and Aya told us the story.

'During the war the women of the village would come up here to offer prayers for their sons or husbands who were serving abroad in the imperial army. Often they never got word of whether their loved ones were alive or dead, but they continued to come to the shrine and offer up prayers. Then one day a mother came up here after dark, only finding her way by the light of fireflies. There at the top of the steps she met her son, wearing his army uniform, but with a terrible wound on his neck. He told her he had been struck down on a battlefield in some foreign country and would not be returning. When she began to cry, he comforted her by saying she could return to the shrine after dark on any day and he would always be there waiting for her. And so she did. Until the end of her life she came up here every night, even in the rain or the snow, to meet with her dead son.'

Neither Sarah nor I spoke for a while. Aya had such a beautiful manner that it was hard not to be moved by the story.

'It's strange,' I said. 'Before I came to Izumi my Professor told me that Japanese ghosts – *yurei*, he called them – tend to be of a certain type. They are young, female and out for revenge. But the ghost you're describing is not just male, but friendly.'

'How can you say that *yurei* are all the same type?' Aya said abruptly. 'Different people see different *yurei*.'

I tried to cover my tracks. 'I'm only repeating what I was told. I'm happy to hear all sorts of stories. There's another unusual thing about that story. As far as I know, ghosts in all cultures are supposed to be location-specific. So, in theory, they're not meant to travel well. If they die in a certain spot, they tend to haunt that spot. This ghost seems to have crossed continents.'

'Maybe if the emotional bond is strong enough,' Aya said quietly, so as not to disturb any ghostly listeners, 'they can travel.'

I could see Sarah looking at us in amusement. 'So this travelling thing is all scientific fact, is it?'

'Not so much fact, as an amalgamation of experiences.' I knew even before I'd said it that Sarah wasn't going to let it pass and, sure enough, she burst out laughing. I'm not sure if Aya had understood, but she followed Sarah's lead and laughed along. I tried to maintain some decorum as we were on hallowed ground, but I gave in and joined them. Even if it was a stupid subject, at least I could say my choice of thesis had provoked a good laugh.

Izumi castle was predictably small in scale compared to its counterpart in Osaka, and like that castle, had been demolished and rebuilt in concrete within the last century. Still, it had a certain presence, perched upon a hillock, stately-white with a pagoda-like roof. There were more ghostly associations as Aya discovered in the explanatory pamphlet. Apparently during its original construction in the mists of the feudal era the builders decided that, for good luck, a young woman should be buried alive within the walls. How they arrived at this decision or who the lucky woman was, the pamphlet didn't tell. It explained simply that the unfortunate victim became an unhappy ghost and had haunted numerous inhabitants of the castle.

This was more familiar territory for me. Young, female ghost with good reason to be pissed off, wreaking havoc on the living. I insisted that we take the full tour.

Inside it wasn't that spectacular. A few exhibits of samurai armour and headgear, with a collection of swords and early muskets. But the real story of the castle and the one for which it became famous throughout Japan, occurred in 1870, in the early years of the Meiji era. The local lord, a man by the name of Wakamatsu, refused to yield his title and came under siege from imperial forces. Rather than give himself up, he committed ritual suicide, but not before butchering his entire retinue of servants, as well as his wife and children. Notwithstanding the brutality of this act, his uncompromising attitude won him great admiration in the country at large.

We followed the events of that fateful day in a sequence of prints around the wall, a kind of Japanese Bayeux tapestry, which ended with a grim depiction of the aftermath of his heroism: the rooms of the castle strewn with twisted corpses and severed body parts. Aya and Sarah made their excuses at this point, while I lingered in front of this last print, trying to fathom what would move a human being to act in this way. I wondered if the ghost of the woman in the wall had anything to do with it, whether Wakamatsu was acting on voices heard in the air, whispered to him while he slept, feeding him thoughts of foul and bloody murder.

We left the castle and its dark history behind and made our way through acre upon acre of farmland to see the strange and wonderful burial mounds. I had read about them both in Charlie's notes and my own guidebook: a collection of thirty or forty grassy mounds, ranging from fifty feet in diameter to a few hundred. I knew there was no other place like it in Japan or indeed anywhere else in the world. Here was evidence of Izumi's greatest mystery. How did it become such a centre for the construction of burial mounds? Was it just a fortuitous accident? Did people really believe that the gateway to the next world was to be found in Izumi? Or, as the Buddhist monk believed, the gateway to hell?

Whatever the answer, the tumuli were impressive to behold. It was hard to imagine that by the seventh century, when the arrival of Buddhism put an end to their construction, the entire village was covered with them. That would have been quite a sight. For a while, the three of us sat in the car, staring at them through the window in silence.

'I wonder who's buried there,' Sarah said.

'No one knows. There are no records.' Aya opened the car door to get out.

'I suppose you have to assume that the more important your status, the bigger your hillock,' Sarah said, following Aya's suit and getting out of the car.

We started walking around the mounds. It was incredible to think that these grassy tombs, some of which rose to twenty feet, had stood there for fifteen centuries with almost no erosion to speak of. I wondered what they had found when, over the centuries, they'd gradually razed them to the ground. Fully-formed skeletons? Funereal artefacts? Everyday objects the deceased might find useful in the afterlife in the style of the Egyptian tombs? I couldn't remember Charlie going into detail on ancient burial practices and, when I put the question to Aya, she didn't know either.

For a while we lingered in that strange graveyard and I couldn't deny its power and majesty. It made me realize why Izumi was special, why it attracted thousands of visitors every year and why I had followed in Charlie's footsteps on this bizarre pilgrimage. And the idea that the destruction of so many of these mounds over time could have awoken some dark spirit now seemed more compelling.

'Is it all right to walk on them?' Sarah asked, breaking the spell. 'In England you're not supposed to walk on a person's grave. It upsets them.'

Aya seemed a little bemused by this titbit, but accepted it with a polite nod. As to whether we could walk on them or not, she didn't say.

'Have you heard any legends or stories about this place?' I asked.

Aya smiled. 'Actually, for Izumi, it's quite a peaceful place. In fact it's famous for fireflies. In the summer they come here in such big numbers that the whole area is lit up. No one knows why they come here in particular, but they say if you stand in the hills at night and look down over the village, everywhere will be dark except for this place. They say it's as bright as a football stadium under floodlights.'

We ate lunch in a traditional inn in the hills. We had our own little *tatami* mat room with good views from the window. There we removed our shoes and sat cross-legged at a low table. A little old lady in a silk kimono served us a set menu of clear soup and an assortment of traditional delicacies, some of which even Aya had trouble identifying. She excused herself by saying she was a city girl by upbringing and was un-educated in country cuisine. Both food and presen-tation were first class, but somehow I couldn't muster an appetite. Though my headache had eased after the morning's activities, my tummy was still feeling the effects of Mrs Azuma's hospitality.

For most of the meal we chatted amiably about Aya's time studying in the States, swapped stories on cultural misunderstandings and took lessons in bowing etiquette. Keep your eyes on the floor, not on the person, and the more important they are, the lower you bow. As we expected Aya was far more relaxed outside of the workplace. It was no wonder that the male teachers at the school queued up for her company. She was lively, witty and had note-perfect English. Sarah seemed almost subdued by comparison.

But it was Sarah who eventually brought up the subject of the high school tragedy. I had resolved not to mention it, having cast a pall over enough conver-sations during my short time in Izumi. And now that the protagonists were invading my dreams, it was time to take a step back and get some perspective. It had never been my intention to awaken Sarah's interest in the distressing events.

She waited for a lull in the conversation, then put down her chopsticks and waded in with a loaded question. 'Are you suspicious of any of the teachers at the school?'

Aya took a moment, carefully weighing up the question. 'Suspicious, how?'

'I can't stop thinking about what happened yester-day, seeing Shirakami-san in the room. Then, last night, we were eating at Mrs Azuma's house – you know her, don't you? – and she was talking about what happened. I know you can't really talk about it in school, but I just wanted to know if there's anyone I should be careful about.'

Aya looked round, as though considering how thin the walls were, or whether someone could be standing on the other side of the sliding screen door, listening. 'It's a difficult question.'

'It's not because I want to hear all the gossip, because I don't. I don't even know most of the teachers, beyond saying "hello" in the morning.'

Aya still seemed to be wrestling with her conscience. This went beyond the usual office gossip about illicit romance and other personal peccadilloes. Sarah was asking about one of the darkest episodes in modern Japanese history.

'You don't have to say anything,' Sarah said, touching Aya on the arm.

'There have always been rumours,' Aya said suddenly. 'Ever since I arrived at the school, I've heard rumours. No one says anything directly. That's not the Japanese way and this subject is too serious. But you come to understand what people are thinking.'

'Are there any rumours you believe?' Sarah asked.

'No,' Aya said, without hesitation. 'I don't think any of the teachers are capable of anything so horrible. But that's my opinion. Of course there were other teachers, who left before I arrived. I can't make any comment about them.'

Sarah seemed relieved. 'I completely agree. I think you'd know if you were faced with a murderer.'

We sat in silence for a few minutes, sipping our green tea and gazing out of the window at the blossom trees dotting the hills and woods around the inn. Sitting up there on a peaceful afternoon, the warm spring air floating in through the bamboo blind, it was hard to believe that the village could have seen so much brutality. Hard to believe that evil could have ever taken such deep root there.

Aya had clearly been reflecting on what Sarah had said. 'I don't know much about this kind of thing, but there's one peculiarity I've noticed about murder cases in Japan. When the murderer is named, he is often a very ordinary person. Sometimes, he has a respectable job and a family. Even in very brutal cases, he is polite and well-mannered and is very sorry for what he has done. There is no outward sign of what is going on in his head. When I saw cases in America, there were always clues. The murderer had a history of violence and abuse, he lived on his own, was aggressive to people and had clear behavioural problems. You saw their photographs in the newspaper and you could see the evil in their eyes. In Japan it's different.'

'So you're saying it might be difficult to spot a killer.'

Aya nodded. 'Not that I've ever met one. At least, I hope I haven't. What I mean is, there may not be any obvious signs.' She stopped, thinking her thesis through. 'Although I'd guess there would be some clues.'

'What about the teachers?' Sarah asked.

It was the question Aya had been trying to avoid by hinting that everyone was a potential suspect. She sighed. 'Well, there is Shirakami-san. I've already told you about him. He was the students' homeroom teacher. Until it happened he was a very popular teacher and now he walks around like a ghost and sits on his own in their old classroom.'

'His behaviour might be weird, but I can't say he's threatening,' Sarah said.

Aya nodded in agreement. 'Numata-san was their English teacher. He's never spoken about the incident to me, but he never speaks to me about anything. Apart from English lessons.'

'He's married though, isn't he?'

'Divorced. His wife left him ten years ago.'

Sarah looked genuinely shocked. 'But he told me about his wife just the other day.'

'I know. I only heard about it from one of the other teachers. He still acts as though he's still married. It may be a cultural thing. Divorce isn't as common in Japan, so he may be ashamed.'

I remembered that Numata-san had been pointed out to me briefly in the staffroom. He might have been in need of a fashion makeover, but he didn't have the air of a serial killer. On the other hand, if Aya's theory were correct that might not be necessary.

'I can't believe he wouldn't tell me he isn't married anymore. Like I care whether he's married or not.' Sarah folded her arms in annoyance.

Aya took a deep breath, as though she needed the oxygen to continue.

'Then there's Odagiri-san, the chemistry teacher.'

I wasn't sure if she was just systematically listing the teachers, or actually naming potential suspects.

'He's quite creepy,' Sarah said.

'They say he was in love with Reiko.' Aya's voice dropped to a whisper and she leaned forward, leaving us in no doubt that she was talking about a prime suspect. 'Odagiri-san used to talk to Reiko after lessons and sometimes he would offer to walk her home after school. He tried to be like a father to her, but I've heard that she found him annoying. Shortly before she disappeared, she even started receiving anonymous flowers left on her doorstep. They couldn't find out who sent the flowers, but some people say it was Odagiri-san.'

'I thought that most of the boys were in love with Reiko. So it could have been anyone,' Sarah said.

Aya nodded emphatically. 'I don't know what evidence they had against Odagiri-san. I know he was taken in for questioning by the police, because he had been one of the last people to see her before she disappeared. They found love letters from many boys in Reiko's bedroom, but I think it's unlikely there were any from Odagiri-san.'

Aya ran through a few more teachers past and present over the next half hour, while Sarah listened intently and chipped in occasionally with observations. Not knowing the characters, it was hard to form opinions about these people, but it was clear that in the absence of a credible suspect, everyone came under suspicion. It seemed that almost every man or boy who'd known her had come under her spell, and all had been turned away the same as the last. I thought of her picture, her chiselled features and searing eyes. And I was sure that whatever had happened to the other four students, Reiko was the key to the mystery.

It was late in the afternoon by the time we paid our bill, gave thanks to the kimono-clad serving lady and traded slippers in for shoes. The other customers were long gone and we realized the entire establishment had been patiently waiting for us to finish up.

Aya didn't know if there was any sightseeing left to do in Izumi, but thought it might benefit our religious education if we saw a Buddhist cemetery. I agreed that now we'd seen the Shinto shrine, it was only right that we should see a temple belonging to Japan's other national religion. Apparently there was no Buddhist temple in Izumi, only a cemetery. Aya explained that while the Christian tradition preferred to have church and graveyard in the same plot, the two were usually separate in the Buddhist tradition. This sounded like a useful area to look into for my thesis and I made a mental note to research it further.

Izumi's cemetery was tucked just out of sight behind a bend in the hill, and could not be seen from the village. Accessible enough to be part of the community, but not so obvious as to provide a constant reminder of human mortality. Not being a local girl, it was Aya's first visit to the place. I asked her how often people came to visit the graves of their friends and relatives and she told me that New Year's Day was the traditional time for paying a visit. She added plaintively that she couldn't remember the last time she'd visited her own relatives' graves. I assured her that neither could I.

Aya stopped the car at the foot of the hill and we gazed up at an entire area of hillside covered with identical grey stone slabs. Given that cremation was the norm, the grave plots were small, only a few square feet each, just enough space for an urn of ashes, a wire grille for the flowers and a headstone. The hillside was arranged in tiers to allow visitors access to the graves further up, giving the effect of a terrace at a sports stadium. It was a strange experience seeing the graves sandwiched so close together. Whereas the Christian dead could usually look forward to a little space, at least enough to stretch their legs, as well as an ample blanket of moss or grass for warmth, there was no such luxury here. Your ashes sat snug against the next person's.

We sat in the car for a while, while Aya gave us some handy tips on graveyard etiquette. None of us really felt the need to get out of the car and walk among the graves. Though my parents had dragged me round many a country churchyard in my youth, enthusiastically reading the headstones, I'd always considered it a morbid pastime. We could see all we needed to without opening a car door.

The place was completely deserted except for one middle aged man, making his way down the steps in the centre.

It was Aya who reacted first, with a sharp intake of breath. I was about to ask what it was when I heard the exact same sound from Sarah in the back seat. The man was balding and paunchy and appeared preoccupied as he reached the bottom of the steps. He turned away quickly, not once looking towards us, and made his way to a car parked nearby. We watched him in silence.

'Who is it?' I whispered.

'Odagiri-san,' Aya said.

'What's he doing here?' Sarah asked. 'Visiting relatives?'

'He's from Tokyo,' Aya replied in a low voice. 'He has no relatives here.'

We watched as Odagiri-san's car pulled away and drove off. Aya opened the door and got out, visibly upset by this chance sighting, and Sarah and I followed suit.

'So whose grave was he visiting?' Sarah asked.

Without responding, Aya started off towards the central steps, on a mission. She trotted up, taking two steps at a time, the first time all day I'd seen her in a hurry.

'Do you think we should follow?' Sarah asked.

I couldn't honestly answer, but curiosity got the better of us and we took off in pursuit.

I saw Aya reach a tier half way up the hillside and make her way along the row of headstones, examining them as she passed. Halfway along, she found the stone she was looking for and stopped, staring down at it with folded arms.

We caught up with her and looked down at the simple grey slab, bearing a short inscription in Japanese characters. In front of the slab was a fresh bouquet of white flowers.

We stood there in silence for several moments, unsure whether to disturb Aya's thoughts.

'Chrysanthemums,' Aya said at last, pointing at the bouquet. 'Chrysanthemums are said to ward off evil spirits.'

'Whose grave is this?' I asked, although I was sure I already knew the answer.

'It's not a grave. It's a commemorative stone. After all, she was never found,' she said in a deadpan voice. 'Shimura Reiko's stone,' she whispered, giving the family name first in the Japanese fashion.

'Are we sure this was the one he was visiting?' Sarah asked.

Aya knelt down and lifted the flower to show their stems still moist. It was obvious they'd just been placed there. 'As we drove up I saw him standing up here.'

Both Aya and Sarah were silent as we walked back towards the car. Now we knew that Odagiri-san, the teacher who had allegedly had a crush on Reiko and had even been taken in for questioning over her disappearance, was also leaving flowers at her grave. It was hard to know what to make of it. On the one hand there was nothing wrong with a teacher visiting the grave of a student he had been close to. But given the circumstances of her disappearance and the suspicions levelled against him, it did seem an odd thing to do. Of course, bringing flowers to a grave in full daylight was not the action of a guilty man and I said as much to Aya and Sarah. In any case, since her body had never been discovered, it was hardly a grave at all.

Back at the car Aya and Sarah began to discuss what we should do next. I was about to say something when my blood turned to ice.

As I glanced casually at the car window I saw reflected there, standing amidst the graves on the hill, the figure of a schoolgirl.

For a few seconds I didn't move. There it was, as clear to me as the sky above: the figure of a schoolgirl, dressed in a sailor uniform, with a crimson ribbon tied in the middle, her face turned down and in shadow.

I spun round to look, but she was gone. The hillside was empty.

I reached for the bonnet of the car, unsteady on my feet. I knew what I'd just seen. It hadn't been a trick of the light. Had it come to this already, that I was hallucinating in broad daylight?

'What's the matter?' Sarah asked, coming over. 'You're white as a sheet.'

It took me a moment to regain my balance. Both Sarah and Aya were looking at me with concern, but I couldn't take my eyes off the spot where I had seen the figure.

Finally, with trembling voice, I said: 'I think it's something I ate.'

'Do you need anything?' Aya asked.

I shook my head. I didn't know what I needed. I just wanted to know what it was I'd seen. I lent on the bonnet and took a few deep breaths, trying to pull myself together, if only for the sake of my companions. The last thing I wanted was for them to think I was a head-case.

I tried to banish the image from my mind, but it was there, scratched onto my retina in indelible ink.

And there was no doubt in my mind that the apparition I had seen was Reiko.

Do You Believe?

'Will you tell me what it is?'

I was sitting with Sarah on the floor of her room, watching the last embers of the sun dissipate over the hills. She had lit some scented candles and put her Gregorian chant on to create a relaxed ambience. Feeling the cool evening air on my skin and hearing the twilight chorus of cicadas, I felt my strength returning.

'It's nothing.'

I knew my answer lacked conviction. I'd never been good at hiding my feelings. The incident in the graveyard had hit me hard and left me nervous, jumpy and irritable. Ever since we'd left Aya at the Seven-Eleven with muted goodbyes, I knew I'd been moody and uncommunicative. It wasn't fair to take my feelings out on Sarah after all the generosity she'd shown me, but I couldn't help myself. A part of me wanted to tell her what I'd seen and a part of me was anxious not to appear insane.

Perhaps she sensed that I was wrestling with something or other and changed the subject. 'One thing I haven't got straight in my head – why did you agree to investigate supernatural phenomena?'

'I'm sure I told you. I got the funding to do it.'

'Is that really the only reason?'

'Pretty much. Honestly, I never had any interest in that kind of stuff. But then I've never had much passion in anything I've studied. I think I'm probably just avoiding real life.'

'Are you religious?'

The question took me by surprise. She had turned to the window and her face was in shadow. I felt twelve years old again, sitting in the cold confessional after church, reluctantly listing my bad deeds for the day to my disapproving priest. 'No,' I said, after some consideration. 'My parents are religious and the idea was that I should be too. It just didn't work out for me.'

'You never felt guilty about that? About abandoning the faith?'

'I guess I never really had it in the first place. I was only ever going through the motions.'

'A bit like your thesis, then?' She turned her face towards me with a mischievous smile.

'Yes, if you like.'

'So, if you don't believe in God, do you believe in ghosts?'

A few days before, I would have answered the question without a moment's hesitation. Now, I didn't know what to say.

She was quick to sense my unease. 'You saw something, didn't you?'

'What do you mean?'

'At the cemetery. I saw your face change. Either you saw something, or you thought you saw something. And ever since then you've been acting weird.'

My first instinct was to deny everything, but what she said was absolutely true. What was the point in lying to her? She deserved better than that. 'I don't know,' I said finally, passing my hand over my face. 'I don't know anymore.'

'I'd rather you talked to me about it. I'm not going to judge you.'

And so I told her. I described exactly what I'd seen reflected in the window of Aya's Nissan Micra, down to the crimson ribbon round the neck and the number of stripes on the collar of the sailor uniform. I told her I was convinced it was Reiko I'd seen, how I'd seen her photograph amongst Charlie's notes and how her eyes had burned a hole in my soul. I told her I thought Reiko still exerted the same power in death as she had done in life.

Sarah listened quietly to everything I said, not commenting, not reacting.

Emboldened, I went on to tell her about my dream of the previous night, how I'd returned to the corridors of the high school leaving a trail of bloodstained footprints on my way to the third floor, how I'd seen the two doomed lovers lying dead on the school forecourt amid a shower of cherry blossoms. I included every detail I could recall, relieved to get this weight off my chest.

Then, as the light over the hills faded to black, I began to tell her about Charlie's file, about the transformation in his handwriting from measured copperplate to messy scrawl, about the paranoid detail with which he'd recorded every aspect of the village's history, about his last days when he'd written nothing but gibberish.

And finally I told her about Yoshi, about our brief conversation by the drinks machine, the journey up in the lift. I dredged up every detail of our brief encounter. I told her how I'd turned to look casually out of the window and seen him fall. A flash of white and a human life extinguished. The first time in my short life that I'd seen tragedy up close.

Sarah listened carefully to everything I had to say, respectful of my need to unload a heavy burden. Now I'd finally confessed all and laid myself bare, I felt something I'd never felt in the mildewed confessional box all those years before: a sense of relief. For a while, she didn't speak and I began to fear that I'd said too much, that she'd declare me insane and dangerous and pack me off to the nearest guesthouse with immediate effect. I only hoped she could appreciate my honesty. After all, I was a certified ghost-hunter.

'I'd like to see his file.' Her voice was calm, as though she were only asking for a cup of tea.

'It's quite distressing.'

'I'd still like to see it.'

Sarah sat very still while she read, occasionally pausing to refill her glass with *ulon* wheat tea. Though she had a desk lamp, she preferred to read by candlelight – maybe she felt it better befitted the material and, of course, she kept the Gregorian chant on auto-repeat. I sat on the other side of the room leafing through a pile of women's magazines, all the while looking at her for a reaction.

For the most part she didn't react at all. Once or twice I saw the trace of a grimace, a nod of the head or a furrowed brow. Fully aware that she was reading the private notes of a suicide, she was treating them with due respect. She read, with only a short break to replenish her tea, for a couple of hours. But it was not until she got to the last pages – the Izumi pages, the ones that scared the life out of me – that I finally saw her flinch. She looked up and met my gaze. Then, without reading further, she shut the file with a deep sigh.

'I can't read any more.'

'You got to those pages?'

She nodded. 'What happened to him? Have you read them?'

'I've looked at them. I thought of burning them. Actually, I should've done that. We've no business looking at them.'

Sarah winced. 'Something happened to him, didn't it. You can tell he was a bit uptight from the handwriting and the style and the attention to detail. But something happened to him while he was here.'

'I know.'

I looked out at the dark hills silhouetted against the night sky and tried to imagine what Charlie's state of mind had been as he faced his last few days of life. Then I thought about my own state of mind, my feeling of anxiety after the experience in the graveyard, the disturbed dreams, the memory of Yoshi, and it reminded me how much I had in common with Charlie.

Sarah interrupted my morbid train of thought. 'So, Japanese ghosts have certain characteristics then?'

'So it seems. They tend to be young, female and out for revenge. Don't ask me why.'

'Ah, Charlie wrote about that.' Sarah said. 'It goes back a long way, to outdated Buddhist ideas of the spiritual inferiority of women. And Taoist ideas of yin and yang.' She opened the file and leafed through to the relevant section. 'Yin represents female, darkness, passiveness, cold and moon. Yang on the other hand represents male, light, activeness, fire and sun. So, whichever way you look at it, women get the raw deal.'

This was another area I knew I would have to research some more, but for the moment I was too distracted to think about it.

'So what's your thesis then?' she asked.

I felt I was no longer sure what I believed, that my convictions had been dented. 'I believe that when people claim to see ghosts, they see only what they think they should see. In other words, what they see is culture-specific. An English person or a Western person will see an amalgam of all the ghosts they've seen over the years on TV or in movies or in stories they've heard. That's all.'

She wasn't satisfied. 'So if different cultures see ghosts in different ways, does that prove to you that what they see is a product of their imagination, that they're all making it up?'

'Basically, yeah.'

'Couldn't it be that a ghost appears to the viewer in a guise that the viewer recognizes?'

I wasn't sure how serious Sarah was being, but I decided to play it straight. 'I honestly don't know. My guess is that the undead don't consult their wardrobe before making an appearance.'

Sarah lowered her eyes. 'I've read what Charlie had to say about ghosts. He seems to accept that there are a lot of differences between different cultures. And he notes that in Japan vengeful female ghosts seem to get the most press. But he also said that there are a lot of similarities and sometimes the differences are just differences of emphasis.'

I lent my head back against the wall, growing weary of the subject. 'I don't know Sarah.'

'I was thinking about this. Say you saw something. How are you going to describe it to people? You're going to do it in ways you think they'll understand. You're going to adjust what you see to conform to the accepted view of these things.'

She seemed satisfied with her thesis and as I had nothing to counter with, I just nodded my head. I had felt okay while she was reading the file quietly, but all this theorizing was making me dizzy.

'What did you see today?' she asked suddenly. 'In the graveyard, what did you see?'

'I told you.'

'She was young, female, dressed in a school uniform?'

'Yes.'

'If that was a ghost, then it's not the traditional Japanese view. According to Charlie, ghosts here tend to wear long white dresses and have long, dishevelled hair covering their faces. So your ghost didn't quite conform. She appeared to you exactly as she appeared in life.'

I felt annoyed that what I'd told Sarah in strictest confidence was being used to illustrate a point. I tried to look pained, but Sarah wasn't paying attention.

'She was young and female. She ticked some of the boxes,' she said.

'Look, let's assume it wasn't a ghost. I've been under emotional strain. There's been the jet-lag, the culture shock, the suicide, the bad dreams. I've been immersing myself in this whole business about the high school deaths and it's all got a bit much. That's all. It was a hallucination. Just my mind playing tricks on me.'

Sarah wasn't ready to let it go just yet. 'I'm sorry, but I've read this damn file and I need to talk about it. I accept your mind was playing tricks, but I want to know what you saw. Just for argument's sake. For instance, was she floating?'

'I couldn't see. It was a reflection in a car window. I saw it for a split second. I don't know if she was floating.'

'It's another thing Charlie put down about Japanese ghosts. They float. Being ethereal beings, they don't make any contact with the ground.'

I began pulling at my hair, wishing to God I'd never brought up the subject of Charlie's file.

'Okay, here's another question: let's assume Japanese people see Japanese ghosts according to their cultural standard. What if a Western person, with all their cultural baggage, sees that same ghost? Do they see the same thing?'

This was going too far and I put my head in my hands. 'Ghosts don't exist, Sarah. If they existed, then maybe I could give you a scientific answer. But they don't. Crazy people see ghosts. People on the brink of insanity see ghosts. Ghosts aren't real.'

She held up her hands in apology. 'Sorry, I'm being provocative. Just one more thing and then I'll shut up. Japanese ghosts are supposedly hell-bent on revenge. That thing you saw, whatever it was, did it look annoyed?'

'No.'

'Not particularly vengeful?'

'No. Why would it be vengeful towards me anyway? I haven't done anything to offend it.'

This seemed to satisfy her and she smiled. 'Sorry, I was just thinking things through. I'd never really thought about it before.'

'Nor me,' I muttered.

I got up, feeling the need to stretch my legs after sitting for so long on the *tatami* mat floor. I also needed to get away from any more of Sarah's questions. 'I'm going to the toilet. I'll be right back.'

She started to laugh. 'You're not meant to say that.'

'Why not?'

'Haven't you seen the movie *Scream*? It's one of the cardinal rules of horror films. If you say "*I'll be right back*", it's like signing your own death warrant. You're a dead cert for the meat truck.'

She was on a roll. I had no idea what I'd started by giving her Charlie's file to read. 'Sarah, I know this is a weird place. But we're not in a horror film.'

I left her chuckling to herself and made my way to the bathroom. With my mind frayed and my stomach still unsettled, I lent over the sink and splashed cold water onto my face. This had an immediate restorative effect and I continued splashing for half a minute. I breathed in deep and watched the water disappear down the plughole. I thought again about how far I'd come in such a short space of time, how many new psychological challenges I'd faced. It was something to be proud of. Then I thought about my parents sitting at the kitchen table, reading the Sunday supplements, wondering how I was faring so far from home. I determined to pull myself together, to defy whatever fate threw at me and to come out the other end a better and stronger person. I would return to England more experienced, more confident and more equipped to deal with the emotional and spiritual challenges ahead.

But even as I made these resolves, staring down the plughole in Sarah's bathroom, fate had me in her sights.

It was just as sudden and just as horrible as before.

The door to the cabinet above the sink was slightly ajar and I peered in, curious to see if there was anything in there to treat my indigestion. I scanned the row of creams, ointments and other products, but could see nothing for indigestion.

I flipped the door closed and the reflection of the wall behind me swung into view.

She was there.

Standing against the wall, hanging her head in the same manner, but only a few feet away from me. I saw her clearly – saw the dark shadows under her eyes, the high cheekbones, the pale lips slightly parted. And I saw the crimson ribbon tied around her neck.

I stood frozen to the spot, staring past my pale, frightened face at this apparition.

Slowly, very slowly, I raised my hands to my face and covered my eyes, praying to the god I'd abandoned in my youth. And when I lowered my hands, she was gone.

I turned, gripping the sink for support, and surveyed the empty bathroom. In the place where she'd been standing only a towel hung limp on a hook. She was gone.

I was taken by a sudden wave of nausea and turned to the sink to be sick. I retched painfully for a moment, but nothing came up. I then stood there, stooped over the sink, trying to compose my mind. What was happening to me? Was I so emotionally frail that I was seeing things that weren't there? Was my mind so fixated on this high school tragedy that the ghostly protagonists were haunting my waking hours?

Maybe I really was sick. Maybe I was living in denial. Maybe all these uneventful years of study and relaxation were only distracting me from the fact that I was ill, that I needed help. And I had come all the way to Japan to finally face this truth.

It took Sarah the best part of an hour to convince me that I wasn't a basket-case. She made me a cup of hot cocoa, laid out her futon to act as a couch, then listened to me as I poured my heart out all over again.

It was the tonic I needed. Lying there wrapped in her bedclothes, warmed by her cocoa, the world began to make some sense again. She told me she was distressed to hear her bathroom was haunted, but that it was most likely the mirror that needed cleaning. To illustrate the point, she'd gone off to the bathroom and come back to tell me she'd seen the exact same thing, right down to the crimson scarf. But a quick once-over with detergent had erased all traces of my ghostly visitation.

Then she did something I hadn't expected. She opened Charlie's file and took out the pictures of the high school students and showed them to me. I told her I didn't want to look at them and she replied that it was better I faced my fears than build them up into something more than they were.

For a while we looked at them quietly, Sarah explaining that they were just like the students she taught. There was nothing evil about them. They were just tragic victims, nothing more. Certainly, there was no reason to fear them.

Then she came and reclined next to me on the bed, supporting herself on her elbow. I didn't know if I should read anything into this display of intimacy, but I felt an unrelenting desire to lean forward and kiss her. If anything was going to dispel my fears and set my head right, it was a passionate kiss.

But Sarah seemed preoccupied with the picture of Reiko, continuing to study it with an attention she hadn't given the others.

'She really was a stunner,' she said at last, showing me the photo again.

I glanced at it and looked away quickly. I was only thankful that I hadn't seen her eyes looking at me in the mirror.

'Was that it?' Sarah said quietly. 'Was that what killed her in the end? I don't think I'd like to be so beautiful that men are driven to despair.'

'You've never driven anyone to despair?'

Sarah laughed bitterly. 'Not in that way, no. I suppose I've had some passing interest. Men with realistic expectations. Steady types, sensitive to my feelings, not too showy. Men who remember my birthday, know that a girl likes a few flowers now and then, or a well-timed compliment. But not men with grand passions.'

'That's pretty much how my relationships have been. Except I've always had the feeling that I like them more than they like me, that somehow I should be grateful for them being with me. I guess it's a confidence thing. From the first night, I'm just waiting for that conversation – the one where they tell you what a nice considerate guy you are, how you deserve much more than they can give you, how they're going through a period of self-discovery or some other bollocks, how it's not you, it's them.' I checked myself, realizing I'd gone too far. For a while after my last relationship had broken down, these rants had been more or less continuous. Only in the last year, had I begun to put the past behind me.

Sarah seemed to take it in her stride. 'It's what people say. It's a way of not telling the truth, which is usually far more hurtful.'

'It still hurts, however they say it.'

She reached over and gave me a comforting pat on the arm. 'I guess you're still recovering then.'

'It was more than two years ago and I'm still brooding over it. Sometimes I wonder if I'll ever stop.'

She continued to pat me on the arm with motherly concern. 'You will. You have to have some faith.'

If only I could. That feeling of complete rejection was still with me. That feeling of being cast adrift from all warmth and love, without any hope of recovering it again.

'You have a lot of good qualities,' she said, lying down beside me with her hand still touching my arm.

I appreciated her kind words, but I didn't for a moment believe them.

'You just have some things you need to resolve,' she said. 'You have a lot of light in you and a lot of darkness.'

I turned to look at her, her face close to mine, her eyes fixed on me. I wished I could read her mind. I wished I could muster the courage to lean forward and take her in my arms. 'What do you mean, light and darkness?'

'I know all about it. I read it in Charlie's notes. Yin and Yang. Light and darkness, active and passive, male and female. It's the natural order of things.'

I didn't know how much of this was serious. 'So you're saying it's the same for everyone?'

Sarah turned onto her back. 'Yes, but in you it's more pronounced.'

I could see that she was starting to tire. The candles had been burning down and going out one by one, leaving the room in semi-darkness. I was still tucked under her duvet lying at her side, but I wasn't sure what to do next. Should I slip out and go back to my own futon? Or should I stay and fall asleep next to her? She'd made no move to push me out or send me back to my own quarters. I wanted to stay with her. On my own I felt vulnerable, but lying next to her ensconced in her bedclothes I felt that nothing could hurt me.

For a while I lay awake, watching the shadows dance on the ceiling, listening to Sarah's rhythmic breathing next to me. I thought again about what I'd seen first in the cemetery, then in the bathroom mirror. And then I wondered what Sarah had meant when she described my character as a mixture of light and darkness? Was it the light side that implored me to forget everything I'd seen and heard in Izumi and take flight while I still had the chance? If so, it was as nothing compared to the dark voice which compelled me to stay and find out for myself what horrible secret this picturesque little village held.

NOWHERE TO RUN

I found myself standing at night in the deserted entrance hall of Izumi high school. A solitary shaft of moonlight crept across the floor from the stairwell.

I didn't know how I came to be there, but I did know that I wasn't alone. Somewhere in the shadows, something was watching me. Something with intent to harm.

I also knew that the danger was pressing and if I lingered any longer I would die. I turned and fumbled for the main entrance door, but it was locked.

I turned and hurried down the corridor, through the shaft of moonlight, past the spot where I had seen the pool of blood the night before. I glanced over my shoulder, but all I saw was darkness and shadow.

I passed the staffroom, the Headmaster's office, the various administrative offices, all pitch black. I glanced over my shoulder again and this time my fears were confirmed. At the other end of the corridor a dark figure crossed the patch of moonlight with quick, stealthy strides. There could be no mistake this time. Someone was pursuing me.

I picked up my pace, heading for the double doors at the end of the hall which opened on to the playing fields. I shoved at them, but they were fastened with a padlock. With no time to lose, I turned to the first door on my right and pushed it open.

It was a storage room, cluttered with stacks of chairs and other junk. At the back there was a window and I headed for it, aware that my pursuer would be gaining on me. I reached for the latch, pulled it towards me and slid the window across. I clambered up and hurdled the window frame.

I found myself on the gravel pitch at the back of the building. A bright moon cast a ghostly pall over the surface. A high fence surrounded it on all sides, but I spotted a gate and sprinted towards it.

Even before I reached it, I could see it was no good. It was secured with a heavy chain and I rattled it in vain. There was no way through.

I looked back to see the figure drop from the window. I didn't know why they were pursuing me. I knew only that my life depended on my ability to run.

And run I did.

Spotting a rupture in the fence in the far corner, I bolted in that direction. As my feet pounded the gravel underfoot, I knew my best hope was to disappear into the woods.

I reached the hole and, grappling with the wire, managed to twist myself through. This time I didn't pause to look round.

I plunged into the woods, knowing I must lose my pursuer in the thicket.

I ran swiftly, vaulting over tree stumps, ducking low-hanging branches, weaving through the trees. I didn't know where I was heading. I knew only that I had to keep running.

The woods were dark and the ground beneath me slippery from the night dew and several times I lost my footing. I had no idea if my pursuer was gaining on me. Once I glanced over my shoulder, but saw only the darkness.

Maybe it was a mistake to take my eye off the ground. Or maybe it would have made no difference. The next thing I knew, my foot hit something and I plunged to the ground with a sharp pain in my leg. I didn't need to stir myself to know that I was badly hurt.

I tried to shuffle along the ground using my arms and one good leg, but I soon realized this was futile. My only chance was to lie still and hope my pursuer would lose my scent. Looking ahead I saw a small clearing in the trees where silvery shafts of moonlight illumined the mossy ground. In the middle of the clearing was a large weather-worn rock, whether there by accident or design I didn't know. But even in this moment of impending doom, I was moved by its eerie beauty.

For a while I lay there, gazing at the moonlight on the rock, feeling the moss cool against my cheek. I wondered if it would be my last sight on earth. And suddenly I didn't care. I felt tired. Tired of life, tired of the cruelty and the pettiness, tired of the endless monotony of hours and days which had brought only disappointment.

There was movement in the trees behind me and a figure emerged from the shadows. I didn't move. I no longer had any will to resist. They get you in the end, I thought. They always get you in the end. I didn't look up at my pursuer. I didn't care who it was or what grudge they bore me. It didn't matter. Soon I would return to the earth and all would be forgotten.

Out of the corner of my eye I saw the flash of a blade in the moonlight.

So this is how it would end.

I looked up at the leaves of the trees silhouetted against the moon and felt a rush of homesickness for the world I was leaving.

My executioner moved forward and sunk the blade into my back.

For a while I screamed out in pain and desperation. Then the pain grew less and I found I could no longer scream.

And soon my sight grew dim and darkness filled the world.

Someone was shaking me awake.

For a moment I didn't understand. I didn't know where I was or who it was and I cowered at the edge of the bed, clutching my own shoulders, instinctively trying to defend myself against an assailant. I could feel the tears fresh on my cheeks and a sharp pain in my back. Sarah fumbled for the light switch and the room was thrown into stark relief. The contrast with the dark woods and the damp moss was so pronounced that I recoiled from the sight.

'What is it? What's wrong?' She was looking at me with genuine fear.

Gradually I adjusted my eyes to the light and the release from my dream. The pain in my back, where the blade had entered, began to ease and I breathed more easily.

'I was dreaming,' I said at last, embarrassed at the state I was in.

Her look of fear had become one of concern and she reached over to pat my arm supportively. 'You screamed out. I didn't know what was happening.'

'It was so real. I was in the woods. There was a mossy clearing and a stone. Someone wanted to kill me.'

'To kill you? Who?'

'I don't know. He had a knife and he ran it though my back. I can still feel the pain, here.' I reached round to my back to indicate the spot.

Sarah winced at the thought, then shuffled over and began to massage my shoulders gently. 'You're too tense. You have to relax, otherwise you're going to keep having these dreams.'

'I wish I could make them stop. I don't understand why they're so vivid. Is it something in the water or the air or the food? I've never had dreams like this before.'

'Maybe it's my company,' she said, trying to lighten the mood. 'I think I have this effect on men. Why else would I be living out here like a hermit?'

'Why were they trying to kill me? What does that mean? Is there some Freudian explanation for that?' Feeling Sarah's hands on my back, my balance was returning.

'Well, I'm not trying to kill you, if that's any consolation. You can cross me off that list. Actually, I think it's pretty unlikely anyone else is. Unless you have some dark past you're keeping from me.'

'I'm clean. I've never done anything bad. I'm sliced white bread.'

She continued to massage my back in silence for a few minutes. It was hard to imagine what kind of state I'd have been in had Sarah not been there. Her understanding amazed me, considering I'd been acting like a basket-case from day one: bringing her the garbled jottings of a suicide scholar, seeing the undead in her bathroom mirror, and now dreaming of being murdered in the woods. She deserved some kind of medal.

'Do you want to go back to your futon, or are you happy here?' she asked, with a final flourish of her hands on my shoulders.

'I'm happy here if you're happy,' I said, pleasantly surprised by the question.

'I'm happy,' she said and reached over to turn off the light. 'Safety in numbers and all that.' She stretched herself out on the mattress with a yawn.

'Thank you,' I was unsure what else to say.

She yawned again and within minutes I could tell she was asleep. As for myself, I don't know when or how I slept. No amount of comfort from Sarah could expunge the dream from my mind. The whole sequence replayed itself over and over in my tired brain until the grey fingers of dawn crept in through the slats in the blind. I relived it all: the dark shadows of the school corridor; the moonlit gravel pitch; the hole in the fence at the back where I'd squeezed myself through; the clearing in the woods, with the moonlit rock and the bed of moss. But above all I felt the twist of the blade in my back, the pain to end all pain and the terrible onslaught of darkness.

In the Woods

The morning began quietly enough.

Sarah was enjoying a lie-in and I lay there for a while watching her as she slept. I only hoped she wouldn't suddenly wake and demand to know why I was there beside her.

I got up and went through to the bathroom, averting my eyes in front of the cabinet mirror, then turning it to face the wall. I wasn't taking any chances. I took a long, leisurely shower, scrubbing my body thoroughly, as though to cleanse myself of my troubled dreams. Everything I'd seen and every sensation I'd felt was still with me, down to the aching pain in my back where the knife had entered my body. Though I only had a limited grasp of the power of the mind, the strength of this feeling was unnerving. Had I felt more comfortable with the mirror, I might even have checked my back for marks.

I got dressed, made a cup of coffee and stepped out onto the balcony. Standing there, breathing in the clean air of rural Japan, it was as if I'd been given a second chance at life, as though I had indeed died in the woods, then come back to make good the terrible waste I'd made of my life. And I'd been given this glorious day at this glorious stage of life to show what I could achieve.

I stood there for a long time, drinking my coffee, gazing at the houses and farms beyond the apartment block perimeter. I saw people riding bikes, taking the rubbish to the bins, hanging out washing and generally getting on with their lives. It was the first time since coming to Japan that I'd taken the time to watch people going about their ordinary business. I'd come to Izumi because I'd heard it was haunted: a cursed village with a history of horrific violence. But it now struck me that this was just a place where people lived, raised families and grew old. This was their home. What right did I have to come here, digging for clues, trying to make theories, perpetuating the myths that had dogged it for centuries? Whatever had happened in the past had no bearing on the present. It had just been bad luck. And the last thing ordinary inhabitants wanted was for people like me to come in and make an issue out of it.

I was still considering these worthy sentiments when Sarah came out to join me wearing a silk dressing gown, hair tied back in a ponytail. I wished I could tell her how beautiful she looked, standing there in the morning sun.

'Are you okay?' she asked, coming to lean on the balcony next to me.

'Yeah. Look, I'm sorry about last night. You're right, I've been pretty highly strung since I arrived. A lot of things have happened and I need to take it easy.'

She smiled and tilted her head towards the sun. 'These are days to cherish,' she said quietly.

I took it as a compliment that she regarded days spent with me as ones to cherish. I wouldn't have been surprised if she'd shown me the door after my performance the previous night.

'Pull up a chair,' she said, in a tone that suggested she had business to discuss.

I did as she asked, hoping this wasn't where she sent me packing.

'I've been thinking about something,' she said. 'I wanted to run it by you. I don't know if this is a good time.' There was a definite edge to her voice.

I said that it was as good a time as any. I was intrigued to hear what was on her mind.

She sat back in her chair and knitted her eyebrows, searching for the appropriate words. Then she looked at me with such seriousness that I had to look away. 'A couple of things happened yesterday which you couldn't explain.'

I nodded.

'You told me you were worried you could be losing your mind.'

I nodded again.

'Well I was thinking, what if what you saw was real?'

This time I didn't nod. I looked hard at Sarah and it was her turn to look away.

'I know it's not your preferred theory, but what if it really was there. Not just in your mind.'

I looked for some sign that she was having me on. But there wasn't a flicker.

'What if it wasn't a hallucination?'

'Just say what you mean.'

She lowered her voice to a whisper. 'What if you actually did see a ghost?'

I stared out at the hills. It was the one possibility I wasn't ready to entertain. I'd talked about stress and strain, jet-lag, culture-shock, food-poisoning, hallucinations, but at no point had I talked about ghosts. Here I was studying the damn things and I absolutely refuted them. They undermined the basis of everything I believed in: my conviction that the material world was governed by rational laws and my complete rejection of religion and superstition.

'You have to at least consider the possibility.'

'I don't believe in ghosts,' I said gruffly.

'It's one possible explanation,' she said. 'That's all I'm saying.'

'Not a very good one though.'

She looked at me, irritated. 'Why can't you admit it's a possibility? Can't you accept that there might be something in it? Just say it's a possibility.'

I ran my hand over my face. I wanted desperately to say 'yes', if only to please Sarah, if only to keep her on my side. She was right. Couldn't I just admit it as a possibility? 'I don't know,' I said at last.

Sarah took this as an admission. 'What if this girl, assuming it's the one we think it is, is trying to get in touch with you?'

'Why?' I asked, bewildered.

'I don't know. I remember reading in Charlie's notes about ghosts in the Buddhist tradition. They're usually people who've met some sudden, violent end and don't have enough repose in their last minutes to achieve nirvana. So they stick around with unfinished business. Wouldn't this girl fit the profile? And couldn't that be a reason why she's appearing to you?'

'Ghosts don't reason, they just do,' I said, uncomfortable with the direction the conversation was taking.

'You say these things about how ghosts are supposed to behave and at the same time you say you don't believe in them. You can't have it both ways.'

'I'm just repeating what I've read.'

We sat in silence, Sarah allowing me some breathing space. I knew it was reasonable for her to say these things. God knows I'd been up half the night thinking them myself. But it was in my nature to fight them and I couldn't easily capitulate. And the same question kept recurring: why me? I was just a passing tourist, with no connection to the village. What would a spirit of the dead want with me? What could I do to help her?

But there was another, darker question which I knew Sarah was thinking, but couldn't put to me. Mrs Azuma had already told us that Charlie had been visited by ghosts. I had justified his suicide on that basis. It had never occurred to me that I, who believed completely in my own sanity, could go down that same road. Had the same apparitions that now appeared to me also appeared to Charlie? And had he seen the same dreams that I now saw?

'What are you thinking?' Sarah asked.

I decided to come clean. 'About Charlie.'

She nodded solemnly.

I had no idea what circumstances had driven Charlie to kill himself, but the feeling that our destinies were somehow linked was stronger than ever. Against my better nature, I'd started to believe there were forces in Izumi I couldn't defend against, forces that eventually overwhelmed Charlie. Was I really any different to Charlie? Was I any stronger than he was?

At least I knew there was one significant difference between us. When Charlie had come to Izumi he had come alone, without friend or ally, whereas I had Sarah on my side. Sarah made me feel safe. Whatever happened, Sarah would never let me come to harm.

And however much I tried to pretend that Izumi was just an ordinary place, where ordinary people went about their lives quietly, I knew it wasn't true. Izumi was different. Izumi was cursed.

There was one thing in Izumi beyond reproach and that was the cherry blossom. As we drove through the village, the trees lined the roads and the blossom cascaded over garden fences and peppered the surrounding hills. While I'd known of the cherry blossom as one of Japan's symbols, I'd never imagined how prolific it was, nor how breathtaking.

Sarah and I had spoken little since our conversation on the balcony. It wasn't so much a bad atmosphere, as a cooling-off period. She knew what she'd said had been difficult for me to accept and she was prepared to give me some time.

She'd promised Aya she'd drop in at the high school that morning and had offered me the option to stay at home or go out exploring on my own. The idea of being on my own didn't appeal so I opted to tag along. I didn't say as much to Sarah, but I didn't know how I'd handle another visitation without her to help me through.

As we drove through the school gates, I had an uneasy sense of deja-vu. Since my one previous daylight visit, I had made two nightly visitations which had been every bit as real. Against my better judgement I scanned the third floor windows, but thankfully saw nothing.

We entered the foyer and I was struck by how bright it was. After two nocturnal visits, I wasn't used to seeing everything in such a stark light. We turned left and walked past the stairwell, where I'd stepped in a pool of blood just two nights before. We headed towards the staffroom and I saw that the corridor was just as I'd seen it in my dream, right down to the door at the end with the bar handle. It wasn't a detail I remembered from my original visit and one I'd assumed to be a creation of my imagination.

Perturbed, I followed Sarah into the staffroom to find it a lot emptier than before. Aya was sitting alone at her bank of desks looking dreamily out of the window.

'Working hard?' Sarah said, approaching her with a grin.

Aya emerged from her daydream with a start. 'Hello,' she said with her trademark smile. 'What are your plans for today?'

'More ghost-hunting,' Sarah said and gave me a nudge.

'In the school?'

'No, just out and about.'

Aya looked round as if surprised to see the place so deserted. 'It's very quiet here today. Saturday is always quiet out of term, especially for teachers with families.' She looked a little sad, conscious that she couldn't count herself among the latter group.

'Have you got any work?' Sarah asked.

'No, I just have to be here this morning. It's a formality.'

I'd found myself thinking about my dream again, about the coincidence of the door at the end of the corridor being exactly as I'd seen it in my dream. I had an urge to go and check it out.

'Is it all right if I stroll around for a bit?'

Aya got up with an enthusiastic smile. 'I can come. I need a break. I need a break from doing nothing.'

We stepped out into the corridor and turned left towards the door at the end. I knew that Sarah would've guessed my intentions. But I couldn't explain to Aya why I was suddenly interested in the bar handle at the end of the corridor. The last thing I wanted was for her to think me a basket-case. I may have gained Sarah's acceptance, but Aya might not understand.

'Where do you want to go?' she asked.

'Just out here,' I said, as we reached the door. I could see it was very similar to the door I'd seen in my dream. But then it was similar to most doors of its type. Maybe I was overreacting. I was about to push the door open when I noticed the door to my right, the door I'd used in my dream. It was similar, but again, all the doors in the school looked identical.

'What's in there?' I asked, approaching the door and trying the handle. It was locked.

Aya looked confused by my interest. 'I don't know. A storage room, I think. It's used by the cleaners.'

I nodded, trying to look nonchalant. I hadn't filled Sarah in on all the details of my dream, but I guessed she was piecing it together as we went along.

At least there was nothing strange about wanting to take a stroll round the playing fields. It was a bright day, and they were surrounded by picturesque woods.

'The cherry blossoms are spectacular just now,' Sarah said, getting on to a safe topic.

I was grateful for her help. I was on an unusual quest and I was happy for her to distract Aya.

They continued to talk about cherry blossom and the changing seasons, while I looked about me, reliving the dream in all its awful detail. We passed the gate I had seen in my dream and I noted the chain holding it fast. There was nothing unusual about that. You'd expect a back gate in a school to be chained shut and, besides, I'd noticed it on our previous stroll with Aya.

We walked on, Aya and Sarah deep in conversation. Without thinking I found myself glancing over my shoulder to check we weren't being followed. Even in the full light of day and with the company of Aya and Sarah, I could still see in my mind's eye the dark shadow moving swiftly across the field, intent on harm. I didn't feel comfortable strolling at a leisurely pace. I wanted to run. I could feel the cold fingers of terror prickling at the back of my neck.

'Are you okay?' Aya had noticed my unease.

'I dreamt I was here last night,' I blurted out, suddenly wanting to unburden myself, wanting her to understand. 'I dreamt I was being followed. I dreamt someone was trying to hurt me.'

There, I'd said it. I saw Sarah glance at me, surprised I'd given away so much, so candidly.

'Who was following you?' Aya asked, bemused by my admission. She had just been having a nice chat with Sarah about cherry blossoms and here I was confessing to nightmares. I felt a little ashamed, but at least it was out in the open.

'I don't know. I didn't see.'

We got to the corner of the field and I approached the point where the fences intersected, the place where I'd slipped through in my dream. I pulled at the back fence, just as I'd done in the dream and, sure enough, there was room for me to pass. I tried to tell myself this was coincidence. It was an old fence and hardly surprising that the joins were weak.

'Did you come this way in your dream?' Sarah asked

I nodded. 'You walk on. I might just have a look around here.'

Aya was watching me a little unsurely and I could understand why. My behaviour must have appeared extremely odd. Just two weeks earlier I wouldn't have thought myself capable of acting like this. But times had changed.

'I don't mind coming,' Sarah said, offering welcome support. 'I've always wondered what's out there.'

Aya still seemed unsure. Perhaps squeezing through a hole in the fence was an improper way for a teacher to behave. But curiosity got the better of her and she nodded her consent. I was pleased that they both wanted to come with me. I was starting to develop a fear of being on my own.

I led the way through the fence and into the woods, heading in the general direction I'd gone in my dream, with Sarah and Aya following at a short distance. The woods were dark and the sun struggled to penetrate the dense canopy of branches overhead. Here and there, thin shafts of light pierced the gloom, producing little pools of sunlight on the leafy floor. It all seemed very familiar, but I told myself all woods shared similar characteristics.

I knew what I was searching for. The one thing that I couldn't have known about, that I couldn't have constructed from my imagination. It was a strange, hopeless pilgrimage, but I had to make it.

'What about that clearing you saw?' Sarah shouted to me. 'The one with the rock.'

'It was a dream,' I said, turning round. 'It was a dream. Nothing more.'

She came alongside me with Aya. 'Then what are you out here looking for?'

She knew as well as I did, but she wanted me to say it. She wanted to me to admit what I'd refused to contemplate that morning.

I turned from her and walked on.

I knew it couldn't be. Seeing something reflected in a dark mirror was one thing. There were any number of explanations for it. Insanity was one. Or a hallucination, the product of a tired and unsettled brain. But to see a place in a dream that I'd never seen in life was impossible. It was beyond the realm of ghosts and goblins and other apparitions. It was something I couldn't bear to contemplate.

For a while we trudged in silence and I sensed the unease of my companions. Even Sarah would be wondering how far I was going to go before giving up. She was no doubt worrying about Aya, who would be too polite to say that she'd had enough and wanted to go back. I began to wish I'd gone on my own and never mentioned my dream. But my thought processes were becoming increasingly divorced from my actions.

Just as I was on the point of aborting the quest, I saw something up ahead which gave me pause. I broke into a trot.

The next few moments of my life passed in slow motion. I sunk to my knees and groped for the mossy floor to steady myself. My eyes grew heavy and my head grew dizzy.

I saw everything as it was. I saw the root where I'd fallen. I saw the tree that had sheltered me. And up ahead I saw the clearing as it had been, as it had always been. A luminous carpet of moss washed in sunlight and a weather-worn rock left there by accident or design.

I collapsed face down on the moss, feeling it cool against my cheek, my mind a riot of confused impressions. I saw Sarah kneel down next to me and touch the side of my face. I saw Aya hovering there, her hand over her mouth, looking down at me.

I didn't know how to react. Nothing in my experience had prepared me for this moment and nothing in my life would ever be the same. I had experienced something manifestly impossible. I had been granted a vision of something. I just didn't know what or why. Had I seen something that had already happened or was yet to happen? Had I experienced someone else's death or foreseen my own?

Questions continued to swirl around my head as together we retraced our steps back out of the woods. Aya had mercifully not heard me describe my dream beforehand, but she guessed that something was terribly wrong. But to Sarah I had described my dream in detail and she would now know there were other forces at work, that I wasn't simply deranged.

If I'd had any doubts before, now I had none. Something was terribly wrong in Izumi.

WHAT CHARLIE WROTE

I slept the sleep of the condemned.

Lying on Sarah's mattress in the heat of the afternoon, I slept a deep and dreamless sleep. Emotionally and physically drained, I was asleep the moment my head hit the pillow and, according to Sarah, didn't move a muscle for several hours.

In the moments before I opened my eyes, I imagined I was back in my bedroom at home, that I hadn't come to Japan, that nothing had changed. But that was another life and I was a different person then. I would never again have that simple, undemanding view of the world.

Somehow I had to come to terms with what I'd seen in the woods and I knew I had to take things as slowly and as calmly as I could.

Sarah, to her eternal credit, had continued her Florence Nightingale job from the moment I collapsed by the clearing. She and Aya had helped me through the trees and back to the school, where I'd finally begun to compose myself. Things hadn't been helped by the sight of Odagiri-san watching us as we approached the school across the playing fields. He'd been leaning against the wall, casually smoking a cigarette, and must have seen us emerge from the woods on the other side. He'd given us a deeply suspicious look before stamping out his cigarette and disappearing into the building with nothing by way of greeting. Then as we'd approached the staffroom, we startled Shirakami-san as he was descending the steps. He'd stared at us the whole time we were sat in the staffroom, then, when we left, I saw him standing at the staffroom window watching us go.

I didn't know what to think about the teachers at the school. I desperately wanted to give them the benefit of the doubt. I knew how hard it would be to live with the constant whispers and rumours and questions. In England, anyone even remotely connected to such a heinous incident would have packed up and left long ago. But I'd already perceived a resilience among the Japanese when it came to work, a doggedness to persevere no matter what the personal cost.

Sarah had brought me back to her house and ordered me to get some rest. She made me have a sandwich and a cup of hot cocoa, then pulled down the blinds in her room and ordered me not to come out until I was thoroughly refreshed. If it hadn't been for her, I suspected I would have still been grovelling on the ground in the woods, rapidly losing my grip on reality.

'James?'

There was a soft knock on the sliding screen.

I cleared my throat and looked about me, wondering what time it was. 'Yes.'

The screen slid open and Sarah entered, carrying a mug. 'I thought you could do with a drink.'

I smiled and sat up. 'What time is it?'

'About five. You've had a good sleep.'

'I didn't even dream.'

She laughed. 'Well, things are looking up then, aren't they?'

I took the mug and held it to my face, enjoying the aroma of green tea. As far as I was concerned, Sarah was an angel. She could pillage and murder for the next fifty years and it wouldn't change my view. She had no peer.

'I'm sorry about what happened,' she said. Plainly the events of the day were weighing heavily on her mind.

'There's no way of explaining this one away.'

'Actually, I want to show you something,' she said. 'It might explain what you saw.'

I frowned. What could possibly explain it? It was fundamentally inexplicable. I'd told her about the dream before we went into the woods. The chances of finding the exact same spot were a million to one.

She got up and left the room, returning a moment later carrying Charlie's file. 'How much of this did you read?' she asked.

'Bits and pieces. Why?'

'How about the last part? The part where he loses the thread?'

'I saw a bit of it, yeah. It didn't make a lot of sense.'

'Do you remember reading this?' She handed me the file, marking the relevant passage with her finger.

I began to read with a growing sense of astonishment. Written in broken sentences and chequered with words scribbled out and blotches of ink, the passage described a dream of being pursued through the high school corridor at night, of a flight across the playing fields under a full moon, of escaping through a hole in the fence and plunging into the dark woods. Then in clear unambiguous prose Charlie had written: *'I lost my footing and fell to the ground with a shooting pain in my leg. I saw ahead a moonlit clearing, covered in moss, marked by an old, weather-beaten rock. That was the last thing I saw before I died'.*

I put the file down, aware that Sarah was watching my reactions carefully. Truth was, I didn't know how to react.

'This can't be,' I said, fumbling for something coherent to say.

'You must've read this. Before your dream, you must've read it.'

I shook my head. It seemed like the obvious explanation, if only I could remember. I'd certainly looked at Charlie's file that sleepless night in Osaka. I'd even read bits of the Izumi section. But for the life of me, I couldn't recall seeing the sentences I'd just read. In fact I was certain I hadn't.

'Even if you don't remember it, even if you took it in subconsciously, maybe your brain reconstructed it for your own dream.'

'I just can't remember it.'

'You said yourself that you've been under a lot of emotional strain. You've not been yourself. You've been forgetful. Isn't it possible that you simply forgot that you'd read it?'

It was ironic that now Sarah was the one trying to rationalize, and it was I who needed convincing. I should have been delighted that here was a perfectly rational explanation for something that had challenged everything I believed in. But I wasn't happy. Even if my brain had managed to reconstruct events from Charlie's description, the clearing I'd seen in the woods was just as it had been in my dream. There was no way I could have constructed such a precise image from Charlie's brief description. He mentioned a moonlit clearing, moss, an old stone, but that was all. I shook my head, despondent.

'It's the only explanation,' she pleaded. 'You can't both have had exactly the same dream.'

I looked up at her, dismayed by the suggestion. A week ago, I would have said the same thing. But too many things had happened in the intervening period. This matter had only reinforced the growing fear that Charlie and I shared some common destiny. I still didn't know how or why this could be, but the evidence was slowly starting to mount.

She opted to change her line of argument. 'Okay. Supposing the dream means something. Leaving aside whether you had the dream independently, or whether you picked up on Charlie's description, the fact is you both had the same dream and it was pretty explicit. What do you think it means?'

I looked back down at Charlie's file to see if there was anything in the preceding or following passages to suggest a theory, but without success. There were what looked like descriptions of his breakfast and accounts of conversations about the weather. The man's mind had been wandering far and wide. Or maybe those were just his attempts to escape the encroaching darkness by focusing on the mundane.

I closed the file. I didn't need Charlie to tell me anything. I already knew the answer. And I also knew that I was throwing all rational thinking to hell by saying so.

'It's about Reiko,' I said and lowered my eyes to avoid Sarah's reaction.

'I think so too.'

I looked up. 'She was murdered in the woods.'

Sarah nodded gravely.

'She was at school. Whether at night or not, I don't know. She tried to escape by losing her pursuer in the woods. But they caught up with her by the clearing. And they killed her.'

A sudden wind rattled the blind, startling us both. Sarah got up to close the window.

I realized there was no longer any point trying to avoid dealing with the topic straight on. I had come too far now. 'They say in Japan that when you talk about the unquiet dead, they will hear you. That's why people are afraid to talk about ghosts.'

'Do you think she's here now?' At least Sarah seemed strong enough to accept the idea.

'I don't know. I'm not supposed to believe in ghosts, so I guess I'm not qualified to say.'

'What would convince you, other than reflections in mirrors and dreams?'

All of a sudden I felt strangely calm, as though I really was coming to terms with the possibility that there was something out there. Maybe if I accepted the idea, it would no longer seem so terrible.

'I've always worked on the assumption that ghosts – at least the popular perception of ghosts – do things according to a prescribed set of rules. They appear at the scene of their death, or where they lived, or where they were happy. They don't have any business with the living. They just appear, mope around and then go away. My plan was to show that ghosts in Japan have a different rulebook.'

The wind rose up again outside the window and we listened to it for a moment in silence. Even if there was nothing ghostly about it, it was adding to the atmosphere.

'The thing that always bothered me about ghosts in general is their lack of purpose. They kind of just appear, give people the willies and then nothing. They're so passive. Then I found out that the traditional Japanese ghost seems to have a purpose. There's a dynamism that traditional ghosts in the West don't have. Japanese ghosts want something...'

'And that is?'

'Revenge.'

The word hung in the air for a moment, buffeted by the wind. Sarah struck a match and lit a candle, relieving us from the encroaching gloom.

'Let's say for the sake of argument that Reiko is appearing to you. Then what I don't understand is, why? Why you? There's a village full of people here. Does she appear to them as well? Is it because you're a ghost-hunter, she thinks you might understand?'

I shook my head, equally at a loss. 'That's what frightens me. There's nothing special about me at all. There's no reason to appear to me.'

Again I thought about parallels with Charlie. She had appeared to him and the consequences were tragic. But was that the intended effect? Were her intentions evil? Did she mean for him to die or was it a terrible mistake? I thought again about Japanese ghosts having a purpose and another question occurred to me. Did they act intentionally? Or were they completely blind? Did a ghost choose who to reveal itself to or was it dictated by some other force? Suddenly these abstract questions had assumed a critical importance. Suddenly they were a matter of life and death.

THE VIDEO FOOTAGE

We continued talking for a long time, until the sun had dipped below the hills and Sarah had lit a full compliment of candles. I was in surprisingly good spirits considering my experience in the woods earlier. Talking to Sarah had restored a sense of normality. I vowed that for the rest of my time in Izumi I would keep my head, no matter what dreams or visitations came my way. I owed it to Sarah.

It being my penultimate night in Izumi, she wryly predicted I would probably make it back to Osaka in one piece. She went on to reassure me that there was no possible comparison with Charlie's case. Having read his ramblings, she was certain the guy's state of mind had been questionable from the outset. I replied that the only real difference was that Charlie hadn't had a companion like her to keep him on the straight and narrow.

Sarah had accepted an invitation to have dinner with the amazing Mrs Azuma, host mum and master chef. We both admitted to a sense of trepidation as we made our way over, the memory of the last banquet still fresh in our minds and stomachs. Apparently Mrs Azuma had apologized in advance, saying she hadn't had time to prepare anything special and she hoped we wouldn't mind eating something very simple. For our part, we prayed this wasn't false modesty.

She greeted us at the door with the same frenetic energy that had swept me off my feet a couple of days earlier. She gave us kisses on both cheeks, helped us out of our shoes, took our jackets, then frog-marched us through to the sitting room, with its inimitable blend of the sublime and the hideous. She left us sitting there side by side and darted off to attend to the kitchen production line.

I took the opportunity to reacquaint myself with the bizarre décor: the beautiful wall-hangings depicting scenes of nature and the changing seasons; the macabre French dolls, watching me from their glass cases with dull lifeless eyes; the small ancestral shrine where the incense was ever-burning. I also saw the row of framed certificates on the wall, a constant reminder that her sons had achieved something in life, even if one had amassed a lot more frames than the other. I couldn't imagine my own parents hanging a certificate of mine on the wall, even if I ever managed to earn one.

Mrs Azuma returned with a saucer of rice crackers and sat down next to us.

'Are you enjoying Izumi?'

'Yes,' I said after a brief hesitation. I wasn't about to weigh in with an account of my experiences to date.

'What have you been doing?'

Again a tricky question, and I found myself looking to Sarah for assistance.

'We've seen all the sights of Izumi, like the castle and the burial mounds,' she said.

'And have you found any ghosts?' Mrs Azuma asked, getting to the crux of the matter.

'I'm afraid not.'

Mrs Azuma looked disappointed, as though she'd been hoping for something spicy. After all, Charlie had sat in the very same room telling tales of ghosts. But I had no stomach to talk about the things I'd seen both in full consciousness and in the shady realm of sleep. Sarah had already warned me that, good-natured though Mrs Azuma was, she could gossip for the Olympic team.

A part of me wondered what she'd actually say if I did decide to tell all. Would she smile politely if I said that I'd seen Reiko at the graveyard, standing as she was in life, reflected in the window of the car; that I'd seen her in the bathroom mirror in Sarah's apartment, her head bowed in sadness; that I'd been pursued in a dream to a clearing in the woods, which I was convinced had been Reiko's last resting place?

'No, no ghosts.'

Mrs Azuma sighed. I was clearly a lot less psychic than the unfortunate Charlie.

'Don't worry,' she said with a smile of encouragement, 'you still have some time in Izumi. When are you leaving?'

'The day after tomorrow, I'm afraid. It's not long.'

'That's a pity,' she cried and drummed on the table with her hands. 'Now, it's time to eat.'

Without wasting a breath, she jumped up and whizzed back to the kitchen to continue her preparations, leaving Sarah and I to prepare our stomachs.

In the event, Mrs Azuma did exercise restraint, perhaps understanding that two banquets in a week were too much of a good thing, even for strapping foreigners like us. She warmed us up with a bowl of traditional *miso* soup with succulent shreds of *wakame* seaweed and *tofu* mixed in. Then she treated us to a *shabu-shabu* main course, which involved boiling various shreds of meat and vegetables in a central pot of boiling water. There were plenty of complimentary dipping sauces and the idea was to eat as much or as little as we wanted. Naturally, as the beer flowed and the conversation got going, the temptation was to eat more rather than less. With communal plates to choose from and a never ending supply of meats, cabbage, *shiitake* mushrooms and other things to boil, there was no logical place to stop.

The conversation was much lighter than the previous evening and my decision to lay off the subject of ghosts seemed to pay off. I felt better for it and I expected that Mrs Azuma did too. She spent some more time explaining what her sons had done to merit the certificates on the wall, then gave a detailed account of her future aspirations for them. The elder was studying medicine and looked certain to become a doctor within the next few years. The younger was a little less focused about where his law degree was going. It was very hard, she said plaintively, to become a lawyer in Japan. She didn't feel that poor Kenji had a chance. If her elder son had wanted to be a lawyer, then he would surely have succeeded, but not Kenji. I knew she only wanted the best for her children, but I couldn't help feeling a little sorry for the lad, sadly unable to live up to his mother's expectations.

It was the way a dinner date should go. Plenty of beer, aimless conversation and compliments to the chef. In fact, it was getting towards ten o'clock when Mrs Azuma suddenly announced we should see some video footage of her sons. Sarah looked at her watch, I looked at mine, and we both made it clear that we were tired and, appealing though the proposal was, it would be better to leave it for another time. Mrs Azuma didn't seem to mind, then suggested we take a disc with us to watch at home.

It seemed odd to send us home with some of her son's home video footage, but we had no special reason to refuse. Mrs Azuma selected a disc from the cabinet and Sarah slipped it into her bag, promising to watch it when we got home.

'So, you're leaving on Monday?' Mrs Azuma asked.

'Yes. Monday morning.'

'It's a pity. You should stay longer in Izumi.'

'I'd love to. But I have to get back to Osaka. I need to do some research before the start of term.'

'Then, you must come and spend the night with us before you go. Sarah often spends the night. You should both come.'

Sarah nodded, amenable to the suggestion, though I guessed she had learnt from experience that it was easier to agree with everything. Mrs Azuma had a persuasive manner about her. If she wanted you to take a disc home, you went ahead and took it. If she wanted you to stay the night, you said 'yes'. My only reservation was the prospect of some kind of 'farewell' banquet. I didn't want her pulling out all the stops again.

As we stepped out of the door, saying our 'goodnights', Mrs Azuma seemed to remember something.

'That disc,' she said, gesturing towards Sarah's bag, 'contains film that Kenji took on his school-trip. But there are also pictures of the students we were talking about. The ones who died.'

This knocked me back a bit. Having scrupulously avoided any mention of the high school tragedy all evening, here she was handing over video footage of the victims. It was unsettling.

'Why would she give us that?' I said as we made our way through the front gate.

'I suppose you were asking about it last night. It's not unreasonable to think you're interested.'

'You don't think it's weird?'

'A bit. But she does that kind of stuff. She just wanted to show us some footage of her son. I've seen some of their home videos before. She probably thought that you'd only sit down to watch it if you knew there were dead people in it.'

'I hope she doesn't think that of me.'

Sarah unlocked the car and flashed me a smile over the bonnet. 'It's true though, isn't it? Admit it.'

She was right. Against my better judgement I couldn't wait to get back and put the disc in the machine.

On the way back Sarah pulled in at the Seven-Eleven to pick up some groceries.

In contrast to the previous day, the shop was completely deserted except for a bored-looking young man behind the till who regaled us with a formulaic greeting as we entered. Sarah picked up a basket and wandered off to look for some food staples while I set up next to the magazine stand and started to flick through some of the wares on offer. There were several categories of *manga*, from the overtly childlike to the overtly adult. I picked up one of the latter to see a double spread of a woman trussed up in leather bondage being straddled by a drooling businessman wearing shirt and tie. I glanced over my shoulder to check that Sarah hadn't noticed my choice of reading matter, but she was at a safe distance. I flicked through a few more pages and saw more sado-masochistic images. In some the man was the aggressor and in the others the woman held sway. There was a whole other thesis hidden in those pages – a whole bizarre world I knew nothing about. I put the magazine down quickly and moved away.

I watched Sarah in the reflection of the window make her way round the shop and I felt a rush of sadness at the thought that I would soon be leaving Izumi. I hadn't left her side in days and it was the kind of constant companionship I hadn't known in a long time. I wondered how I would adjust to being on my own again, with only Josh to keep me company until the new term started. I thought of my Spartan room in the dormitory, a far cry from Sarah's candlelit sanctuary with hot mugs of cocoa and Gregorian chant. Then I thought of Yoshi, of his body laid out on the asphalt covered in a bloodstained sheet. And I thought of Charlie all those years ago, making the long trip back from Izumi and deciding that, on balance, he didn't want to live.

'What are you thinking about?'

Sarah had appeared at my side.

'Nothing,' I mumbled. 'Away with the fairies.'

We wandered over to the counter and Sarah handed the basket to the bored cashier.

'Oh, can you get some beer,' she said, pointing to the fridge on the far wall.

I walked over, opened the glass door and bent down to grab some cans.

I don't know what made me glance up at that precise moment. Maybe the devils on my shoulder, a slight tingling at the back of my neck, a primeval intuition. But even before I looked, I knew she was there.

Reflected in the glass door of the fridge, she was standing in front of the magazine rack wearing her school uniform tied with a blood-red ribbon. Whereas before her eyes had been downturned, now her head was raised and she looked straight at me. And for the first time I saw her from head to toe, down to her pleated skirt and knee length white socks.

I looked straight at her and she looked straight at me and I knew beyond all doubt that it was Reiko.

The beer cans dropped to the floor with a clatter and the door swung shut. I turned to look, but she was gone.

I sank down onto the cold tiles and leant back against the fridge door as the room spun around me. My stomach churned, my sight grew dim and, in a daze, I saw Sarah lurching towards me with arms outstretched. I saw the cashier emerge from behind the counter, alarmed. And I saw the beer cans roll slowly across the floor.

The next thing I knew, I was sitting on a bench outside the shop with Sarah's comforting arm on my shoulder. It was good to feel the cool evening air in my lungs.

'You saw her, didn't you?'

I nodded wearily. Compared with the two previous occasions, I felt more numb than afraid. This time she had been more distinct, more rounded, the outlines clearer and the colours stronger.

And then there were her eyes. Those same eyes I had seen in a photograph in Charlie's file one night in Osaka. Those eyes which had peered into the black depths of my soul.

It was eleven o'clock by the time we got back to Sarah's apartment. We had sat outside the shop for a long time, talking about what had happened, sifting the clues and evidence, agreeing to take whatever came without passion or prejudice. The main crumb of comfort that Sarah continued to offer me was that I would be leaving Izumi within thirty-six hours and that I need never return again. I told her that I would be sad if I couldn't see her again and she told me she only had another three months before she herself would be leaving forever. She went on to remind me of the universal law that ghosts do not travel. I'd told her myself that ghosts were absolutely location-specific. They might be able to follow you around within a limited radius, but once you got on a train and travelled halfway across the country, they had no way of following. I said I only hoped there were no exceptions to this rule.

We were neither of us particularly tired, despite the full and hearty meal Mrs Azuma had given us, so we decided to make a cup of hot cocoa, settle down on the mattress and watch a bit of the footage she had sent us off with. It probably wasn't the ideal way to relax after seeing what I'd seen in the Seven-Eleven, but with three sightings under the belt, they were beginning to seem commonplace. And, as Sarah pointed out, with only thirty-six hours before I left, we didn't have much time if we were going to solve the mystery of these ghostly apparitions.

Sarah wasn't much into audio-visual entertainment and both TV and DVD player had to be dragged out of the cupboard and wired up from scratch. While I did this Sarah told me she'd spent her first week desperately looking for something to watch. TV shows in Japan, she said, seemed to fall into three categories: live baseball, bizarre variety shows featuring wacky male presenters and women in bikinis laughing at their jokes, and Samurai dramas. The rest of the time there were adverts. I asked if she had any better opinion of British TV and she said 'no', but that she still lived in hope of finding a tele-visual nirvana somewhere in the world.

The DVD player hooked up and the television turned on, we settled down side by side to watch Azuma Junior's school trip diary. Seeing myself and Sarah reflected in the blank screen immediately set my nerves on edge. What would I do if I suddenly saw a dim figure standing at my shoulder or a ghostly white face peering through the window behind us?

I fumbled for the remote control and started the disc. I don't know if I was still suffering the after-effects of the Seven-Eleven experience, but the mere sight of static at the beginning of the disc seemed to ratchet the tension up another notch. I shifted to get a little closer to Sarah, then waited.

The footage started with a grainy shot of a school bus waiting in the forecourt of Izumi high school. It appeared to be early morning and the students were gathered around in groups, chatting excitedly about the trip ahead. Everyone was wearing school uniforms, except for the teachers who were busy doing a headcount. It was impossible to make out any of the students from the opening shot. It seemed the camera operator, who I took to be young Kenji, was still grappling with the zoom and focus functions. I did, however, identify both Odagiri-san and Shirakami-san among the teachers.

The footage cut to a shot taken inside the bus, after they'd set off. Kenji seemed to have mastered the camera now and offered a slow sweeping shot from the front of the bus, taking in all the students. They were seated in orderly fashion and I spotted Kanae Kubota and Jun Takada, the doomed lovers, side by side and smiling happily. I thought I also spotted Saori and Hideki, sitting near the back, but I was less sure. The only one I couldn't see was the one I most wanted to see: Reiko. I was going to suggest that we play the disc back to get a better look, but I didn't have to bother.

The very next shot was a full close-up of Reiko herself, sitting in the seat at the front, face turned to the window, ignoring the camera. In the seat next to her with arms folded and a serious expression was the increasingly suspicious Odagiri-san.

Sarah and I exchanged looks. I felt as though we were part of a jury assigned to investigate a series of suspicious deaths and here we'd been granted access to a confidential piece of evidence. I wondered if that had been Mrs Azuma's intention all along. Had she wanted us to see these images and draw our own conclusions? It seemed a far-fetched idea, but I'd seen enough of the far-fetched over the past week to believe anything.

Seeing Reiko like this was almost more than I could bear. Only months or even weeks before her disappearance she was there, in the pride of youth, displaying an almost unearthly beauty. No wonder the camera lingered on her. It was equally disturbing to see the dubious figure of Odagiri-san next to her, positioned like a sentry between her and the rest of the bus, warning all who approached to keep their distance. In fact, it was he who eventually looked up at the camera and said something in Japanese that I couldn't understand. From the tone we guessed he was telling Kenji that he had filmed enough.

The scene changed and Kenji was getting down from the coach with his classmates and heading towards a grand temple complex in the hills. We surmised this from the few flashes of scenery we were granted as Kenji was having difficulty pointing the camera and walking at the same time. One minute we were looking at the shoes of the person in front and the next minute we were seeing leafy hills and the cloudless sky above. We went on to a series of exterior shots of the temple, which Sarah guessed was the shrine at Nikko, a popular attraction for high school excursions and one of the few major tourist spots within striking distance of Izumi.

We cut to inside the grounds of the temple with a series of shots of students standing around chatting noisily, enjoying their freedom. For the next ten minutes we followed this cast of characters, Kenji's intrepid camera guiding us in and out of the temple and its various outbuildings. But there was one constant in all of it. Wherever he went, whatever he was focusing on, Reiko was never far away. Others came and went, flashed the two-fingered peace sign in the camera's direction, pulled funny faces, or ducked out of view. But Reiko neither acknowledged the camera nor avoided it. She seemed to hover around the edges of the shots, either chatting quietly to her friends – mainly the four ill-fated students we already knew about – or to the teachers. Odagiri-san certainly seemed to spend a lot of time standing next to her, making jokes and observations, pointing to the architecture. Shirakami-san, the shyer of the two, also made a number of cameo appearances at her side. And there were other boys too, coming and going, happy to occupy her personal space.

Throughout the whole thing, my eyes never left her for a second and nor, it seemed, did the cameraman's. At one point, there was a shot of a carving of three monkeys, illustrating the motto *'hear no evil, see no evil, speak no evil'*. One monkey had its paws clamped over its ears, another had its paws over its eyes, and the third had them over its mouth. The camera moved down to catch Reiko, face upturned, looking with a mixture of soulful reflection and amusement. The camera lingered there, until she moved away and the moment was gone.

There was then a poignant shot. Kenji had chanced upon the five friends in a group together, talking together happily. Jun turned to see the camera on them and flashed a broad smile in its direction. Kanae turned and did likewise, brandishing the peace sign – the standard Japanese student's response to a photo opportunity. Then they all turned and struck poses for the camera – even Reiko, who seemed to acknowledge it for the first time. Kenji framed them perfectly underneath a glorious red arch. And then they turned, as though with one mind and began to walk through the arch, casting glances over their shoulders and laughing.

Kenji tracked them all the way, using the zoom to keep up with them, until they were no more than grainy blobs on the screen. Then the scene cut to a tranquil shot of a tree. The students were gone.

Sarah reached for the remote control and paused the disc.

'What do you think?' I said.

'I think he was in love with her.'

I was in complete agreement. 'He never let her out of his sight.'

'He was following her like an obsessive. No wonder she wouldn't look at the camera. He was stalking her and she knew it.'

I felt I had to stick up for the guy. 'You don't think that's a bit harsh? The guy had a crush. It's what teenage boys do when they like a girl. They follow her around, while she ignores them. Of course you try not to do it as an adult, because by then it's weird. But didn't you ever have a crush on someone, then constantly obsess about them? Didn't your hormones ever go haywire?'

I was surprised by how reasonable I was sounding. Maybe it was because I recognized the impulse so well. I identified with teenagers, identified with their prob-lems, with their insecurities and roller-coaster emotions. I used to think I would never leave my teenage years behind. But what I didn't like to admit to Sarah as the images unfolded was that I shared Kenji's fascination with Reiko. Ever since seeing her photo in Charlie's file that night in Osaka, I hadn't been able to get her out of my mind. Little wonder that I was seeing her every-where, standing as she was in life, like an avenging angel.

Sarah lay back on the mattress and sighed heavily, staring up at the ceiling.

'It's not so much Kenji I'm worried about,' I said. 'He's just a horny teenager. It's those teachers, clamping themselves on to Reiko, like they own her.'

'Agreed. They're fucking creepy.' She bit her nails irritably. 'I can't ever look at them in the same way.'

'So what made her give us the disc?' I asked.

'That's what I don't get. She must have seen it. She must have noticed that her son spent most of the time following Reiko about. And she must have known that we'd notice, after all our questions.'

'Maybe she didn't look at it that way. We'd asked her a load of questions about the case, so she gave us some footage to see. Her son shot it, so she probably thought we'd admire his technical skill as a film director or something. I don't think there was any other motive.'

Sarah yawned and pulled the duvet over her legs. 'I'm pretty tired. Are you going to watch any more of this?'

I wanted to say 'no', but the attraction of the disc was too great. I needed to satisfy myself that there was nothing more to see. 'Do you mind if I continue?'

'No, just prod me if anything interesting happens.'

Sarah settled in under the duvet and I moved across and propped myself against the wall to catch some more of the show. I knew I would have been better off getting some kip, but I needed to go the distance on this one.

I pressed 'play' on the disc and watched as Kenji took some more footage of trees. I guessed Reiko must have given him the slip and he was filling in time with some nature shots.

Sure enough, within a few minutes she was back, the camera caressing her fine-boned features once more. Maybe Sarah had been right. Maybe the kid's obsession was unnatural. I tried to remember if I'd ever done anything of the sort myself. I'd never taken video footage of a girl I liked, so I couldn't make an exact comparison. I recalled sending tremulous love poems to a girl in my class for several weeks, before she told me she hated poetry and that I should stop. I guessed that if I'd had the guts I would have happily spent all day filming her.

After a while my eyes began to droop. It was more of the same stuff: students standing around talking and Reiko somewhere in the margins of the shot. The images on the screen soon merged into a continuous blur of school uniforms and shaky camerawork. Once or twice my head nodded and I lifted it with a start. The candles were burning low and Sarah was sleeping peacefully by my side. I resolved to turn in, but I'd somehow managed to mislay the remote. Not wanting to disturb Sarah rooting around for it, I decided to let the disc run on.

My head nodded again and when I lifted it, the footage had ended and the screen was blank, even though the disc still seemed to be running. I knew I should turn it off, but Sarah was lying right up against me and I didn't want her to move.

I let my head drop and this time it didn't come up. Sitting upright against the wall, my head down on my chest, I dozed to the faint hum of the disc, while the candles went out one by one around me, leaving the room in darkness.

A sudden noise broke the silence and I lifted my head with a start.

At first I didn't know what was happening. Sarah stirred from sleep and sat up. The television was showing grainy footage of a news presenter reading a story.

It took me a moment to realize that the disc was still playing.

'What's this?' Sarah asked, her voice sleepy.

'I don't know.' I found the remote control where Sarah had been lying and pressed the 'pause' button.

'Is this the same disc?'

'Someone must have taped this on the end. Sorry, I would've turned it off, but I couldn't find the remote.'

I was about to press the 'off' button, but Sarah stopped me. 'Let's see what it is.'

'It looks like the news.' I pressed 'play' and we watched a po-faced newsreader addressing the camera. By his demeanour, I guessed it wasn't happy news, but I couldn't make out the details. The only word I heard with any certainty was '*Izumi*'.

Suddenly the scene cut to an exterior shot of Izumi high school with dramatic titles running along the bottom of the screen and a monotone commentary. Then there was another cut, and this time it was Reiko's high school portrait, the same one that had been in Charlie's file.

'They're reporting her disappearance,' Sarah said, horrified. 'He's taped the report of her disappearance.'

I didn't know what to make of it. How strange to record the report of Reiko's disappearance and tack it on the end of the tape of the school trip. But it wasn't just tacked on the end. There was a half-hour or so gap between the end of the school trip footage and the beginning of the recording, as though it had been added in secret. After all, if I hadn't left the disc running and fallen asleep, we would never have got to this part.

'Why do you think he recorded this?'

I shook my head. 'It's all a bit creepy. I guess he was a hormonal teenager and the love of his life had gone missing. Maybe that's what you do.'

Sarah looked unimpressed.

'He then stuck it on the end of a disc he didn't think anyone would see. It's the natural teenage need for secrecy.'

'Do you think his Mum knew about this?'

'Probably not. Otherwise she wouldn't have handed it over so willingly.'

The scene had cut to what appeared to be a rescue operation, with volunteers scouring the undergrowth around the hills, while men in uniforms directed operations. There followed a gratuitous aerial shot of the field of burial mounds before we were passed back to the po-faced newsreader and a link to a different story.

I was about to say something to Sarah about what we'd just seen when there was a break in the recording followed immediately by another news story.

This time, two newscasters, one male and one female, were reporting a different incident and again their tone signalled that this was another difficult story. By the time the scene cut to the portraits, I'd already guessed what it was. First Kanae's portrait came up, followed by Jun's, and again they were the same photographs that Charlie had put in his file. This time the cut to the exterior of the high school revealed a sea of activity in the forecourt. There were police cars, flashing lights, ambulances and a small crowd of concerned onlookers. Then the camera moved in to see a body under a white sheet being wheeled towards the waiting ambulance. This prompted a policeman to usher the camera away and the scene cut back to the newscasters, one of whom started talking about Reiko Shimura, clearly making the connection between the two cases, then bringing up her photograph.

'Honestly, what do you think of this?' Sarah asked.

'I don't know. I don't think we were meant to see it. I'll stick by what I said before. Kenji taped this stuff because the people were in his class, he knew them, maybe they were even his friends. It's a morbid thing to do, but he was a teenager. He's gone off to university now, hopefully got a girlfriend and got a life. It'd probably embarrass the hell out of him if he knew his Mum was handing this out.'

'You don't think we should tell his mum? I assume she doesn't know.'

'No. No way.'

Sarah was about to say something else, when the recording broke to yet another newscaster and we were treated to a similar sequence surrounding the case of Hideki Sano, run over on the highway. There was the obligatory portrait, the scenes of chaos on the road and the monotone commentary. Then we saw a group photo of class 3C, but four heads were now circled, highlighting their demise. This was followed by full-size portraits of the previous three victims.

By now we knew what was coming next. The last victim, Saori Kumano, found dead in her bedroom, and a fifth head was now circled on the group photo. I began to wonder what it must have been like for the remaining pupils seeing their numbers dwindling so rapidly, wondering whose head was up next for circling.

For a while after the disc ended we sat and said little. Sarah said that she'd given up smoking aged eighteen, but this was the first time she'd felt a craving since that time. Neither of us really knew what to think about the sequence, and both of us were too tired to come up with any theories. Sarah agreed that, weird though it was, Kenji maybe deserved a little slack. He was a screwed-up teenager with a pushy mother, who had witnessed his classmates dropping dead around him. After all, he'd been in love with Reiko and all of a sudden she'd disappeared without trace. Dead or alive, no one knew.

'Will you sleep here?' Sarah said, as she settled under the duvet. 'I don't want to be alone.'

I echoed this sentiment wholeheartedly. I switched off the disc and ejected it, fearful perhaps of what else might be lurking further down the line, then got under the duvet next to Sarah. It was comforting to feel her close to me. I was sure that as long as she was there nothing could touch me. Nothing could ever touch me.

I was wrong.

Night Encounter

It was just after two when Sarah woke me. I felt her tug at my sleeve under the duvet and turned to see her propped up on her elbow next to me.

'What is it?'

'I thought I heard something.'

'What?'

'A scrabbling sound, like someone was clawing at a door somewhere. It's stopped now.'

The moon shone in through the partially open blind revealing her features to me. The sight of her in the moonlight tempered the alarm I felt at being woken so suddenly.

'It could've been an animal,' I said.

'That's what I would've said. But after what I've seen tonight, I'm not feeling very trusting. We know that a murderer could still be out there somewhere in the village.'

'Come on, it all happened years ago. Anyway I'm the one who has the nightmares.'

'It's all right for you. You can leave on Monday. I'm stuck here for another three months. Anything could happen in that time.'

I reached out and began to pull Sarah down towards the bed, telling her she needed to relax. But the next thing I knew I'd pulled her into my arms and she was kissing me.

I didn't know how it had happened or who'd made the move, and my reactions struggled to keep up. I found my hands reaching for Sarah's waist, caressing her warm skin and feeling the smoothness of her back. We kissed, softly at first, then with increasing firmness. Two years of pent-up emotion were quickly finding their release.

I fumbled with her nightdress and in a moment it was over her head. She propped herself on her elbow and I caught sight of her naked body for the first time, alabaster white in the moonlight. Passion had me in its grip and I swooned with the sheer exhilaration of it. I felt her hands grapple with my T-shirt and pull it over my head. Then they travelled down and freed me of my boxer shorts.

She sat upright and her profile was perfectly silhouetted in the window frame. Pushing her hair back with her hands, she manoeuvred herself on top of me.

I didn't know if I was ready for what was about to come. After so much time out of action I was hesitant at first, but Sarah bent down and whispered in my ear, telling me to let go and enjoy it, that I should leave everything to her.

I lay back and gazed at her nakedness, made more mysterious by the delicate play of light and shadow. And I whispered that I would follow wherever she wanted to lead me. In that moment she was more beautiful than anything I'd known, more feminine, more sensuous.

I gave myself up to my senses. There was no nervous fumbling, no embarrassment, no fear of consequences or an inability to perform. It felt as I always hoped it would feel: the most natural thing in the world.

I closed my eyes, letting these sensations wash over me, but when I opened them again, my heart turned to ice.

It was only a split second, but it was enough. It wasn't Sarah looking down at me, it was Reiko, wearing the same dispassionate expression I'd seen in the home video, looking at me, looking straight through me. Only there was no love there, no emotion, nothing.

I winced and looked away and when I looked back Reiko had gone and Sarah was there in her place. She caught the sudden change in me and stopped, concerned.

I tried to put the image out of my mind, to give myself up to my senses again, if only for Sarah's sake. But the spell was broken, the passion gone.

'Are you all right?'

I caressed her shoulders, cursing myself to hell. What was wrong with me?

'What is it?' she asked, leaning forward and stroking my face. I thanked God there was still affection in her touch. At least I still had that.

'I'm sorry. I'm so sorry. It keeps happening. I can't help it.'

She looked at me, bewildered.

'Why doesn't she leave me alone?'

Sarah came and lay down next to me, continuing to stroke my face and hair.

'She's in my head and I need to get rid of her.'

Sarah pressed a finger to my lips. 'You don't have to say anything.'

I marvelled at her attitude. She wasn't showing the slightest sign of irritation at the sudden change in my behaviour, the rude interruption of our intimacy. She'd taken it in her stride. I could have declared my undying love for her there and then.

For a while I lay there listening to her rhythmic breathing at my side and I realized she was fast asleep.

For the next couple of hours I tried my utmost to focus my mind on Sarah, what had just happened between us and the feelings I had for her. But every time I closed my eyes, I saw Reiko staring down at me, dissecting me with her cold eyes. What was this hold she had over me? Why had her unearthly beauty disturbed me so much? It was the first time in two years I had been intimate with someone and here I was having to battle against this impostor from some dark, unknown place. What did she want of me?

These questions circled my head until the first light of dawn appeared at the window and allowed me, grudgingly, some sleep.

KIMIKO

I woke up to a heavy stomach and an aching sadness.

I lay there with Sarah asleep beside me, knowing that this would be my last day in Izumi and that I would be leaving her behind. I wondered if there was any hope for the two of us after what had happened in the night. She had been more than considerate after I'd broken things off so abruptly, but she couldn't have been pleased. Maybe if I had a few more days to smooth things over, I might have some hope. But at the rate I was going I'd probably be certified within that timeframe. There was no way of getting round it: I had to leave Izumi.

It seemed unlikely there was any chance of a long-distance relationship. She only had a few more months left on her contract and would then be heading straight back to England. I couldn't see her calling on me in Osaka. By the time I left Japan in a year's time, she would have started a new life, no doubt complete with new boyfriend.

However I looked at it, I couldn't see it happening. She had said herself she'd been starved of social contact during her time in Izumi and she hadn't exactly been fighting them off. She had admitted to feeling lonely and isolated and that my coming here was a big event for her. It seemed likely that under different circumstances she would never have gone this far with me. And given the chance to make something happen, what had I done? I'd blown it completely. I would be relegated to a cringeworthy anecdote in a beery pub. I could hear her now, telling her friends of the night she slept with a ghost-hunter psycho who had to break off from sex because he'd just seen a ghost. Thinking about it in the cold light of day, it sounded truly awful. What was wrong with me?

She stirred in her sleep, opened her eyes and looked at me. I was expecting her to look shocked or embarrassed and tell me what a mistake it had all been, but instead she stroked my hair and smiled.

'Good morning, sunshine,' she said cheerfully. 'Sleep well?'

'Not too bad, considering.'

'Considering what?' she asked, looking at me with wide eyes. 'Considering I'm not wearing any clothes?'

It took me a moment to realize she was joking. I was feeling too frail for humour. I needed things spelt out in clear, unambiguous English. 'You know, the video footage, the newsreels, everything.'

'Yeah, I know. Don't worry.' She locked her hands behind her head and stared at the ceiling.

'Look I'm sorry about acting weird last night. I shouldn't have watched that footage. It can't have helped.' With only one day left in Izumi I needed to work quickly to salvage some dignity.

'You said you saw her again?'

'Yes.'

'You saw her appear in the room?'

I nodded, pleased that she wasn't trying to avoid the subject. I'd wanted the opportunity to clear the air as quickly as possible and she seemed to want the same. The only thing I couldn't tell her was that Reiko hadn't just been in the room, she had actually taken Sarah's place. I didn't think she'd want to know that.

'So, it wasn't a reflection this time?'

'She was just standing there.' I thought it best to leave it vague.

'Right, you've got one more day here. I'd better make sure you leave in one piece.' She sat up, not at all embarrassed by her nakedness.

I smiled, ashamed that I'd ever doubted her.

'Your last day,' she said to herself, considering the prospect quietly. I hoped I could sense at least a tinge of regret in her voice.

'Your life will be able to return to normal.'

'That's one way of putting it. Before I thought it was just the village that was haunted, but now I know my apartment is too.'

Sarah stretched her arms and slipped into her dressing gown. I felt a pang of sadness, as though this were the unofficial end of whatever had happened between us. The act of dressing represented a return to normality, a return to the old routine. I wished we could have lounged in bed all day and let the world get on with its business without us. I wished we could have forgotten that anything had ever happened in Izumi, expunge its dark history from our memories and carry on as though it were just a quaint old village in the country. In that moment I wanted to forget everything about what I did and why I'd come.

'Do you want low key or high octane today?' she asked from the door.

'Low key. Definitely low key.'

'Agreed. We need to get you out of here alive.'

The sun was still shining, so we decided on a short drive in the countryside followed by a quiet lunch or picnic somewhere. In the afternoon we would come back to the apartment, avoid all reflections on the way, then vegetate until dinner. It was a shame that we'd arranged to have dinner and a sleepover at Mrs Azuma's, as I guessed sleeping at the Azuma home would involve sleeping separately. I felt I needed another night with Sarah to repair the damage I'd done.

Driving through the village on a glorious Sunday morning, the beauty of the place struck me all over again. It was inconceivable that these peaceful streets had witnessed such a bloody history. The cherry trees lining the streets were bright with blossom, children rode their bikes along the pavements, while their parents tended to their gardens on their day off. All round the village the hills provided such a picturesque backdrop that I couldn't imagine how evil had ever taken root.

We arrived at a popular scenic spot in the hills overlooking Izumi and surrounding villages. We found a patch of grass and lay there looking up at the sky. It was liberating to be out in the fresh air, lying next to Sarah, and it was just the tonic I needed after the difficult night. I desperately wanted to ask the question, the one that people dread the most, the *will I see you again?* poser. The conversation continued for a time along light-hearted lines and I realized the folly of trying to change direction with questions about relationships.

But there was another topic we had been avoiding, which little by little crept into the conversation.

We started by talking about my thesis and about how my views had changed since coming to Izumi. Then we got on to the high school tragedy and what we thought had really happened and whether the video footage really had any significance. And then we got on to why I was seeing things, why the brooding sprit of a dead student was disturbing my waking hours. We had nothing new to add to what we'd already discussed, but one thing was abundantly clear: this wasn't a subject we could let lie. We both wanted to know more, even if we had to suffer for it.

Sarah had an idea. One of her students had lived in the States for a year and was always nagging Sarah to meet up at the weekend to practice her English. So far she had resisted, but this girl's elder sister had either been in Reiko's class or had known Reiko. She might be able to offer us some more clues.

She got on her phone and within minutes had arranged for us to meet up. The girl's name was Kimiko Ando and, according to Sarah, was quite a talker. It was a long shot, but perhaps she would be able to help us. We felt we had nothing to lose by making a social visit.

Sarah had agreed to meet at Kimiko's house since her parents were away for the day and she had the run of the place. She told me it would be the first time she'd ever ventured into a student's home and she was aware she was setting a dangerous precedent. As soon as the others got wind, they'd all want her round.

The place was close to Mrs Azuma's home, a sizeable property at the foot of the hills, protected by a giant gate and a pair of unfriendly Dobermans chained to a post near the front door. As we stood on the porch waiting for Kimiko the dogs strained frantically at their leads, barking and salivating like the hounds of hell. It was a relief when the door finally opened and Kimiko appeared.

Bright and bubbly, with a wide toothy smile, she was stars and stripes through and through. Her cheerful welcome was in complete contrast to her dogs and I felt compelled to point this out to her.

'Oh, they're for protection,' she said matter-of-factly.

'Protection? I can't imagine there being much crime here.'

'Not ordinary crime. People do get murdered, though.'

This came out of the blue. But since we'd come to pick her brains about suspected murders, we couldn't argue.

She took us into the living room and we sat down on the plush sofas. In contrast to Mrs Azuma's house, this place was almost entirely Western in appearance. No scrolls on the wall, no ancestral shrine, and certainly no ornamental dolls in glass cases.

'So nice of you to come.'

I could see from the way Kimiko looked at Sarah that she worshipped her teacher. To have her in her home was something she'd be bragging to her friends about come Monday morning.

'Nice of you to have us,' Sarah said, adopting her schoolmistress tone. 'We're not disturbing you?'

Kimiko shook her head emphatically. 'I wasn't doing anything. There's nothing to do around here anyway.'

Kimiko fetched us a drink, then joined us on the sofa beaming from ear to ear.

Still in school teacher mode, Sarah got right to the point. 'I thought I'd bring James round to meet you. He's here studying ghosts.'

Kimiko gave me a quizzical look and I gave her a nod as though to say: 'yep, it's as weird as it sounds'.

'He's been finding out about the Reiko Shimura case and wanted to talk to someone about it. You're one of about three people in Izumi with fluent English, so I thought you might be able to tell us something.'

Kimiko flashed Sarah a broad smile. 'Thank you. You're always helping me out at school.'

'Is she a good teacher?' I asked, already knowing the answer.

'She's the best. She's the best teacher in the school by miles. Everyone thinks so.' Kimiko flapped her arms around wildly and for a moment I thought she was going to lunge forward and throw her arms round Sarah. Whatever her intentions, she managed to restrain herself.

'You told me your sister was in the same year as the students who died,' Sarah said, returning to the purpose of our visit. I appreciated that she didn't want to get too touchy-feely with her students.

'Yeah, that was our first year, after we came back from the States. We had no idea anything like that could happen here. We thought we were coming from the most dangerous country in the world to the safest.'

'Did your sister know Reiko?' Sarah asked.

'Yeah, but she wasn't a big friend or anything. She knew her to say "hello" to.'

I felt a bit sorry for Kimiko. I was certain she would have been happier playing cards with us or talking about boys or whatever teenage girls liked to do.

'Did she hear any rumours about Reiko after she disappeared?'

'Some people said she was having an affair with an older man. But that was just a rumour. My sister didn't believe it. She said Reiko wasn't that kind of girl.'

'What about the boys in the class? Were there any rumours about them?'

Kimiko looked unsure about this. 'Some of the boys were in love with her, I think.'

'Anyone in particular you remember?'

Kimiko shook her head.

'What about Kenji Azuma?'

I was surprised Sarah had come out and named the poor lad, especially to a student. What would her doting host mother think? But Kimiko shook her head. The name didn't ring a bell and I was quite relieved that it didn't.

'I did hear a story from my sister about the time after Reiko disappeared.' She trailed off and looked around anxiously, as though to check no one was listening in on our conversation.

'What was it?' Sarah was sitting on the edge of the sofa, a little impatient now. Of the two of us, it seemed to be her showing the greater urgency.

'Well, it was something that Jun said to her just before he died.' Kimiko leaned in, her smile gone and her voice lowered to a whisper. 'He'd said he'd seen Reiko.'

'Seen her?' I exclaimed.

'Yes. He said she wasn't dead.'

'Where did he see her?' I asked, leaning forward, so we were all huddled in a little group round the coffee table.

'He said he saw her more than once, as though she were following him. But whenever he tried to speak to her, she disappeared. And there was another thing.'

I felt a sinking feeling in the pit of my stomach.

'He said that his girlfriend had seen Reiko too. She was Reiko's best friend, but Reiko still wouldn't speak to her. She disappeared as soon as she saw her.'

'What about the other two, Hideki and Saori? Do you know if they saw anything too?' Sarah asked.

Kimiko shook her head. 'I don't think my sister knew them so well. But people said they were quite depressed before their death, so maybe they saw the same thing as Jun and Kanae.'

'Reiko?' Sarah whispered the name, as though she too was convinced she could be overheard.

Kimiko nodded her head solemnly. 'People were frightened. The school was shut, some students refused to come to school for months and some families moved away. It's like there was a curse.'

'Is that what they said?' I asked.

'Yes. They said that anyone who saw Reiko died within a week.'

I leaned back on the sofa, feeling faint. I now knew for certain that all the people who'd followed Reiko to the grave had one thing in common. They had all seen her in the week before their deaths.

First Jun and Kanae, her closest friends, dying in the grounds of the school. Even if she didn't know what had happened to Hideki and Saori, it was easy enough to infer. And then there was Charlie. I had always assumed he was on the edge of sanity even before he set foot in Izumi. I had assumed that the visions he saw were the product of a sick mind. But even if that were true, I had no reason to believe I was any saner.

Kimiko's words reverberated round my head, making me dizzy. *Anyone who saw Reiko died within a week.* My rational self told me it was nonsense. Superstitious nonsense. The usual drivel teenagers come out with to explain something they don't understand. A cock-eyed theory to explain away a series of tragic events. They couldn't have seen Reiko. Reiko was dead.

Anyone who saw Reiko died within a week. Jun claimed to have seen her. As did Kanae. As did Charlie. And all of them were dead within a week.

I tried to steady myself, but I felt sick – my stomach was heavy, as though I were carrying a dead-weight. I saw Sarah look over at me with concern.

Anyone who saw Reiko died within a week. It was ridiculous. It lay in the realms of the absurd, along with goblins and leprechauns, mermaids and sirens, orcs and elves. It lay in the realms of fairy tales told at bedtime, Jack climbing the beanstalk, Cinderella going to the ball and Snow White choking on the apple. I never believed those stories, so why should I believe this one? There was no curse, no visitor from beyond the grave. Everything could be explained, even my dream of the woods. Everything was in the mind. Everything.

I would be on the first train out of Izumi in the morning and I would leave it all behind. I would look back and laugh about it in years to come, laugh about how I bought into the whole idea of ghosts and goblins. How I actually believed for a moment that I was cursed.

In any case, I had no possible connection to Reiko. I hadn't known her in life like Jun or Kanae, and she hadn't known me. There was no possible reason for me to be cursed, any more than there had been for Charlie.

I collected myself and sat up. I wasn't going to die within the week. I wasn't going to give in so easily to these poisonous ideas. I had more than a few days to live, more than a few years. And one day the village of Izumi would be a distant memory.

I didn't feel well as we left Kimiko's house. I felt a crushing anxiety as we waved goodbye to her, ran the canine gauntlet and returned to Sarah's car. The conversation had been illuminating, but not in a com-forting way. Of course Kimiko had no way of knowing that I too had seen Reiko, that the curse she spoke of could equally be applied to my case.

Sarah asked if I wanted to go home and have some rest and I said that I did. I didn't really want to be out and about, at least not with a curse hanging over my head. However much I tried to discredit the thought, I found myself counting the weight of evidence. The first thing I'd wished for on waking up was for a longer stay in Izumi, so I could sort things out with Sarah, but I was now counting the hours until I got on that train. I wanted to get away from Izumi, to put miles between myself and Reiko, to return to the safe haven of Osaka. The sight of Yoshi hurtling to his death no longer held any fear for me. In fact, my whole time in Osaka seemed like a distant age of innocence and simplicity.

In the car on the way back to Sarah's apartment I closed my eyes. I wanted to avoid any further sightings of Reiko. I was fearful now of anything that produced a reflection: car windows, shop fronts, the rearview mirror in the car. I wondered how I'd react if I saw her sitting behind us on the back seat. I didn't want to find out.

'What are you going to do?' Sarah asked, after we made it in. 'I really need to get some things from the shop. Do you want to stay here or come with me?'

I didn't want to be left on my own, but nor did I want to go out. 'I'll stay,' I said finally. 'I'll just lie low and hope for the best.'

'Just stay away from anything with a reflection,' she said, like a mother warning a wilful child to keep away from the road.

For a while after Sarah left, I lay on her bed and stared at the ceiling, tying to devise a strategy for getting through my remaining time in Izumi. I was working on the absolute certainty that once I left Izumi behind, I'd be in the clear, that whatever was happening was specific to Izumi. I'd discussed it with Sarah: one of the cardinal rules of ghostly behaviour in all the literature was that they did not travel. They had their haunting patch and that was that. Of course, Charlie had returned to Osaka and killed himself, but judging by his notes, he'd already lost his mind by the time he boarded the train. Whatever had been out to get him, had already done its job.

My greatest asset in surviving my remaining time in Izumi had to be Sarah. If it hadn't been for her, I might have already gone the way of Charlie. She had provided protection from whatever demons were undermining my mental stability. She had shown understanding and sensitivity far beyond the call of duty. She had also provided a roof over my head. If she hadn't been there to distract from the visions and explain away the dreams, the monsters might have got me already.

I decided my best strategy was to lie there and wait for Sarah to get back, then when Sarah got back, to lie there some more and not let her out of my sight. Then to go to Mrs Azuma's and eat, drink and try to forget. The only thing that genuinely frightened me was sleep and what dreams might come visiting. I remembered Edgar Allan Poe calling them '*little slices of death*'. I had died once already, in the dark woods, and I didn't want to die again. I could of course drink so much that I lost control of my faculties, but then I was afraid of what I might do in my senseless state. I could try not to sleep, but lack of sleep might make me vulnerable.

Stay calm, I told myself, and think pleasant thoughts.

Sarah arrived back laden with shopping bags, relieved to find me in good spirits. I explained that I'd been lying there thinking pleasant thoughts, and outlined my strategy to her.

After unpacking the bags, she came and sat down beside me with a cup of tea and we chatted about inconsequential things. Showing genuine affection, she linked her arm in mine and rested her head on my shoulder.

And there we stayed, not moving, not even speaking much, just huddled together, seeking comfort in one another's company. I felt none of the embarrassment I'd felt the night before, none of the frustration at my inability to perform, but only a sense of wellbeing, knowing that Sarah was with me, that she was an amulet against all misfortune. With her at my side I would see out my last night in Izumi and return to the old life with my sanity intact.

THE LAST SUPPER

In 1143, a tax-collector from the imperial court paid a visit to Izumi and recorded a frank opinion in his journal. He wrote that Izumi lived under an ancient curse and that the spectre of death haunted every wretched house in the village. He described seeing rotting corpses in a field, the result of some bitter local feud. It was a sight which made him long for the comfort and safety of the capital.

In 1621, the fifth year of the reign of emperor Genraku, an itinerant Buddhist monk, entered the village of Izumi, just north of the Great Shirakawa gate. He stopped for the night at a small inn and there the devil came to him in a dream and took him to the house of a local lord where he showed him the gateway to hell.

More than two centuries later, in the year following the opening of Japan to the West, the local lord made a last ditch stand against the advancing imperial army. Seeing that all was lost, he retreated to the sanctuary of his castle and there butchered his entire family and retinue in cold blood, sparing no soul.

Then, in the first decade of the 21st century, five high school students died in mysterious circumstances within the space of a month. A year later a foreign research student came to Izumi to learn more about its turbulent history for his doctoral thesis. He cut his visit short, made the long journey back to his dormitory in Osaka and hung himself that same night.

Four years following Charlie's death, I found myself on the eve of my own departure, trying to understand what the fates had in store for me and whether I too would enter the pantheon of Izumi legends. In years to come, I too might become a cautionary tale for foolhardy research students.

It was dark as we set off to see Mrs Azuma for my last evening. Sarah had packed her overnight bag and I had brought all my belongings, with the object of going straight to the station in the morning. Sarah assured me it would be a fun evening, though I suspected she was glad we would be spending my last night in separate rooms. No doubt she wouldn't want to go through a repeat of my previous night's performance. I had to accept that our brief fling was coming to an end. Whatever happened, I would be getting on the train in the morning and leaving Sarah behind. I told myself I had to get used to the idea.

We didn't speak much on the way to the house. I kept my head down, still fearful of what I might see caught in the headlights or sat in the backseat of the car. Sarah, for her part, seemed preoccupied.

'Mrs Azuma told me on the phone she was having some people round,' she announced as she stopped the car in front of the house.

'Anyone you know?' I wasn't in a very social mood, even it might prove a distraction.

'She wouldn't say. Actually she was all mysterious about it. Said you'd be interested in them too.'

Mrs Azuma opened the door before we'd even reached it and clapped her hands in excitement at our arrival. 'Welcome, welcome,' she cried, patting us both on the back.

She ushered us in and hopped about while we removed our shoes and stepped into the courtesy slippers already laid out for us. She was even more hyper than usual.

'I'm so sad you're leaving. You've been a good friend for Sarah,' she said, as though Sarah were her socially challenged daughter. 'So tonight is a special evening. Tonight is your last supper.'

I didn't know if she'd intended the religious reference, but it did seem an unfortunate choice of phrase. At least Sarah was amused, flashing me a con-spiratorial wink as we made our way into the sitting room.

I'd been warned there were people coming to dinner, but I was still unprepared for the row of faces greeting us. Shirakami-san, the man we'd found pining away in Reiko's old classroom, sat at the extended table looking up quizzically as we entered. Next to him, wearing a dark jacket and unable to muster a greeting sat Odagiri-san, the man who had loved Reiko in life and become one of the suspects in her disappearance. Finally, adding a little class to the line-up was Aya, smiling warmly, presumably relieved to see us join the grim little gathering.

209

I was struggling to understand why these people had been assembled here and for whose benefit. I presumed it must have had something to do with me. I couldn't believe these people were Mrs Azuma's special friends.

Sarah and I exchanged fumbled greetings with Shirakami-san and Odagiri-san, neither of whom looked pleased to see us. We said our hellos, they said theirs, but it was up to Aya to provide a bridge.

'Odagiri-san and Shirakami-san are shy about speaking English,' she said. 'I've been trying to encourage them.'

Neither of the two looked particularly encouraged. Odagiri-san grunted something inaudible while Shira-kami-san looked at the table.

'We didn't know you'd be here,' Sarah said.

'Neither did I,' Aya replied. 'I only got a call this afternoon. Mrs Azuma said you were coming for dinner.'

Shirakami-san spoke for the first time, making an attempt to join the conversation. 'Azuma-san is a famous cook in Izumi.'

'Is this the first time you've come here?' I asked him, doing my own bit to be sociable.

He nodded his head. I looked at Odagiri-san to see if he was going to join in and he followed Shirakami-san's lead with the briefest of nods. I got the impression he was deeply suspicious of me. Perhaps it was understandable after he'd watched me snooping around the school. I assumed they knew the reason I'd come to Izumi – from what I knew of the place, word travelled fast.

For a while we sat in embarrassed silence. Aya looked inhibited by the presence of her male colleagues, while Sarah was still coming to terms with the weird congregation Mrs Azuma had assembled for our benefit. As for Mrs Azuma, she was beetling around in the kitchen in her usual frenetic manner. The sounds of food preparation reached us loud and clear, providing a welcome distraction from the stilted atmosphere round the table.

She was back after a few minutes bearing some starter dishes which looked just as sumptuous as the first time she'd cooked for me, but with more of everything. The food relieved some of the pressure to make conversation and it was quickly followed by bottles of beer, which no one wasted any time in pouring. For her part, Mrs Azuma seemed happy to leave us to our devices.

Aya did some more sterling diplomatic work, starting to explain some of the delicacies to us. She pointed to the *natou* fermented soy bean dish, explaining that foreigners had trouble with it. Mrs Azuma had given it to us on the first night and we had indeed had trouble with it, but we played along and gave it another try, hoping to lighten the atmosphere. Shirakami-san mustered a smile, but Odagiri-san wasn't so easily won over.

We continued in this vein through a variety of dishes, keeping the focus firmly on the food. Aya led the charge, Sarah and I came up with appropriate responses and the other two sat there looking subdued. Eventually Mrs Azuma finished in the kitchen and came to sit down and, before she'd even tasted the food, she brought the forbidden subject up. It seemed as if this had been the plan all along.

'James is studying ghosts,' she said to the three teachers. 'He's interested to know if there are any ghosts at the high school.'

I was mortified that she had introduced the subject so bluntly. I could see Shirakami-san and Odagiri-san looking at me sternly.

At first no one said anything. Aya looked down at the table. Shirakami-san and Odagiri-san continued to look impassive. Surprisingly, it was Shirakami-san who spoke first. His voice wavered slightly, but his English was precise.

'Why are you studying ghosts?'

'Well, I'm not studying ghosts in particular. I'm studying the difference between Eastern and Western attitudes to the supernatural. Izumi has a long history of hauntings, so I'm interested in everything. Obviously I've heard about what happened at the high school.'

Mrs Azuma immediately began to clarify what I was saying in Japanese. It was too fast for me to understand properly, but I distinctly heard the word '*yurei*' come up.

Whatever she said didn't seem to appease them and I saw that Aya looked especially uncomfortable.

I felt I needed to explain myself. 'I didn't have any plan to research what happened at the school. I just wanted to research people's attitudes. I don't mean any disrespect.'

For a while, that was the end of that. Mrs Azuma left the room and came back with more food, this time some large platters of different meats, some cooked and some raw. I politely enquired if horse meat was on the menu and Mrs Azuma laughed and said it certainly was. Aya, like Sarah, found the idea disgusting and declined to try any, but both Shirakami-san and Odagiri-san tucked in without hesitation.

'Do you like raw horse now?' Mrs Azuma asked.

'It's a bit chewy, but I like it,' I said, trying to sound enthusiastic. Truth was, I didn't like it and I didn't want to eat it. I only wanted the dinner party to be over.

Then, just as I thought we were safely back to talking about food, Mrs Azuma waded in again. 'Have you found any clues about the ghosts you were searching for?'

It was abundantly clear she had only convened the little gathering in order to help me prise some information from the teachers. Perhaps she thought I should be doing more to push my agenda.

'No, not really,' I lied. 'I haven't heard any stories. But I know it's a sensitive subject and, as I said, I don't want to be disrespectful.'

Mrs Azuma looked disappointed. She turned to Shirakami-san and Odagiri-san, asking them in Japanese if they had anything to contribute. Again the word 'yurei' came up, followed by Reiko's name. I was no expert in Japanese etiquette, but judging by their outward demeanour, she wasn't being very tactful.

Odagiri-san looked at Mrs Azuma so long and hard that I was worried we were in a stand-off situation. Finally he put his chopsticks down and spoke in English for the first time. I had assumed that it would be basic at best, but it turned out to be as accomplished as Mrs Azuma's.

'Reiko had no peace in life. Now she has no peace in death.'

He said it so eloquently and with such feeling that both Sarah and I were stunned into silence.

But he hadn't finished and he now directed what he said at me, as though it were I who had brought the subject up. I guessed he hadn't forgotten seeing me emerging from the woods together with Aya and Sarah. 'Someone hated her, so they killed her. That is all.'

'Maybe it wasn't hate. Maybe it was love,' Sarah said a little unexpectedly.

Odagiri-san looked at her for a long time, weighing his response. 'People don't murder for love. They murder for hate.'

I was intrigued to know what he meant by this, but I didn't have the courage to ask. Instead it was Sarah who ventured a question.

'Do you have any suspicions about what happened to her?'

Odagiri-san stared into the distance, leaving the question hanging in the air, unanswered. It wasn't clear whether he was considering the question, or simply ignoring it. None of us moved a muscle for those few moments. We just sat there watching Odagiri-san, who sat as motionless as the dolls in their glass cases, staring at us from across the room.

Even as the three teachers were preparing to leave, I was still wondering why they'd been invited and why they'd agreed to come. They didn't seem particularly close either to Mrs Azuma or to one another. Both Shirakami-san and Odagiri-san had begun to open up a bit more towards the end of the meal, helped perhaps by the beer, or the arrival of Mr Azuma, who at least wanted to speak to them in Japanese. They both seemed to be there out of a sense of obligation. Was an invitation to one of Mrs Azuma's dinner parties something no self-respecting villager could refuse? Shirakami-san had said her cooking was famous in Izumi, but there had to be more to it than that.

To their credit, both Shirakami-san and Odagiri-san had dealt well with the delicate subject of the school's past. They had maintained their composure in the face of Mrs Azuma's persistent probing and I didn't feel they had acted at all suspiciously.

As Odagiri-san was getting up from the table to leave, he leant close to me. 'Leave Reiko. She's dead now. Let her have peace.'

There was nothing I could say. After all that had happened there was nothing I wished more than to let her have peace.

'I will.'

Looking round, I saw Shirakami-san watching the exchange. He nodded at me, as though acknowledging my response. I felt I could see into his eyes and into his tortured soul. Here was someone who had loved Reiko, spiritually if not physically. With no family of his own, he had put Reiko on a pedestal and now spent the days sitting in her classroom, pining.

Odagiri-san and Shirakami-san went out into the hall, put on their shoes, gave thanks to Mrs Azuma for the meal and left without another word.

Aya was the last to leave, pausing to kiss me on both cheeks by the door, 'continental style' as she termed it. She looked as though she had something to say to me but wasn't sure how to say it. At last she lifted her head and looked me in the eye.

'Be careful.'

She turned briskly and disappeared into the night.

A Discovery

A hush descended on the house after the teachers had left. Sarah and I lounged on the sitting room floor, nursing our heavy stomachs and listening to Mrs Azuma crashing about in the kitchen, clearing up after an evening's entertaining. We'd pleaded with her to let us help, but she'd given us short shrift. As distinguished guests we had no business in the kitchen and she was adamant that I, in particular, needed to rest my feet before my long journey home in the morning. Anyone would have thought I'd be walking back to Osaka.

Neither Sarah nor I felt much like talking. We had the taciturn company of Mr Azuma, sipping an after-dinner *sake*, but our attempts at conversation soon petered out. The entire evening had left me drained. The two teachers had responded to Mrs Azuma's probing with a mixture of calm and disapproval. They'd come across as defensive, but ultimately harmless and, after all our analysis and speculation, there was a feeling of anti-climax. They'd simply told us to let the matter rest, which was the sensible and appropriate thing to say.

The dishes all safely loaded into the dishwasher, Mrs Azuma came out rubbing her hands and asking us how we felt. I told her I was pleasantly full and Sarah patted her stomach with a satisfied smile.

'Are you ready for your bath?'

The idea of having a bath after such a heavy meal seemed ludicrous to me, but Mrs Azuma explained that it was traditional in Japan. In fact, it was strange to get into bed without first washing and bathing. Strange to carry the dust and grime of the day to bed with you. Sarah nudged me and told me it was actually rather relaxing, so I agreed.

'First, let me show you my house.'

With some effort we got up and followed Mrs Azuma into the kitchen, which was large, modern and spotlessly clean. This was clearly her domain and she gave us a whistle-stop tour of her white goods: top-of-the-range fridge, dishwasher, microwave and even a talking toaster, which she kindly demonstrated for us.

Next, she led us through to a series of utility rooms, one with an exercise bike and treadmill, another with a washing machine and tumble dryer. Then, along a dark corridor we came to what she announced was her pride and joy: the freezer room. It was a cavernous storage room with an obscene number of chest freezers, two or three on either wall. She opened one up to reveal more frozen products than your average supermarket. She stood there proudly for a moment, looking for some sort of reaction from us. I had never been asked to admire a chest freezer before, but I tried my best to look impressed.

'I do a lot of entertaining,' she said by way of just-ification.

I was glad to leave the freezer room and move on to the comparative warmth of the garage, where we admired Mr Azuma's people-carrier for a few minutes. From there we went on upstairs and looked in on the master bedroom, a sterile Western en-suite which res-embled an upmarket hotel room. Then we were shown to the boy's rooms, where Mrs Azuma announced we would be sleeping.

'Kenji's room. You can sleep here,' she said, addressing me. It was a large room, fairly typical for a boy in his late teens, with posters of rock bands, baseball stars and a map of the world. With a feeling of dismay I saw that the wardrobe boasted full-length mirrors on both its doors. Having avoided reflections all day, it wasn't what I needed.

Osamu's room across the hall would be Sarah's for the night. It was almost identical to Kenji's both in size and furnishings and like Kenji's room it was metic-ulously clean.

The one comfort I derived from the tour was that though Sarah and I were in different rooms, she was only a short distance across the hall. There might yet be some hope for us.

The bath was every bit as good as Sarah had predicted. I sat for over half an hour up to my neck in the self-heating tub, letting the strains of the day grad-ually leave my body. On reflection, the day hadn't been quite as harrowing as I'd anticipated. I'd expected stress levels to rise to some kind of crescendo, but it hadn't happened. So far my ghostly stalker had kept quiet. Either she had let me off the hook or was fattening me up for the kill. Allow me to relax completely, lull me into a false sense of security, then strike when I least expected.

I wasn't wrong.

Returning to Kenji's room, bathed and buffed and looking forward to sinking into soft linen sheets, I did what I'd managed to avoid doing prior to my bath. I looked up at the mirrors on the wardrobe doors.

She was there.

She was there standing on the other side of the bed next to the desk, wearing her uniform. Her face was turned down, her features in shadow, and her left hand was touching the desk, as though marking it for attention.

Light-headed from the bath, I sank to my knees, clasping my hands together in an attitude of prayer. She didn't look at me, just continued staring at the desk.

I closed my eyes and, when I opened them again, she had gone.

I sat on the floor by the door for several moments, my heart beating a hole in my chest, trying to bring some order to my emotions. There had been something about her posture that was different this time. The first times I'd seen her, in the graveyard and in the mirror in Sarah's apartment, she hadn't been looking at me, but she had been facing towards me. Then, in the convenience store, she had both been looking at me and facing towards me. The same could be said of her appearance in Sarah's bed. But this time was different. She was both looking away and facing away: she was looking at the desk.

It seemed idiotic, but I'd seen too many horror films not to think that she was trying to show me something. Equally idiotic was my next thought – that this wasn't a defining trait of Japanese ghosts. It was at odds with the single-minded revenge she was supposed to be plotting.

Pulling myself together, I opened the door and tiptoed across the dark hall to Sarah's door and rapped on it lightly. She'd had her bath before me and I prayed that she was not only awake, but inclined to see me. I was relieved to hear her voice from the other side of the door, inviting me to come in. I knew she wouldn't desert me in my hour of need.

She was sitting cross-legged on the bed, attempting to dry her hair by running her fingers through it. 'Did you have a nice bath?'

'Yes, thanks. You?'

She pointed to her hair. 'I forgot my brush. I should have asked Mrs Azuma, but I didn't really want to go knocking on her door.'

I sat down on the bed next to her with a weary sigh. She immediately read my expression.

'It's those mirrors on the wardrobe, isn't it?' She motioned to a carbon copy wardrobe in her room.

'I was caught off my guard. I relaxed too much.'

She stopped brushing her hair and got up. 'Would you feel more comfortable kipping down on my floor?'

It was an offer I would certainly be taking up. But sleep was far from my mind.

'Actually, I wanted to ask your opinion about something.'

There was nothing on Kenji's desk except for a neat pile of stationery in one corner. There were three drawers underneath, all of them locked. We briefly considered forcing the lock, but decided it would be uncharitable considering all Mrs Azuma had done for us. That left us to search for a key, which we set about doing methodically, Sarah taking one side of the room and I taking the other. She asked me where a young man might hide something important and the only thing I could think of saying was 'under something'. This turned out to be unexpectedly good advice. Within a few minutes of lifting everything in sight, she found a key on the young scholar's shelf, underneath a stack of encyclopaedias.

But standing in front of the desk holding the key, I suddenly felt unsure. I took a step back and thought about the young man who we'd never met and whose life we were prying into. What did we have to go on? Just a vision, a trick of the light, the product of an overwrought brain. What were we expecting to find?

'Are you okay?'

'I think I might be going mad,' I said.

Sarah smiled. 'Maybe you are. Maybe you were already mad before you got here. Maybe you'll end up strapped to a bed getting electric shock treatment three times a day. We just don't know.' She pressed the key into my hand. 'Remember, you're not the first one to see her.'

'I know. And they're all dead now.'

Sarah looked at me sternly. 'Whatever you saw or think you saw, it can't hurt you. It could drive you mad, but it can't hurt you. If you can believe that, then you'll be okay. You're not the same as Charlie. I've seen his file and you're not the same. He was vulnerable.'

'He didn't have you to protect him.'

'Exactly. You really think I'd let something happen to you? You think I'd let some miserable spirit touch you? I'd like to see them try.'

The way she was standing there, in her white silken dressing gown, arms akimbo, I would have laid down my life for her. I took the key and it turned immediately. Pulling open the first drawer we found nothing but loose stationery items and other odds and ends, thrown in willy-nilly. It was probably the one place where Kenji could be untidy, where he wasn't subject to his mother's obsessive cleanliness.

The second drawer contained bits of paper – probably fragments of schoolwork – thrown in without order. The third drawer was more of the same, but fishing beneath reams of white paper a flash of red caught my eye. Reaching in, I pulled out a bright red folder, tied with a black ribbon.

I carried the folder over to the bed and slowly untied the ribbon. Sarah watched in silence by my side. I paused before opening the file, dimly aware that we were not alone in this, that there was another presence in the room, peering from the shadows, watching our progress.

I did the deed, letting the contents spill out onto the bed – the private possessions of Mrs Azuma's absentee son. For a while neither of us spoke as we realized what we had found. A secret treasure chest, testament to Kenji's adolescent infatuation. There were photographs, drawings, newspaper cuttings and they all had one subject: Reiko. There were photos of Reiko in her sailor uniform at school, unaware that she was being photographed; pictures of her in her tracksuit playing volleyball; pictures of her in plain clothes, walking down the street with friends. All the pictures seemed to have been taken without her knowledge. The sketches were mostly pencil drawings, some of her profile, but mainly of her head bent in thought. The artist had paid particular attention to the contours of her face, with delicate shading to bring out the high cheekbones and almond-shaped eyes. Kenji had been in love with Reiko and, judging from the photographs, the love had not been reciprocated. The newspaper cuttings were all taken after her disappearance and most of them displayed the same school portrait I'd first seen in Charlie's file. The cuttings had been dated, but otherwise were in no particular order. In fact this whole stash of Reiko memorabilia had been thrown in without any care.

'My God,' Sarah said finally. 'He really was obsessed.'

'You're right, but like you said before, half the boys in her class felt the same.'

'This stuff is pretty sick.'

I had to admit that the hidden camera was creepy. But there was nothing unusual about the sketches. In fact, they showed a touching sensitivity and I was sure some girls would have been flattered by them.

'What do you think? Is this what Reiko was trying to show you?'

I sifted the evidence, trying to reconcile the face in all the photographs with the fleeting figure I kept seeing in mirrors. 'How can I know?'

'One thing's for sure. This girl could drive men half-mad.'

It was true. I'd never seen her in life, but I was still unable to get her out of my head. If that was the effect she had in death, imagine what it must have been like in life. Here in Kenji's drawer was evidence of an extra-ordinary power over people. And it hadn't just been Kenji. There was Odagiri-san, Shirakami-san and, according to Aya, several other mature, responsible teachers.

Had this apparition really been pointing to the desk, guiding us to Kenji's secret stash? After all, the desk was the only logical place to keep something like that. We knew already that he'd been madly in love with her and it was hardly unusual for love-struck teenagers to keep some kind of evidence of their infatuation.

'We should put this back,' I said, stuffing the photographs back in the folder. 'Imagine how mortified the poor lad would be if he knew we'd had this out.'

'You don't think he could've done anything, do you?' Sarah asked, a little hesitantly. 'I know he was only a young lad, but you don't really think he could have anything to do with it?'

'He was just a teenager in love. No different to everyone else.' I tied the ribbon and took the folder back to the drawer to lock it away again.

She sat on the bed chewing her nails. 'It's a frightening thing, isn't it? Someone was responsible for killing those kids and they're just walking around, going about their business. Someone is carrying that burden around. How do they manage to live with that? How can they go around doing ordinary things, when they know they've done something so completely evil? How can they live like that?'

'Because they're insane. That's why.'

She shivered. 'It hurts my head to think of it. It hurts.'

I sat down on the bed next to her and, feeling bold, slipped my arm round her waist. She laid her head on my shoulder and for a long time we sat there, holding each other, drawing mutual comfort and support. I suddenly felt stronger than I had done all week, ready to meet any obstacle, to fight any battle and to slay whatever beast hell could throw at me.

ANOTHER DREAM

In a dream I awoke to a strange sound from deep within the house. I sat up, taking stock of my surroundings. A solitary shaft of moonlight cut the floor like a knife, illuminating the sterile landscape of the room. By my side Sarah slept soundly, her hair dark upon the pillow and her naked breast stained silver by the moon.

I didn't know what the sound was or where it had come from, but something drove me to explore. I slipped out of bed carefully, so as not to wake Sarah, and tiptoed slowly across the room, passing in and out of the shaft of light. I opened the door and entered a long corridor, with doors leading off on either side. At the end were the stairs, bathed in silvery light from a high window. As I made my way forwards, I noticed that my footsteps made no sound. Passing the room where Mr and Mrs Azuma slept, I heard their heavy breathing from within.

I headed down the stairs, out of the light and into darkness. I still didn't know where I was going, but my feet led me past the front door and into the sitting room where the porcelain dolls and ancestral spirits watched my passage with indifference. I continued through the kitchen and into the utility area where the racks of clothes were hanging out to dry.

Suddenly I realized where I was going. I paused at the entrance to that dark corridor, filled with a terrible fear of what lay in wait at the other end. I saw light seeping out underneath the frame of the door and, slowly, fearfully, I edged towards it, feeling my way along.

The door responded to my touch, opening with a painful creak, like every door in every horror film I'd ever seen, and I stepped in. The freezer room was larger than I remembered it and my eyes took in five large chest freezers lining the walls. All of these were open, flooding the room with light.

I stood there, feeling the chill in the air. Why had they all been left open? How could Mrs Azuma have been so careless?

I moved forward into the room, thinking I should close the lids to the freezers. Then I saw her.

I knew straight away it was Reiko, lying full stretch, her eyes closed and her face deathly white, her arms folded over her chest: a freezer for a coffin. There was a delicate frost on her face and lips, but the blue of her uniform and the red of her ribbon stood out bold against the white walls of the box.

Without emotion I turned from the box and stepped over to look at each of the other freezers in turn.

There they were. Each of the other students: Kanae, Jun, Saori, Hideki, dressed as they were in life, in their standard-issue school uniforms, lying in state with their arms folded over their chests, their faces frosted over.

I stumbled back towards the door, a scream forming on my lips. The horror of the scene threatened to overwhelm me and I reached for the wall to support me.

From the corner of my eye, I saw something move.

'Please,' I said under my breath, appealing for clemency.

There was a stirring from Reiko's coffin and I saw her raise herself slowly to a sitting position, the back of her head white with frost.

'Please,' I said again, appealing to her. 'Please don't.'

Slowly she twisted her frozen torso towards me and turned her face to look straight at me. And while her forehead was dusted with frost, her eyes were filled with fire.

'What do you want?' I stammered, stepping backwards. 'What do you want of me?'

She didn't answer. She just looked at me with the same blank expression. And then the expression on her face changed and a half-smile began to form on her frosty lips. And in that smile I saw all the poison and contempt in the world. For the first time in my life I caught a glimpse of hell.

And this time I did scream.

Sarah was shaking me awake.

'James! James!'

Coming to my senses and realizing where I was, I clutched her for support.

'James, are you all right?'

I stared round the room with wild eyes, taking stock of everything around me. I didn't know how I'd got from the freezer room to the bedroom, but I did know I'd been down there. I could still feel the chill in my bones.

'She's in the freezer,' I said with finality.

Sarah lifted me up and put her arms round me for support.

'I saw her downstairs. I saw them all. In the room with the freezers. Reiko was there. She sat up and looked at me.'

I stared into the room, at the shaft of light cutting across the floor, which I had walked through in my dream. I recalled every detail from leaving the room, to the journey into the dark bowels of the house and the freezer room. And I had an absolute conviction that if I were to walk down right now, Sarah at my side, I would find exactly what I'd found in my dream. I would find Reiko.

Reiko was close. That much I knew. Reiko was within touching distance. And come morning, I needed to board that train and leave Izumi far behind. I needed to leave and never come back, because if I didn't, I was certain I would die. And if the train didn't arrive, I would leave Izumi on foot. I would crawl on my hands and knees if I had to, but I needed to get out.

ODAGIRI-SAN

We woke to the sound of heavy rain outside. How I'd managed to sleep through till dawn, I don't know. Perhaps it was Sarah's protective embrace that helped me find peace after such a horrible dream. I felt shaken, but determined. I had seen things in Izumi that I never wanted to relive, but it was now time to leave. I would put it all behind me and resume my life. Whatever secrets the village harboured and whatever I had witnessed, it would all be past history. It had been a doomed expedition from the start. I should have learned from Charlie's tragic mistake and stayed in Osaka and hung out with Josh.

As we dressed I thought again of my conflicting emotions. There was real relief at leaving Izumi and its dark secrets behind, but also sadness at the thought of leaving Sarah. There had been no passion between us, but she had held me close to her all through the long night. Neither of us said anything about what would happen, about coming to visit me in Osaka, about somehow keeping the flame alive.

'You made it,' Sarah said, as we stepped out of the bedroom for the last time. 'You made it through safely.'

'I suppose I did.'

I forced a smile, but I still felt the chill grip of the dream. I had tried explaining it to Sarah during the night, but I didn't know if my descriptive powers had done it justice. I'd had many vivid dreams over the past few days, but none as vivid as that one.

Mrs Azuma seemed in exceptionally good spirits when we appeared for breakfast. She proclaimed herself to be a morning person, which was an ominous sign in itself. She bustled around preparing breakfast, eager to know whether I'd slept well on my last night in Izumi. I told her I'd slept very well, thank you very much, which seemed to be the right thing to say. She said I needed feeding up before my journey and slapped a huge portion of bacon and eggs in front of me. My stomach still felt leaden from the previous night and it was with a heavy heart that I tucked in.

As I sat there, force-feeding myself fried eggs, I thought again of the freezer room and the bodies lying in their icy coffins, still wearing their uniforms, with their hands folded across their chests. Then I thought of Reiko standing by Kenji's desk, pointing to the secret red folder documenting his obsession. Watching Mrs Azuma beetling around in her inimitable way, I wondered how much she had known of her son's feelings. But it wasn't something I was ever likely to know. Later that morning I would be leaving Izumi, never to return. Never again to receive Mrs Azuma's fine hospitality.

It took a lot of perseverance to stop Mrs Azuma from accompanying us to the station. I needed the time alone with Sarah to say my 'goodbyes' and, more importantly, gauge whether she ever wanted to see me again. Mrs Azuma had set me up with a lunchbox, which she packed into my bag, even though the breakfast had probably done me for the day. Then as I was bowing deeply and humbly and thanking her for everything, she suddenly remembered something and began rummaging around in the drawer of a side cabinet. She pulled out a photograph and pressed it into my hand.

'A souvenir of Izumi,' she said.

The picture showed a group of high school students in their school uniforms sitting round the table in the Azuma sitting room.

'This is Kenji,' she said proudly, pointing to a glum youth with a bowl haircut. I realized this was the first time I'd seen a photograph of the lad. Since he was the cameraman in the school video, I'd only ever seen the world from his point of view. I was about to say what a nice young man he looked when I realized who the other students were. Kanae, Jun, Saori and Hideki sitting round the table with a spread of food in front of them. All of them, including Kenji, looked at the camera without enthusiasm, as though they'd all rather have been somewhere else.

'This was taken just after Reiko disappeared,' Mrs Azuma added. 'I invited them round for dinner to comfort them.'

I wasn't sure what to say. Why was she showing me this photograph now?

'It's a terrible thing,' she said finally.

We stood there at the door to Mrs Azuma's house, looking at the picture in silence, as though out of respect for the dead students. I didn't know if I was meant to be moved that her son was the only one in the photograph still alive. I didn't even know if I was expected to comment on the photograph or keep it. I just stood there patiently waiting for some sign.

We arrived at the station more than an hour before the train was due to leave. Sarah had suggested one last tour of the town, but somehow the station seemed the safest option. The rain was falling steadily and I was happy to sit in the little shelter and wait. There seemed less chance of bumping into wandering spirits there amidst the cigarette stubs and graffiti.

But if I thought that nothing more would happen to unbalance my equilibrium, I was mistaken. As we approached the small waiting room on the platform we saw a solitary figure sitting there, hunched in a raincoat.

It wasn't until we entered the room that we realized it was Odagiri-san.

'Hello,' he said, as if he'd been expecting us.

'Hello,' Sarah said, with impressive composure. 'Are you waiting for a train?'

Odagiri-san got up with a heavy sigh, walked over to the window and looked out. 'No,' he said firmly.

This was a conversation stopper and Sarah and I looked at each other for help. We took the easiest course of action, which was to go over to the bench and sit down, as we'd planned to do all along. On the wall opposite the bench was an old police poster featuring mugshots of wanted criminals, photographs too blurred to be of any use. I wondered who they were and what dark crimes they were wanted for. What if one of those blurred faces was Odagiri-san or someone else we'd met in Izumi?

'I expect Azuma-san has told you many stories,' Odagiri-san said suddenly, not turning from the window.

Again, Sarah and I could only look at one another and wonder where he was going with this.

'I expect she told you some stories about her sons, about the school, about the tragedy that happened there.' This time he turned to look straight at us.

We both nodded in unison, unable to speak. Odagiri-san had come with a clear agenda.

'What has she said to you?'

'I don't understand,' Sarah said, feeling her host mother's integrity was being questioned. 'Why is it important?'

Odagiri-san sat down opposite us and leaned forward, choosing his words carefully. 'It's very important. Maybe you don't understand the position of the Azuma family in Izumi. It is a very old family. A samurai family, which in the past ruled over Izumi. She thinks of herself as an aristocrat. She feels superior to other people in Izumi.'

Sarah raised her voice, unwilling to let this pass. 'I don't know why you're telling me this, because I'm not interested.'

Odagiri-san shook his head. 'You don't understand.'

'What don't I understand? Mrs Azuma has been kind to me from the day I arrived. She's helped me out with everything. She put me up in her house, she showed me around, she made me feel welcome, made me feel at home. She didn't have to do any of that. I don't care what you think of her.'

Odagiri-san weighed up Sarah's words and looked away. At least his speech confirmed that he'd appeared at Mrs Azuma's house the previous evening out of a sense of duty towards one of the village elders. And it also explained his surly attitude over dinner. And all along I'd thought it was me he didn't like.

'Why did you come here?' I asked.

Odagiri-san looked at me, a little more conciliatory now. 'I came to defend my name.'

'Your name? From what?'

He sighed and looked at the ground, wringing his hands together nervously. 'After the tragedy involving my students, some people in the village suspected me, suspected that I had some involvement. There were a lot of rumours and I suffered a lot. Maybe I should have left Izumi, but it is my home now and I won't be chased out. Not by Azuma-san. Not by anyone.'

'You blame her?'

'She started rumours about me. I know that she told the police. I know that she told many people.'

'Why?' Sarah asked, adopting a more conciliatory approach herself.

Odagiri-san got to his feet abruptly, his nervous energy palpable, his emotion breaking through the impassive exterior. He turned towards the window again and looked out at the rain pelting against the glass. 'You must understand that Azuma-san is very ambitious for her sons.'

'That's not so unusual,' Sarah said.

Odagiri-san shook his head. 'I was their home-room teacher. I taught them both and I knew them well. Osamu was a strong student, but a very unhappy boy. He couldn't wait to leave Izumi and go to Tokyo. Kenji though was a weak student and Azuma-san couldn't accept this. She blamed me for his performance.'

Given all we'd heard about her two golden boys over the past few days, it was strange to hear them described in this way by their teacher. I thought of the row of certificates on the wall, of their mother's pride at their achievements. Was it so wrong, I wondered, to boast about your sons' achievements, even if Kenji wasn't setting the world alight? What was Mrs Azuma supposed to do? Bemoan his failures? Pretend he didn't exist? Wish he'd never been born?

'She couldn't accept that Kenji was getting bad grades. She came to me frequently and told me I wasn't doing my job. I should pay more attention to him and then he would start getting better grades…'

Sarah stopped him in his stride. 'Why do you care what we think?'

'I want you to know I had nothing to do with what happened four years ago.'

'No one said you did. And it's normal for a mother to care about her son's education.'

Odagiri-san folded his arms. 'She doesn't care about their education. She only cares about her reputation. If they get good grades at school, it reflects well on her. If they get bad grades, it reflects badly. And Kenji always got bad grades.'

I was still no nearer to understanding where this was heading or why he had apprehended us here. He seemed to be on a personal mission to discredit the Azuma family in return for the suspicions Mrs Azuma had raised against him. That he could accept an invitation to dine with her at the same time seemed remarkable to me. It was a fascinating insight into Japanese village politics.

Odagiri-san appeared to sense our scepticism and sat down with a heavy sigh, while the rain began to beat even more furiously at the window.

'I know some things,' he said, abruptly. 'I know some things you wouldn't believe.' His voice was flat and mournful and he stared out of the window as he spoke. 'Azuma-san is an educated woman. She attended a prestigious university, she studied in America, she had a good job in Fukushima City. Maybe if she'd stayed there, things would have been better. But she had an arranged marriage to her cousin. You know her husband.'

He turned to look at us and we both nodded.

'He doesn't talk much and likes to drink. He's not an educated man. And maybe Kenji was like him. Maybe he didn't inherit his mother's academic mind. Maybe that's why she was cruel to him.'

'What do you mean?' Sarah asked.

'She was cruel to Kenji when he got low grades. When he got low grades, she hurt him.'

Sarah's eyes opened wide in disbelief and astonishment. 'She hurt him?'

'She hurt him. Sometimes she made cuts on his arms or back. Sometimes she gave him bruises on his body. All the teachers knew this. She thought it would encourage him to concentrate on his school work. Some teachers were frightened to give him bad grades for this reason.'

'Didn't anyone speak to her?' Sarah looked unsure whether to believe him or not.

'No one wanted to challenge the Azuma family. As I said, they are aristocrats in Izumi.'

'But to abuse your child. That's a serious thing.'

Odagiri-san bowed his head. 'I know.'

For a moment, we sat there in silence, listening to the rain, trying to take in what he had just told us. Mrs Azuma was cheerful, friendly and energetic and I couldn't believe she was capable of doing what Odagiri-san had described. One thing was true however. While she'd been generally enthusiastic about her sons' achievements, she had said harsh things about Kenji, repeatedly claiming that he was less gifted than his brother.

Then I remembered my dream of the previous night. I remembered the descent into the bowels of the Azuma home, down dark corridors to the freezer room. I remembered the cavernous chest freezers laid out like coffins and the five students lying in state, their faces tinged white with frost. And I remembered Reiko, rising slowly from her icy coffin, her dark eyes looking at me. And I felt a chill creep through my veins.

'Of course, Kenji was in love with Reiko.'

Odagiri-san said this so suddenly that I started. It was as though he knew what I'd been thinking about, had seen what I'd seen.

'Why do you say that?' Sarah said.

'Kenji was in love with Reiko and Azuma-san hated it.'

'Why?' Sarah looked further unsettled by this statement.

Odagiri-san got up, signalling his intention to leave.

'Why do you say that? All the boys were in love with Reiko.'

'Not like Kenji. Kenji was obsessed with Reiko and his mother knew that. How could he concentrate on his studies when he was thinking about Reiko all the time? How could he sit and do his homework when he was out taking pictures of Reiko?'

Odagiri-san opened the door to leave, but Sarah was adamant that he stay to explain himself.

'What do you mean? What does that have to do with anything?'

Odagiri-san shook his head, as though suddenly regretting everything he'd said. 'I don't mean anything. It's time to go.'

'You think Mrs Azuma had something to do with it? Is that what you're saying?'

'I'm saying nothing.' Having come entirely of his own accord to plead his case, he was now anxious to leave.

'You can't just say those things,' Sarah said, but it was too late.

The door swung shut and we watched Odagiri-san walk swiftly down the platform, his shoulders hunched, his coat flapping in the wind and rain.

'I don't know anymore.'

Sarah was standing on the platform, her face wet and her hair dripping with rain. I'd wanted to stay in the waiting room or at least sit in the car, but she'd preferred to go out and stand in the rain. She said she needed a good soaking to clear her head.

'Maybe it's best to forget about it.'

She turned on me aggressively. 'I can't forget about it. How can I forget about it? He's telling me my host mother is a monster. I can't just go away and forget about it.'

'That's just his take on things. It's his opinion.'

'Why would he lie about it? He said she abused her sons. How can I face her knowing that?'

I didn't know what to say. I searched around for something comforting to say, but in vain. I was the one about to get on a train and leave Izumi far behind, leaving Sarah to deal with everything I had dredged up.

The rickety train approached the platform slowly and I knew the time had come. I had imagined a send-off straight out of a Hollywood movie: the fumbled embraces, the hurried promises and the heroine running alongside the train as it moved off. Instead I had a torrential downpour and a heroine in a state of mental turmoil.

'I need time to think,' she said.

The train pulled up at the platform and I still couldn't think of anything appropriate to say.

'So, will I be able to call you?' I asked, pathetically.

She wasn't listening. My leaving was no longer of any significance in light of this latest twist.

'What?'

'Can I call you?'

The train had stopped and I opened the door, hoping that she would at least acknowledge my departure. She continued to look away, distracted, so I stepped onto the train and hauled my bag up with me.

Then she did something I hadn't expected.

She got on the train and pulled the door shut.

'What are you doing?'

'I'm coming with you.'

I looked at her in astonishment, convinced she was having me on, merely getting on to take shelter from the rain. Then the whistle blew and the train began to move off.

'Why?'

'I need to get away,' she said. 'I'm coming to Osaka with you.'

I couldn't prevent a smile spreading across my face. This was the one event I hadn't foreseen.

'If it's okay with you, that is.'
I could barely speak with relief.

To Osaka

We said little on the short journey to the bullet train terminal in Shirakawa. We sat side by side watching the rain sheeting against the glass, as the train passed through a series of non-descript villages where no soul either joined or left the train. We were completely alone in the carriage and each time the driver announced our arrival and departure from the little stations it came as a comfort. For all we knew, we were riding a ghost train into some rain-sodden underworld, never to return. Thank God I had Sarah's company.

I was still stunned that Sarah had got on the train with me. Was it purely down to Odagiri-san or had the idea already occurred to her? And what would she do once she got to Osaka? How long would she stay? She was deep in thought and it wasn't the right time to probe.

As we alighted at Shirakawa I was convinced she'd announce a change of heart. She would tell me that it was a silly spur of the moment thing and now that she'd had a chance to dry off and think about it, she'd be heading back. After all she had no change of clothes and was expected in work the next day. But I followed her to the ticket office and watched as she bought a ticket to Osaka with an open return. Only then did I believe it.

'I'm sorry. I hope I haven't freaked you out,' she said as we stood on the terminal platform. In contrast to Izumi, we were mercifully under cover.

'I've seen enough this past week never to be freaked out again.'

'It's been bothering me. You going back, after what happened to the other guy.'

'Charlie?' This took me by surprise. After all that had happened, I hadn't given him much thought.

'Yeah. Call it my maternal instinct, but I need to know you'll be all right.'

She could call it whatever she liked. I was just pleased to have her with me. Even if my relief at leaving Izumi had been soured by Odagiri-san's revelations, I felt a renewed sense of vigour. I knew that I was leaving Reiko and the strange circumstances of her death far behind me. Wherever I went and whatever I did, she could no longer touch me. I was out of reach.

Not surprisingly Sarah couldn't put Odagiri-san's words out of her head.

As the bullet train began pulling out of Shirakawa station, with the rain pelting the concrete walls of that grey city, she took out the photograph Mrs Azuma had given us of Kenji and the four dead students.

'There's something about this photograph,' she said, studying it intently.

I couldn't help looking at Kenji, seated in the middle, looking sombre and ill at ease. My perception of him had undergone some dramatic changes over the past week and I no longer knew what to think. He'd gone from the model son filling his mother's wall with certificates of achievement, to an obsessive loner with a secret stash of pictures of Reiko, to a victim of parental abuse. And here he was, flanked by four fellow students who obviously weren't really his friends. Four young students about to die horrific deaths.

'Why did she give it to us?'

I shook my head. If there had been an ulterior motive, I didn't know what it was. It was certainly no weirder than lending us Kenji's home video. And in the light of Odagiri-san's accusations, my perception of Mrs Azuma had also changed dramatically. I knew now she possibly wasn't the model citizen and all-round do-gooder I had assumed. So what could you read into this gift of a photograph? Possibly nothing. It was just a picture of five high school students posing reluctantly for a photograph at a meal none of them were enjoying. Maybe she took a perverse pride in knowing that her son was the only one left standing. They might have scored better grades than him at school, but those grades hadn't saved their lives.

'And if they weren't really friends with Kenji, why were they over there?' Sarah asked, continuing to stare at the photo.

'The same reason Odagiri-san came to dinner yesterday. Mrs Azuma invited them and no one turns down her dinner invitations.'

She leaned back in her seat, dissatisfied. The train had left the outskirts of Shirakawa and plunged back into the countryside.

'Maybe she thought they really were Kenji's friends. He probably talked about them, so she just assumed they were. He's not going to tell his mum he doesn't have any friends, is he?'

'The timing seems a bit odd, doesn't it.'

'One of their friends had disappeared off the face of the earth. I presume she wanted to cheer them up.'

She started to laugh sarcastically. 'Looks like she failed on that count. Look at them all.'

'You have to feel sorry for them.'

It was an unfortunate choice of phrase. Was I sorry that they were having to put up with an unwelcome dinner invite or that four of them were about to die?

'They're eating exactly the same stuff as we did,' she said, pointing to the plates on the table. 'Raw meat. That could well be the horse meat right there.'

I let out an involuntary laugh. The food did look eerily familiar and I felt a shudder down the spine as I cast my mind back to that first night with Mrs Azuma, being overawed by the sheer force of her enthusiasm and devouring every dish she set before me, raw horse meat and all. I thought about the incense stick burning before the shrine, the porcelain dolls staring out from their glass cases, the incongruous meeting of East and West in the décor and furniture. And I was overcome with relief to be putting that unholy place far behind me.

In a while Sarah was asleep, the photograph of the unhappy diners still lying on her lap. I turned to the window and watched the rain pelt upon the glass as we passed through more non-descript towns and villages shrouded in semi-darkness. I tried to settle my mind, to put some emotional distance between myself and the hell I was leaving behind. I tried to tell myself that what had happened in Izumi was not my business and it was useless to think about it. I should have heeded Professor Atami's advice and stayed well clear of the place, but what was done was done. I had to look forward and enjoy my time in Osaka. God knows I needed some relief.

But if I hadn't gone to Izumi I would never have met Sarah and, as I watched her asleep beside me, I was overcome by my feelings for her. She had admitted that her motivation for getting on the train was to protect me from harm and it choked me to think that she cared that much.

She had been thinking about Charlie, my tragic predecessor. And now, as I embarked on the same journey, I started to think about him too. What was it he had seen in Izumi? Had he seen everything I had seen? Was it really that which finally caused him to break? It struck me as strange that he had made a six-hour journey before ending his life. Leaving Izumi behind, I could feel my spirits lifting and by the time I reached Osaka, I imagined I would feel completely restored. So why hadn't Charlie felt his spirits lift? Why hadn't he felt restored?

At Tokyo Station, we made our way to the Tokkaido bullet train terminal through a maze of tunnels and afternoon crowds carrying umbrellas. It was comforting to see so many people, all hurrying about, going about their business. Sarah still seemed preoccupied and spoke only to point out the signs directing us to our terminal. I didn't know exactly what was on her mind, but neither did I want to ask. I simply kept my head down and let her have some space.

It was on the train that she was finally ready to talk. 'Do you ever wonder why Charlie killed himself?'

We were gliding through the endless Tokyo suburbs, a concrete jungle submerged under a tropical
deluge. The bullet train had begun to feel like a sub-
marine passing through some industrial Atlantis.

'I guess he was depressed.'

'Do you think he saw the exact same things you
did?'

I breathed in deep. 'Yes, I do.'

'Have you ever thought you were capable of doing
it?'

'Suicide? Never. I don't have it in me.'

She stared at me hard. 'How do you know? How
can you be certain? He saw her too…'

'Listen, I don't know why Charlie killed himself.
But I know what I'm feeling now. I'm feeling elation
that I'll never see Reiko again.'

She wasn't done with me yet. 'How do you know
you'll never see her again?'

'There's something evil in Izumi. I wouldn't have
believed it before I went, but I believe it now. There's
something unholy and awful and Charlie and I both
seem to have got mixed up in it. I accept that. I accept
that totally. Maybe what I saw was a ghost. If so, I'll
have to live with that. But I'm absolutely certain that
what I saw in Izumi will stay in Izumi.'

'You're sure about that?'

'Because ghosts don't travel – we've talked about
this. It's funny, but my whole thesis was meant to
challenge the accepted wisdom on the supernatural and
here I am finally accepting it. It's the same in all
cultures and all traditions. Ghosts don't get on trains
and travel cross-country. They haunt those places
where they have unfinished business.'

She shook her head. 'I'm just trying to get everything out in the open, so I know what to expect. It just seems to me that whatever it is you see – and I only know what you tell me – is inside your head.'

'Look, I'm just starting to get over it. Give me a break.' It annoyed me that she was saying all the wrong things. I wanted her to cut me a little slack.

'I know it's not what you want to hear. But I'm trying to look at this rationally. I want to know what's in your mind.'

'Nothing. There's nothing in my mind. Whatever I saw, whatever it was, I left behind in Izumi. Reiko, or whatever it was, is gone for good.'

I turned away, letting Sarah know that I had nothing more to say on the matter. How could I explain what I knew to be true? Maybe Sarah was right and I was just making childish assumptions. Maybe Reiko would follow me to the ends of the earth and back. I just didn't believe it. I believed that what I'd seen in Izumi would stay in Izumi.

I glanced over and saw that Sarah had folded her arms and closed her eyes. I had the clear feeling of being in the dog-house. Not to be outdone I closed my own eyes and took refuge behind their dark lids.

Within minutes fatigue got the better of me and I fell into a deep, unquiet sleep.

I dreamt I was still on the train, travelling through a bleak, featureless landscape. I watched as the rain lashed the window, while Sarah slept peacefully by my side. Up ahead I could see the lights of a station emerge through the gloom.

The train began to slow and I realized we would be making a stop at the station. As we slowed to a halt, I saw queues of people, standing with their luggage waiting to join the train. I was a little surprised as I'd thought the bullet train was non-stop to Osaka. I craned my neck to make out the name of the place, but there was no obvious sign.

I sat back and watched as the train stopped in front of a long queue of people, all preparing to board. But my eye was caught by someone else, standing on the other side of the platform, watching the train pull in. He was wearing beige chinos and a white T-shirt, not dressed for the weather.

At first I couldn't see him clearly through the bodies of people waiting to get on the train. But I was curious, as he seemed to be smiling in my direction. Then the queue began to move and I saw him properly. It was Yoshi.

Unsure how to react, I lifted a hand in salutation. On the other side of the platform, he lifted a hand to return the gesture.

But what was he doing there, standing on a platform, somewhere between Tokyo and Osaka, when only a week ago I'd seen him fall from a seven-storey dormitory tower?

Yoshi seemed to think of something and fished around in his pocket, eventually pulling out a one thousand yen note. He began rubbing it between his hands, much as he'd done that night in Osaka. Satisfied, he held it up with both hands so I could see it, as if he wanted to make sure I remembered him. As if I could ever forget.

I still didn't know what to do. Should I take advantage of the train's stop and go over to greet him, ask him how he came to be here. I attempted to suggest this with another hand gesture, but Yoshi shook his head firmly and pointed up the tracks. I realized he must be waiting for an approaching train.

He gave me a thumbs-up and a wave and then turned away from me to wait for his train.

I heard and saw the train at roughly the same time. And I realized two things. The train wasn't stopping and Yoshi wasn't getting on. It thundered into the station and, with immaculate timing, Yoshi stepped off the platform into its path. The train struck him with a stomach-wrenching thud and a shower of blood.

I didn't scream. I was beyond that now. I simply closed my eyes in pain and despair at the frightening waste of life. I closed my eyes and felt myself spiralling downwards into darkness.

I woke suddenly and alertly and looked about me.

Nothing had changed. The rain still beat against the window, Sarah still snoozed at my side and the brightly lit carriage buzzed with the murmur of voices.

It occurred to me that when I'd left Osaka, I'd left with the memory of Yoshi's death still fresh in my mind. I'd headed to Izumi to be refreshed and revitalized. A few days on I was retreating from Izumi a nervous wreck, looking to Osaka for solace. What was happening to me? Only a couple of weeks earlier I had left England searching for escape. Why could I not find peace? Was I spending my life searching for something I could never hope to find?

I turned to the window and strained to make out features in the rainswept landscape, cursing the rain under my breath, cursing myself for sinking so low.

Then I saw her. It was only fleeting, but it was enough.

The train passed into a tunnel and the darkness of the tunnel walls threw the carriage interior into sharp focus.

Reiko was standing in the aisle next to Sarah, head bowed, arms clasped in front of her. She wore the same uniform, with the same blood-red ribbon tied around her neck.

I didn't turn my head, just stared at her, stared at her downturned face, the three white stripes on her collars, the pleated skirt. Of all the visions, this was the most frightening.

The train passed out of the tunnel and the landscape came back into focus. She was gone.

I swivelled round to see the aisle empty and Sarah sleeping peacefully beside me. So she'd been right after all. Everything I'd thought about Reiko being bound by the borders of Izumi was wrong. She'd been with me when we'd left Izumi and she was still with me now.

I now knew she was following me, just as she'd followed Charlie before me.

Over and over I'd wondered what had happened to Charlie that night in Osaka after the long journey home. I'd wondered why his spirits hadn't been lifted after leaving Izumi and why he had despaired so quickly. I'd wondered why he had gone back to the Tower, attached his dressing-gown cord to the window frame and hung himself by the neck.

And now I knew.

RETURN TO THE TOWER

As the bullet train glided into the terminal at Shin-Osaka station, it seemed like a different city to the one I'd left behind. Maybe it was my frame of mind, but under the relentless downpour it resembled something from the lower circles of Dante's inferno. The once proud skyscrapers were shadows in the mist, while the people cowered beneath umbrellas or ran for cover. The elation I'd felt on leaving Izumi behind had gone, to be replaced by a grim determination to see out the next few hours or days or weeks. I didn't know what Reiko's appearance meant for me, but I certainly knew what had happened to Charlie on his first night back in Osaka.

As we made our way across the station complex, through the evening rush hour crowds, I resolved not to mention that I'd seen her again. Maybe it was an unwillingness to admit I'd been wrong. Maybe it was a desire not to burden Sarah further. I sensed she was still coming to terms with what Odagiri-san had told us and her impulsive decision to get on the train with me.

We found a taxi outside the station and jumped in, keen to get back to the Tower before the rain made the roads impassable.

'So this is Osaka,' she said with a hint of irony, as the taxi disappeared into the traffic. Since we could barely see past the next car, it wouldn't have been the best introduction under any circumstances.

'Bet you wish you'd stayed in Izumi now.'

She turned to me with a genuine smile. 'I wouldn't go that far.'

'I'm glad you came,' I said. It was the first time she'd appeared relaxed during the entire journey.

'Me too. I'm sorry I've been a moody cow. It's not you.'

I patted her hand shyly. I wanted to tell her again and again how glad I was she was with me. I wanted to reach over and throw my arms around her.

'I hope you've got some board games in your room. I think we're going to be indoors tonight. Scrabble, Trivial Pursuit, something like that,' she said, before adding, 'maybe not Cluedo.'

I started to laugh. I couldn't think of any better way to while away the hours than playing Scrabble with Sarah. I turned back to the window and saw, standing at a bus stop in the rain, the figure of a schoolgirl.

It was only a brief flash and I had no way of knowing if it was Reiko, but terror took hold of me again. It was out of term time, so there was less reason for any schoolgirl to be in uniform. And she'd been standing there, head bowed in the manner of Reiko, soaked through by the rain. It must have been her. No one would have gone out without an umbrella and stood in the rain like that. She had been with me on the train and now she was with me in Osaka.

'Are you okay?' Sarah asked, catching the change in my expression.

'Fine.' I wasn't going to tell her. Maybe she suspected something, but I was determined not to let on that Reiko had come with us. I was going to keep my head down and will her to go away. I would close my eyes and live the rest of my life in darkness if that's what it took.

We travelled through the opulent Osakan suburbs with their elegant topiarized gardens dripping with rain. And soon we passed under the entrance arch to the university, through the dark and deserted campus, to the Tower standing desolate against the hills. Apart from the entrance, there was only a solitary light on in the building, which I guessed would be Josh. The place had effectively shut down for the holidays.

I paid the taxi driver and we made a beeline for the entrance, where we stopped to shake off the rain.

'We're here,' I said. 'This is where I call home.'

'The one place in Japan more depressing than Izumi.' She smiled mischievously and I mustered a laugh. God knows I needed her to help relieve the knot growing in my stomach. I glanced at the spot where Yoshi had fallen, and had a brief flashback to the thin white sheet covering his broken body, the paramedics talking in low tones, the flashing blue lights of the ambulance.

As we entered the foyer and made our way to the lifts, I glanced over at the drinks machines and thought of Yoshi flattening out the bank note, his last act of kindness. I wondered if I'd ever be able to stand in the foyer and think of anything else. Somehow I had to banish these things from my mind.

We travelled up to the fifth floor and I fished my keys out of my pocket. I felt no elation at returning, not even with Sarah standing next to me. If only I'd returned during the start of term, when the place was milling with activity and people. Right now it felt like an abandoned building, a place that had witnessed too much tragedy in its time to be ever used again.

With only a dingy overhead light to guide us, we made our way down the corridor to my room. Fearful of what might be lurking in the shadows, I kept my head firmly down until we reached my door, like a little boy afraid of the dark.

I unlocked the door and we stepped into the gloom of my room. I fumbled for the light switch, anxious not to be left in darkness.

'What do you think?'

Sarah looked around at the small, sterile room, perhaps comparing it in her mind to her comfortable pad in Izumi. There were no candles, no Gregorian chant, no posters or fabric throws on the wall. Nothing. I suddenly felt ashamed for bringing her back to this prison cell of a room. If only I'd known I'd be returning with someone, then perhaps I'd have made it more presentable.

'Well, it's monastic,' she said, picking her words carefully.

'Sorry. I'll try and find something for you to sleep on.'

She patted me on the shoulder with a smile. 'I came here to protect you, remember. Why do you think I got so much sleep on the train? If I'm going to be guarding you, I can't very well do it asleep.'

As I'd guessed it was Josh burning the dormitory's solitary light and he seemed mightily pleased to have company on such a wild and stormy night.

'Man, I'm glad to see you,' he said on opening the door. He pulled me in for a heartfelt hug, which lasted several seconds. The guy had definitely missed human company. 'I was hoping you'd be back today. Then I thought maybe you'd gone travelling someplace else.'

'Meet Sarah,' I said, extricating myself from his firm grasp. 'I brought her from the provinces to sample some city life.'

'Great to meet you,' he said, shaking her hand vigorously and flashing me a conspiratorial smile. Bringing girls back to the dorm was the kind of thing he approved of.

We stepped into his room, which at least made mine look respectable. It was the room of a single young man with time on his hands and no one to tell him what to do. It was a mess of magazines, pizza boxes, empty beer cans and a tangle of bedclothes.

'Sorry about this. I've been living like a tramp this past week,' he said, kicking some of the debris under the bed. 'The only people I've seen are the pizza guy and the girl at the convenience store. Even the concierge only comes now and then to check the place is still here.'

'So the whole place is…?'

'Empty.' He completed my question with a firm nod of the head, as though his isolation needed emphasizing. 'Right now, we own the building. Did you ever see 'The Shining'? Jack Nicholson in that hotel with his wife and kid and all those demons going round in his head. Well, that's how I've been feeling.'

'Did you get any work done?'

Josh laughed. 'Work? Hell, no. I've been pacing up and down the corridors like some mad person. You get some strange fucked-up ideas all on your own in this place. Any longer and I would've been looking round for that axe.'

Sarah was understandably alarmed at this six foot five American talking about axes, so I quickly changed the subject.

'Some storm we've got here. It started when we set out. It was there in Tokyo. It's followed us all the way across Japan.'

Josh slapped me on the back with a booming laugh. Maybe he really had been going mad. 'So, what's the plan?' he said.

'I don't think we'll be hitting the town tonight,' I said. 'Not really the weather.'

Josh looked a little disappointed. He clearly favoured venturing out. 'We could get the beers in, have a party here.'

This seemed like a good idea and I realized that Sarah and I needed Josh's company as much as he needed ours. Josh knew nothing about what had gone on in Izumi and, while he knew what had happened to Charlie, he probably wasn't thinking about it just now. We needed someone to distract us from our own tormented thoughts.

'Only trouble is, someone needs to go out to the convenience store in this typhoon.'

In the end Sarah and I volunteered to brave the weather. Sarah suggested a good soaking might just clear our heads. I couldn't let on that I didn't want to venture out for fear of seeing Reiko, so I agreed with her suggestion. Josh said he'd try and find out if

Shinichi and Etsuko were around to join us. The more the merrier, he said, and we couldn't have agreed more. With the wind and rain shaking the foundations of the empty dormitory, I'd have pulled strangers off the street to come in and join us.

'He's very highly strung,' Sarah said, as we walked across the foyer towards the wall of rain awaiting us outside.

'He's okay. Just a little lonely here on his own.'

'You sure he was joking about looking for that axe?'

I laughed, but I could see what Sarah was thinking. As my guardian, she had to think of every conceivable hazard. While Charlie might have hanged himself from his window, I could easily fall victim to a giant football-playing American with cabin fever. It occurred to me how difficult it must have been for Josh staying behind after what had happened to Yoshi. The number of beer cans littering his floor were an indication of his struggle.

We started our journey across the campus wrestling with an umbrella, but the wind soon ripped it to shreds and we gave ourselves up to the rain. I didn't really care that I was wet. I was too busy keeping my head down and my eyes fixed on the ground beneath my feet.

As we hurried along I was aware that every shadow could be hiding the figure of a long dead high school student. I neither knew what she wanted of me, nor why she had followed me so far. I just didn't want to ever see her again, in this life or any other.

We proceeded through the dark, deserted campus, under the entrance arch and down a street of residential houses to the bright lights of the convenience store.

I pushed open the door with a sense of triumph that I had avoided my pursuer thus far, but remembered she had confronted me in a convenience store once before. With windows on one side and a wall of glass fridge doors on the other, I would have to keep my eyes firmly on the ground. Out of the corner of my eye I could see the young female shop assistant staring at us in alarm – two bedraggled foreigners leaving a trail of water in their wake.

'How many beers?' Sarah asked, grabbing a basket and heading towards the fridges.

'As much as we can carry, I reckon. What do you think?' The thought of drinking myself into oblivion strongly appealed.

Sarah nodded and, pulling open the fridge door, began filling the basket with cans. I crouched down next to her, trying to avoid looking at the glass door.

'James?'

I looked up, startled at the sound of my name, and saw Professor Atami standing at the end of the aisle, folding an umbrella. 'Hello,' I said meekly.

'When did you get back from Izumi?' he asked, approaching me slowly.

I got to my feet, leaving Sarah to concentrate on the beer. 'Just this evening. We got back to the dormitory an hour ago.'

I realized what abject figures we must have cut. I was standing there, my shirt plastered to my skin, rain still dripping from the tip of my nose. I ran a hand through my hair in a vain attempt to tidy my appearance in front of my supervising tutor.

'This isn't the kind of weather I signed up for when I came here,' I said, trying to keep the mood light.

Professor Atami smiled faintly, but looked troubled. 'It's a coincidence.'

'What is?'

'Meeting you here. On your return from Izumi.'

I frowned, not catching his drift.

Professor Atami took a deep breath. 'I met Charlie here, the night he returned from Izumi. On a night just like this one. Did I tell you?'

He hadn't told me. He'd told me a number of things about Charlie, but not that he'd met with him on the night he died. Perhaps he'd even been the last person to speak to him, just as I'd been the last person to speak to Yoshi.

'Did you have a successful trip to Izumi? Did you find what you were looking for?'

I didn't know how to answer. I wasn't going to tell him what I'd seen. But nor could I look him in the eye and tell him the trip had been successful.

'We had a good time,' said Sarah, getting to her feet. 'I'm the English teacher in Izumi. James invited me back to stay.'

Professor Atami acknowledged her briefly, but he was more interested in getting an answer from me. 'Did anything happen? Anything unusual?' He was watching me closely for a reaction.

'Not really.' I was a bad liar and looking up at his face I could see he wasn't fooled. He knew that I had gone down the same road as Charlie. And now we were reliving the tryst in the convenience store. I wondered at what point history would stop repeating itself. So far the only real difference was the presence of Sarah. As far as I knew Charlie had returned to Osaka alone and I clung to this one crumb of comfort.

'That night,' he continued, 'Charlie told me he'd seen visions of a high school student.'

I shrugged, feigning disinterest. I prayed that my face didn't betray my horror. I had still not admitted to Sarah what I'd seen.

'She appeared to him in Izumi. And when he came back to Osaka, she appeared to him here.'

Now was not the time to show weakness. 'I've seen the file you gave me. Charlie was losing his mind.'

Professor Atami looked at me for a long time, evaluating me. He was dissatisfied, but I could see he didn't want to push the point.

'Don't worry, I had an uneventful stay in Izumi. I didn't see anything to make me believe it's cursed.'

'And I live there,' Sarah added. 'I'm sure I'd have noticed if it was.'

Professor Atami nodded his head, reluctantly accepting our testimony. His concern was understandable. He didn't want a second fatality on his watch.

'One other thing,' he said.

'Yes?'

'When I met Charlie that night, he told me he was being pursued by this apparition. But he also told me he knew what to do.'

I looked up in surprise.

'He told me she was trying to kill him, but he knew what to do. Someone had hurt her once and now she was trying to hurt them. I asked him why he thought that and he told me it was a case of mistaken identity. Then he said he had a solution to the problem.'

This was even more interesting, even if I was trying my best not to look too interested. I began to think I should come clean and tell him everything.

'He said he knew how to stop her.'

I was conscious of an eerie silence filling the convenience store. Even the rain sounded distant and detached. What did he mean about mistaken identity? And what was this about a solution?

Professor Atami stopped suddenly. Perhaps he too feared that spirits might be listening to him.

'What was the solution?' I asked, trying my best to sound nonchalant.

Professor Atami turned away, shaking his head sadly. 'I'm sorry, he didn't tell me what it was. He died that night. Whatever it was, it couldn't save him.'

And with that chilling valediction he left us.

THE RECKONING

All the way back to the dorm, I kept my head down and my eyes on the ground, a carrier bag full of beer cans swaying at my side. Though Sarah walked beside me, the relentless noise of the rain made any conversation impossible. This suited me, as it was less obvious that I was afraid to look up. I looked no different to any other person battling against the elements. Once or twice I thought I glimpsed a figure out of the corner of my eye, though I could no longer say what was real and what was imagined. In the end I shut my eyes and walked blind, letting myself be guided by the presence of Sarah at my side.

As we rounded the corner of the playing fields on the approach to the Tower, I heard Sarah exclaim loudly. I raised my eyes and saw with a horrible sinking feeling that the building was in total darkness.

'Must be a power failure,' Sarah said, shouting above the sound of rain.

'Shit. That's all we need.'

'Maybe lightening struck.'

Now there would be no light in the entrance or stairwells or corridors. I looked up at the Tower with a horrible sense of foreboding. The building, which had seen many a young life snuffed out in its prime, seemed to be waiting for me. Was this how Charlie had felt on the way back from the convenience store and his meeting with Professor Atami, as he faced his final hours?

'It's going to be an interesting night,' Sarah said with bitter irony.

This was no exaggeration. I sensed it was going to be the most interesting night of my life.

We reached the shelter of the dark entrance and paused to shake off the rain and attempt to wring some of the water out of our clothes. The only sign of power was the small emergency light over the fire doors. Otherwise everything was in darkness, even the drinks machines along the wall.

I knew with crushing certainty that she was behind me, watching from the forecourt in the rain. I knew that she'd been with us at the convenience store and that she'd followed us every step of the way. It didn't matter to her that I'd kept my eyes on the ground. It hadn't made me any less conspicuous. All I had to do was turn and I'd see her there, head bowed and hair dripping, waiting for my next move.

'Come on, let's find Josh,' I said, striding over to the lifts.

'Hope he hasn't found that axe.' Sarah seemed to be back to her gallows humour best, but it wasn't what I needed right now. My nerves were too frayed.

We realized that the lifts were out of order along with everything else, so we followed the green emergency exit light over the stairwell. Not only were we

264

soaked to the bone, but now we would have to walk up five flights of steps in the dark.

As we groped our way upwards leaving a trail of water for any would-be pursuers, our state of isolation began to hit home. Apart from us, Josh was the only sign of life in the entire building. The concierge had gone home for the day and wouldn't be back until the morning at best. No one would be coming to restore electricity until then. We were well and truly stranded in a dark building with no one in the immediate vicinity to hear us scream. I thought again of the family alone in the Overlook Hotel, snowbound for the winter with nothing to keep them company except ghosts of winters past. And even if I only had one night to endure, it was stretching out before me like an eternity.

We found Josh silhouetted in the entrance to the fifth floor stairwell, awaiting our arrival impatiently.

'I can't tell you how glad I am to see you two,' he shouted down as soon as he saw us. 'Looks like we're in the dark here.'

'You have to admit, though, it's atmospheric,' Sarah said cheerfully. 'And we've got a load of beer.'

Josh laughed. 'Don't worry, I've got candles.' He held up a couple of large ornamental candles with Japanese calligraphy up the side. 'I got them from some Buddhist temple as a gift.'

We started down the dark corridor towards my room, feeling our way along the walls.

'Looks like you got wet,' Josh said, gleefully stating the obvious.

I unlocked the door, then stood outside with Josh while Sarah went in to change. He'd come across as so confident when I'd first met him that it was a shock to see him so vulnerable.

'I got hold of Shinichi and Etsuko. They're around, so I asked them to come over. That okay?'

It was nice to hear. Never had the phrase 'the more, the merrier' carried so much resonance.

'I told them to bring candles. They're going to stop off at the convenience store and get some.'

Josh crouched down with a box of matches and began lighting his temple candles.

'So, you see any ghosts in Izumi?' he asked, peering up at me.

I knew he was being jocular, but the question still hit home. What should I say? Not only had I seen one, but I'd brought one back with me too. 'Yes,' I said, deciding to continue the jocular tone.

'Girl ghost or boy ghost?' He placed the candles on the desk for maximum light.

'Girl ghost.'

'Good looking?'

'Like nothing on this earth.'

Josh grinned. 'Sounds great. That's one experience I've never had.'

'If you like, I'll introduce you.' Keep the tone light, I told myself. It was the only way to combat the fear.

And then I heard something that stopped me cold. It was a sound carried on the wind, rising above the sound of the driving rain. Maybe I was imagining it, but it sounded like a scream.

'What's the matter?' Josh asked.

'Listen,' I said. 'Did you hear something?'

Josh shook his head. 'What is it? I can't hear anything above this rain.'

He was right. It was impossible to hear anything with any certainty. I wished I could explain what was happening to me. I wished I could tell him of Reiko, the tragic high school girl who had followed me all this distance, with motives I couldn't begin to understand. I wanted to give him fair warning should anything bad happen that night.

The door opened and Sarah appeared, changed and rubbing her hair vigorously with a towel.

'Did you hear anything?' I asked.

'Like what?'

'It sounded like a scream.'

Sarah looked at me oddly. I still hadn't told her that I'd seen Reiko.

'Doesn't matter. Just me hearing things.'

I went into my room to change and found myself drawn towards the window against my better judgement. It was difficult to make out anything much through the downpour, but I knew I had to look. I had to understand what I was up against. With a mounting sense of terror I squinted through the mist of rain to see a figure standing in front of the building, looking up at me. I couldn't make out the features, but there was no mistaking the stripes on the uniform and the crimson ribbon round the neck.

She had come.

Shinichi and Etsuko arrived to find the three of us huddled round a large temple candle in my room. We'd put the other candle in the corridor to spread the light around. Even with the windows firmly shut, draughts were buffeting the flames from all sides and Josh had already re-lit the candles several times, leading to a discussion about what we'd do if the matches ran out.

Start a camp fire, was the general consensus. The beer tasted good and was helping me to keep the image of Reiko from the forefront of my mind. I resolved to drink just enough to relax, but not enough to lose control of my faculties. The one thing I had going for me was this company of friends, this band of brothers. From what I knew of Charlie, I was sure he'd not sought out anyone's company on his last night. Whatever demons he'd faced, he'd faced alone.

Our two Japanese friends were in high spirits, excited by this adventure in a dark building.

'Hello,' they cried in unison, and we all got up to greet them as friends and saviours.

Their enthusiasm was exactly what we needed. The beer had helped, but we had still been on edge. Sarah and I had our own reasons to be nervous, which we couldn't easily share. As for Josh, a week of isolation had left him with other demons to contend with.

For the next few minutes we embraced, exchanged pleasantries, opened beer cans and delved into a big bag of tea-lights. They'd even thought to buy matches. Soon every surface in my room had its own candle and we'd set a row of tea-lights leading down the corridor to the toilets, like landing lights on an air-strip. As far as I was concerned the extra bodies made for extra security and the image of Reiko standing outside the building looking up at me began to seem less menacing. What could she possibly do to hurt me? We had safety in numbers.

Shinichi and Etsuko wanted to know all about Izumi and I focused on all the cool things I'd done with Sarah. I talked about visits to burial mounds, temples and castles; then I described some of the things I'd eaten, starting with Mrs Azuma's terrifying raw meat platters. They found it hilarious to hear what I'd been duped into eating and told me Japanese people were prepared to give foreigners all sorts of stuff just to see the looks on their faces when they found out what it was. Sarah was on great form, cracking jokes about her adopted home, telling anecdotes about the back-wardness of life in the provinces. With the candles giving off a warm glow and the beer showing no sign of running out, the evening was shaping up into some-thing quite pleasant.

I was beginning to think I was in the clear. I was beginning to think I'd make it, that the curse of Izumi would dissolve into the air around me. I was beginning to relax and enjoy the company, the beer, the feeling of being away from home in an exotic country.

And then I heard the scream.

This time it was closer. This time it was inside the Tower. And it was unmistakably human. No wind could ever have made a sound like that.

And this time they all heard it too. The conversation stopped dead and we looked at one another in alarm. There was an initial comfort in know-ing that I wasn't alone. But this was outweighed by the terrible realization that this wasn't just my warped imagination playing tricks. This was real.

'What the hell was that?' Josh said, breaking the silence.

'That's it,' I said. 'That's what I heard before.'

'Who else is in this building?' Shinichi asked.

'No one,' said Josh.

Shinichi got to his feet and went over to the window. He stood there for a moment, squinting out, while the rest of us strained our ears for further sounds.

He turned back to us, saying there was nothing out there.

'We should go and take a look,' Josh said. 'Sounds like someone's in trouble down there.'

Was this where I laid my cards on the table? Was this where I told them all about what I knew was following me, what I'd seen standing outside the building just a short while before? I knew it was hopeless.

After a short deliberation, we agreed that Josh and Shinichi would venture out to look. The idea seemed to empower Josh. As a man of action, this was the kind of challenge he liked. It was my job, he said, to look after Sarah and Etsuko. All the time I saw Sarah watching me carefully. She knew I was keeping something from her. After all, it wasn't her that needed protecting. It was me.

As we listened to their footsteps retreating down the corridor, I had the sickening feeling that they too might be in real danger. So far Reiko had been invisible to everyone but me. But if it was Reiko's scream that we had all heard, then suddenly others had been drawn into the fray. The rules had changed.

I clung to the possibility that it was a real person's scream. All the foreign students might have gone home, but there were still other students on campus who could come in and make a racket in the empty building. I told myself to keep an open mind.

For a while we sat there, huddled round the temple candle, listening to the sound of rain hammering on the window. Without the other two to swell the numbers, the shadows seemed to be closing in.

'James,' Sarah said, her voice grave.

I looked up. I knew what was coming.

'You saw her didn't you?'

I nodded my head. There was no point pretending anymore. I had told her everything up until then. She needed to know that Reiko had followed us. 'Yeah, I saw her.'

Etsuko realized this was a private issue between us and didn't ask who we were talking about.

'Where?'

'On the train. Then from the window of the taxi. Then just now, outside the building.'

'So she did follow you. I thought she probably would.' I was expecting her to react angrily to not being told, but she seemed calm enough. After a few moments reflection she reached over to her bag and pulled out a piece of paper. She looked at it for a moment, in two minds, then put it down in front of her. It was a page of Japanese writing, crumpled and dog-eared.

'I found this,' she said quietly, straightening it out with her hands.

'What is it?' I asked.

She took a deep breath. 'I don't know. But I found it and I had a feeling it was important. I've learnt to read a little Japanese, but I need help deciphering it.' She looked up at Etsuko.

'Sure.' Etsuko reached for the paper.

'At first I didn't want to know what it said, in case it just made matters worse. But after meeting the Professor at the convenience store and hearing what he said, I think we have to know everything.'

'What is it?' I asked, getting frustrated. It wasn't like Sarah to be cryptic.

'It was among the photographs. Kenji's photographs. I took it out and kept it. I think we need to know what it says.'

'Why did you keep it secret?'

'I don't know. I thought you might have enough to deal with. I'm sorry.'

A draught swept through the room, snuffing out several tea-lights and leaving the place darker than before.

'Who's Kenji?' Etsuko asked.

'He's the son of my host mother in Izumi. He was in love with a girl in his class called Reiko Shimura. She disappeared four years ago.'

Etsuko visibly recoiled. Of course it was she who I had originally questioned about Izumi and I remembered her reluctance back then. Now, crouched in a dark building, amidst a dwindling number of candles, with her boyfriend gone to investigate a disturbing scream, she was facing the same subject again. No wonder she looked unhappy.

'Have you heard about it?' Sarah asked.

Etsuko nodded. 'It is very famous in Japan. One girl disappeared. Her four friends all died soon after.'

Sarah leaned over to her bag again and pulled out the photograph of Kenji and Reiko's four friends taken at the Azuma home. She handed it to Etsuko, who received it reluctantly.

'That's Kenji, eating at home just after Reiko died. His mother must have invited them over. That's why none of them look very happy to be there.'

Etsuko nodded faintly.

'I'm sorry to bring this up now,' Sarah said, 'but I need to know what he wrote. Can you help me translate it?'

'It's okay.' Etsuko put the photograph down on the floor and carefully unfolded the piece of paper to reveal what looked like a poem in Japanese: a series of neatly-written lines, inscribed vertically and from right to left according to the Japanese style. Even in the dim light of the candle I could see that this was a careful, studied piece of work.

Etsuko took the piece of paper with a frown, troubled by the task we had set her.

'*Yatto wakatta*,' she read, then after a brief pause, translated. '*At last I am able to understand.*'

Sarah and I watched Etsuko's eyes move down the page, reading the characters.

'*Dare ka Reiko o koroshita ka yatto wakatta… At last I understand who killed Reiko.*' She read this with a sharp intake of breath.

'That's the bit I understood,' Sarah said quietly. 'That's why I needed to know.'

'I can't read this,' Etsuko said, her voice trembling.

'Please,' Sarah said. 'Please. I know it's horrible, but I need to know what he says. This is where I live. I need to know whether I can ever go back there or not.'

With considerable effort Etsuko returned to the page, her eyes flitting about, taking it all in.

'Please,' Sarah said again.

'He says she killed Reiko,' Etsuko said, almost to herself. She didn't seem to be translating any passage in particular. 'He says his mother killed Reiko. He says she followed her to the woods after school and killed her.'

I stared at Etsuko in disbelief. It was a ridiculous statement. Mrs Azuma was manic, but she was no murderer. She was a local dignitary, a respectable citizen, a celebrated host of dinner parties. She was no murderer. I didn't know what drove someone to murder, but it had to be a desperation beyond anything I'd ever experienced. Besides, she was too small – she wouldn't have been physically capable.

'If Kenji suffered from abuse,' I said, 'it's not surprising he says these things about his mother. It's his way of venting his frustration.'

I looked to Sarah for support, but she ignored me. Her eyes were on Etsuko, waiting to hear more.

'*Reiko o tabesaseta. Reiko o tabesaseta.*' I wasn't sure what it meant, but Etsuko read the sentence twice and suddenly her face creased with emotion.

'What does it mean?' I pleaded.

Etsuko's eyes filled with tears and she put her hand over her mouth as though to stifle a scream. 'It says she made them eat Reiko.'

'What?'

'That's what it says,' she cried. 'That's what it says. She made them eat Reiko.'

I could feel a slow churning in my stomach, as though somewhere in the depths of my entrails, the truth was dawning. I glanced at the picture of Reiko's four friends having their dinner at Mrs Azuma's house. What was happening? What was Etsuko saying?

'*Reiko wa yonnin no tomodachi o oikoshite, sorekara koroshite shimatta… Reiko pursued her four friends and then killed them.*' Etsuko's hands were trembling so violently that she couldn't hold the paper still enough to read Kenji's testimony.

Another draught, more violent than the last, swept through the room, extinguishing more candles, including the large temple candle on the desk. Simultaneously a scream echoed through the building, closer and more piercing than the last. Etsuko let the piece of paper fall to the floor and put her head in her hands, sobbing.

I fumbled for the matches and set about re-lighting some of the extinguished candles.

Etsuko was rocking back and forwards, distraught. I reached out and put a hand on her shoulder, painfully aware that I had dragged her into my own private nightmare. As for Josh and Shinichi, we hadn't heard a squeak from them in ten minutes. Surely they'd heard the latest scream.

'What else does it say?' Sarah asked, determined to get what she could in spite of Etsuko's discomfort. 'I'm sorry, but it's so important.'

Etsuko lifted her head to look at Sarah. Then, hands trembling, she picked up the piece of paper again. For a moment she read in silence, taking it all in. Finally she took a deep breath and spoke with a physical effort. 'He says that Reiko's spirit cannot sleep. He says that his mother keeps Reiko's body and spirit. He made them eat her. And Reiko was angry because they ate her. So Reiko took revenge and killed them all.'

'He's insane,' I said. But the knot in my stomach was growing tighter.

Etsuko lifted her eyes. 'He said that now he understands the truth, he wants to die.'

I looked up at Sarah, who had been very quiet and controlled as she listened to Kenji's horrifying testimony, and I saw there were tears rolling down her face. 'Don't you understand?' she said.

'I don't know,' I said.

'You're the ghost hunter. You of all people should understand.'

'You can't believe this stuff. This is a deranged teenager talking. None of it makes sense.'

'Maybe he is deranged. Maybe madness runs in the family. But I don't believe he's making it up. I believe he's telling the truth.'

'That his mother killed Reiko and fed her flesh to her friends?'

Sarah nodded, her face puffed up with tears. 'She hated Reiko, because her son was obsessed with her and his grades at school were suffering and God knows what else. She hated her friends, because they refused to let her son into their circle. I know her. I've known her for nine months. I know she's been kind to me, but I also know she's consumed by hatred. Odagiri-san was right.'

'You think she killed Reiko's friends too? Is that what you're saying?' I felt a wave of anger and frustration. Not at Sarah, but at the sheer insanity of what we were discussing. I couldn't admit to myself that possibly, just possibly, Kenji was telling the truth.

Sarah looked at me, her eyes filled with horror. 'Mrs Azuma didn't kill the friends. Reiko did.'

From somewhere deep in the building came the sound of glass shattering. It sounded like a window pane blown in by the wind.

Etsuko looked about her with wild eyes, ready to turn and flee the room. 'Can we stop talking about this? Can we go and find Shinichi and Josh? They've been so long.'

But things had gone too far. I couldn't think about Shinichi or Josh. I had to hear Sarah out. 'How could Reiko have killed them?'

'You know what happened. You just don't want to hear it. She killed Reiko, just like in your dream, just like in Charlie's dream. She killed her in the woods, by that old rock. She brought her body back and stored it in the chest freezer. Just like you dreamt.'

'It was just a dream,' I cried, willing her to stop talking.

Sarah picked up the photograph of the five students and waved it at me. 'This was no dinner party. Look at those plates of raw meat on the table. That was no horse meat. Don't you get it?'

'No,' I shouted, beginning to strain under the pressure.

'That was Reiko's flesh, served up to her friends. Her son doesn't eat raw meat, she told us. Her body was never recovered because it was served up to her friends.'

I couldn't fight it any longer. Sarah was right. I knew why Reiko was following me, even if I couldn't accept it. I knew why she had followed Charlie before me. I knew why her four friends had had to die. And I knew why Charlie had had to die too.

In that moment, with the wind shaking the foundations of the building and Sarah and Etsuko looking at me with tear-stained faces, I understood.

I closed my eyes and saw it happen.

I saw the five of them sitting round the table in Mrs Azuma's living room, looking subdued and uncomfortable, Mrs Azuma hovering above them, encouraging them to eat. I saw the plate of raw horse meat, that I too had had before me. Except it wasn't horse meat. It was something quite different.

In quick succession, a montage of images flashed before me. Reiko, in the school at night, looking down from the steps, watching impassively as Kanae fell to her death. Reiko, at the door to class 3C, looking on as Jun fought his way across the room, upending chairs and desks, and plunging through the window to his inevitable death. Reiko, looking down at the busy expressway, her red ribbon fluttering in the wind, watching Hideki step into the path of an oncoming vehicle. And Reiko, standing by the side of Saori, as she bled to death at the window of her bedroom.

She took them all, even if she didn't know why she did it. Her flesh for their flesh, a simple enough exchange.

Another image flashed before me like some hellish foretaste of what awaited me. Charlie, in his dormitory room, standing by the window, fixing his dressing gown cord to the handle, his eyes filled with tears. Charlie, looking over his shoulder towards the door, fixing this makeshift noose around his neck with shaking hands. Unknowingly, Charlie had eaten her too.

I opened my eyes. Sarah and Etsuko were still there, watching me, their eyes filled with terror. A draught blew in, extinguishing all but a few of the remaining candles.

'It's not your fault, James,' Sarah said.

'I ate her,' I said. 'I ate her flesh. Oh fuck, I didn't know what I was eating. Oh fuck.'

'You didn't know. You couldn't know'

'She's inside me. I ate her flesh and now she's inside me. That's why she's following me. That's why she followed Charlie and that's why she killed him.'

'It doesn't mean it has to happen to you.'

I passed my hand over my face several times, my stomach churning violently. 'Why me? What did I do? What did I do to deserve this?'

'That doesn't matter now. We have to try and keep calm.'

As if on cue another scream echoed through the corridor, closer than the last. It was Reiko, announcing her arrival. She was close. She had caused the power to fail; she had entered the building; and now she was closing in. I looked to Sarah for reassurance, but for the first time she had none to give. All I saw was fear and confusion, her realization that she was powerless to protect me.

I didn't know whether to stay put or run. But how could I run from Reiko? How could I run from something that was inside me? Where, in all the rule books, did it tell me what to do? Even Charlie, the scholar, had not been able to escape. Even Charlie, with all his learning, had not outwitted her.

And sitting there in this dark room in a strange country, I was overcome with sadness. Sadness for the life that I'd tried so hard to love, sadness for the friends I'd made and lost, for the opportunities seized and then spurned. Sadness for my parents, who'd raised me and guided me and seen me drift away. How would they cope when they heard that the young boy in whom they'd invested so much had come to such a terrible end? If only I could meet them once more and say how sorry I was and how I wished it had all been different. But I was certain I would never see them again. I was certain I would never leave the building again.

I would sit there with Sarah and Etsuko watching the candles go out one by one, waiting for the axe to fall.

REIKO

Suddenly there were footsteps in the corridor.

For several minutes we had sat in silence and near-darkness, huddled in a little group, waiting for something to happen.

'It must be one of the boys,' Sarah said. 'About time.'

The steps were slow and hesitant and it didn't sound like either Josh or Shinichi. But if it wasn't them, who else could it be?

I bowed my head and waited. If it proved to be my pursuer, then I was ready for her. I would not shy away from this confrontation. I may not have amounted to much in my life, but I resolved not to go meekly into the stormy night.

The footsteps drew near and I fumbled for the matches to re-light some candles. Maybe it was a conceit, but light promised security.

'Hello.'

Professor Atami stood framed in the door, dishevelled and dripping wet.

'Hello.' I felt a surge of relief. This was not what I'd expected.

'I'm sorry to come like this,' he said.

'How did you know where to find us?'

'I followed the candlelight.'

'We're having trouble keeping them lit.'

Professor Atami turned to Sarah and Etsuko, acknowledging them with a formal nod of the head. He stood there awkwardly, his shadow flickering on the wall of the corridor, while I tried to fathom why he had come.

'Did you see anything on your way up?' Sarah asked.

Professor Atami shook his head, distracted.

'We heard some sounds downstairs, so our two friends went to look. They haven't come back,' she added.

Again Professor Atami shook his head, then stepped through the door, and surveyed the room uncertainly. Under his arm he was carrying a bag.

'I came to give you something,' he said at last, motioning to the bag. 'I came to give you this.'

We all watched and waited, but he still seemed reticent.

'Can we see?' I asked.

'I told you before that I met Charlie,' he said, with a sudden resolve. 'I told you I met him the night he died.'

As we waited for him to say more, we again heard the sound of breaking glass from somewhere in the building. Etsuko jumped to her feet in distress.

'It's just the wind,' I said, even though I knew it wasn't.

A draught swept through the room and snuffed out the candles I'd just lit.

Professor Atami continued. 'I don't know why I came here tonight. I don't know why I'm bringing you this.'

He paused, still waging some inner battle.

'Charlie told me that night he had found a solution. He didn't tell me what it was, but I think this is it.' Professor Atami took the bag out from under his arm. 'It was found on his desk. Of course his parents didn't want it when they came to collect his personal items. Just like his file, I should have thrown it away, but I didn't. I kept it.'

'Please tell me.' I couldn't bear the suspense.

'Charlie said something followed him back from Izumi. Something was trying to kill him.'

'You believe that? You believe that's what drove him to do it?'

Professor Atami looked me straight in the eye. 'Do you have that feeling? Do you feel that something has followed you?'

'Yes,' I said. All cards on the table.

He didn't say anything, but headed over to the desk and pushed the candles away to create some space. He opened the bag and pulled out what looked to be a homemade rag doll and laid it out flat. It was crude and hideous, sewn together in a hurry from pieces of ordinary fabric with bits of felt stuck on for its facial features.

'What is it?' I asked, dismayed that Charlie's solution took the form of a tattered rag doll. Did Professor Atami really think it could help me?

'It's a doll,' he said quietly.

'What am I supposed to do with this?' It just seemed so stupid. What did it matter if Charlie had left a rag doll on his desk?

'Charlie was trying to do something with this, I'm sure. He said he had a solution. He said he knew how to kill the beast.'

'What beast? What beast was he trying to kill?' I realized I was shouting at him, partly to make myself heard above the din of the rain, partly out of frustration. I knew Professor Atami was trying to be helpful. I knew he'd weathered the storm to bring me this ghastly creation. But I didn't want to spend these vital minutes examining a ridiculous doll.

'I don't know. He didn't tell me. I only know that it was female.'

'Why are you telling me this? Charlie was insane. I've read his file. He'd lost touch with reality. All the stuff about a beast, that's all part of it. He was insane.'

Professor Atami sunk into the desk chair with a defeated air. 'You saw it, didn't you? You saw the same thing Charlie saw. You know what I'm talking about.'

'I don't know,' I ranted, all composure leaving me. 'I don't understand what you're saying. I don't understand what Charlie was trying to do.'

Professor Atami was about to reply when a blood-chilling scream pierced the air. It had come from somewhere close and echoed round the corridor.

Sarah stepped out of the room. 'I don't see anything,' she said.

Professor Atami got up. 'I'll go and look.'

I grabbed his arm. 'You warned me. You told me not to go. I'm so sorry.'

He touched my arm, almost tenderly. 'If this is a Japanese ghost, I'll know what to do.'

'What about the doll?'

'Remember Charlie's thesis. Remember what he believed. All cultures and traditions share common themes.'

Professor Atami patted my back and left the room. I watched him go, wondering what he would find out there, praying to God he wasn't in the same danger as me. As his footsteps retreated down the corridor, I turned my attention to the doll.

Sarah came over and examined it with a grimace.

'What the hell do we do with this?' I asked.

She grasped it in her hands. 'We need to think. We need to think about the beast. We need to know who the beast is.'

'You mean Reiko?'

'I don't think it's Reiko.'

'Why are you saying that? She's followed me halfway across Japan. I know what I've seen.'

'Reiko's not the beast. Reiko was an innocent victim. Her vengeance is blind. She doesn't know what she's doing.'

The conviction in Sarah's tone silenced me. While my thoughts were all at sea, Sarah was managing to be calm and rational, even in the eye of this deadly storm. With her at my side, I still believed there was hope.

'Can I see Charlie's file?' she asked. 'I read something in there about dolls.'

She was right. I remembered it now. I'd seen a sketch of a rustic doll, but I'd paid it no heed at the time.

Another scream rang out from somewhere close, which Etsuko echoed with a scream of her own.

'I'm calling the police,' she said, taking out her mobile phone. She took one look, then cursed and hurled the phone across the room. There was no signal.

It was a terrible thing she'd been drawn into – screams echoing through the corridor and her boyfriend lost in the bowels of the building.

I fumbled in my bag, pulled out Charlie's file and slammed it down on the desk next to the doll. I tried flicking through the pages, but my hands were shaking too violently. Sarah took over and swiftly found what we were looking for – a diagram, with arrows and annotations all round it. At the top of the page the word 'voodoo' caught my eye. At least I realized where Charlie was going with the doll.

I heard some movement from the door and looked round to see Etsuko leave and run down the corridor. She'd had enough and was taking her chances on the outside. I felt desperately sorry, but I remained convinced that I was the only one in mortal danger. I was the one who had eaten her flesh. I was the one she was after. I hoped Etsuko would catch up with Professor Atami on the stairs and together they would escape the Tower.

As I tried to focus on Charlie's annotations, I felt my eyes grow faint so I left Sarah to read what he had written. I tried lighting a match to give us more light, but my hands were trembling too much and the box dropped to the floor.

As the wind grew wilder and the rain more vicious, I saw the room spin around me. Sarah was bent over the file, squinting to read Charlie's impenetrable scrawl. But I had no confidence left. How could we hope to succeed where Charlie had failed? What could we do that he hadn't done?

There was another scream, so close that it must have been somewhere outside in the corridor and it occurred to me that this time it might be Etsuko.

I closed my eyes, seized with the hopelessness of the situation. Maybe now it was time to turn and run. But how do you outrun a ghost? Wherever I ran, she would find me.

I began to prepare myself. Did I have the strength to face death? Would I pass over to other side quietly or would it be with a wrenching pain?

I saw Sarah shaking her head in reaction to something Charlie had written, but I was beyond taking it in. I wanted to say goodbye and have done with it.

'We don't have it,' she said.

I wondered if this was how Charlie had felt in those last moments, as he wound the noose around his neck.

'There must be something,' I heard her say, but whatever it was it no longer seemed important.

I went over to the door, as if drawn by an unseen hand, and stepped into the corridor. She was there just as I expected she'd be, standing in the stairwell entrance, her eyes bearing down on me. Though the corridor was in darkness, she seemed to glow, like a will-of-the-wisp. For the first time I saw her with absolute clarity. I looked straight at her and she at me. She was as beautiful as her photograph and more: an unearthly beauty that brought a sigh to my lips, even in this moment of reckoning. After all the evasion, there was a strange sense of relief to finally come face to face with my tormentor. This was no fleeting glance in the mirror or refection in the window of a train. I had no need to close my eyes or turn away. I saw her high cheekbones, her almond-shaped eyes, her delicate mouth. I saw the stripes on her collar, her pleated skirt and knee-length socks. And the crimson-red ribbon, like her softly beating heart.

It struck me as odd that I should be so calm now I was confronted by the sum of all my fears. I was no longer shaking. I was no longer afraid.

I glanced into the room, wanting to tell Sarah to stop fretting, that everything was all right. I could see her tearing at her hair, still clutching Charlie's weird rag doll. There was nothing to fear from Reiko. Sarah had said so herself. She wasn't the beast.

Reiko began walking slowly towards me and I stood rooted to the spot, waiting for her to come. A strange feeling came over me. A feeling that I was losing a grip on my sensations, that my spirit was preparing itself to leave my body.

Then with a sudden jolt the panic returned and I tried to step away from the approaching figure. But I had lost all sensation in my body. I was paralyzed.

Reiko crept ever closer, her gaze never wavering, her expression emotionless.

Out of the corner of my eye I saw Sarah, oblivious to my plight, rummaging around in her bag. Could she not see what was happening? Could she not pull me inside, away from this approaching figure, away from Reiko? What was she doing?

Then it was too late. Reiko had come within a few yards, her eyes boring into the depths of my being, drawing my soul from my body. In that final moment I realized two things. I realized she was taking possession of me, just as she'd done with all the others. And I realized that her eyes were the last thing I'd see in this life.

Her face loomed before me, my lids grew heavy and darkness swept over my soul.

A New Dawn

'James?'

I opened my eyes. Sarah was kneeling over me, touching my forehead.

'That's quite a fall you had.'

I sat upright, confused and disoriented. I couldn't remember what had happened or why I'd been lying on the corridor floor.

Sarah smiled at me. 'You're living,' she said with a heavy sigh. 'You're living.'

I started to remember things: the wind and rain shaking the foundations, the candles spluttering in the bedroom, my trembling hands, the confusion. But there was something else.

'Reiko,' I said, gripped with panic. 'Where is she?'

I remembered it now. Reiko, walking slowly towards me down the long corridor, her eyes filled with fire; and I standing motionless, powerless to move, as all sensation drained from my body. I remembered the feeling of falling from a great height. And then darkness.

'I think she's gone.'

'Where? What happened?'

Sarah sighed and sat herself down on the floor next to me. 'Where, I have no idea. I really don't. But I know she was there. I know she was walking towards you. I saw your face.'

'What happened?'

'I don't know. I followed Charlie's instructions. That's all.'

She pointed to the homemade doll, lying face down on the floor. It was all flooding back. Professor Atami appearing with the doll, but no instructions on how to use it; opening the file with trembling fingers, finding Charlie's diagram; Sarah poring over it, just as I was drawn out into the corridor to face Reiko.

'I don't understand.'

'It said the doll could be a representation of a living person, if it was made according to certain principles. I suppose Charlie must have made it.'

As I looked at Sarah her face creased up and she put her head in her hands. 'I don't know what I've done, James.'

I leaned forward and put my arms around her, desperate to love and protect her in this ungodly hour. I didn't know what had happened or why she was sobbing, but I held on to her with everything I had.

After a while she raised her head and looked at me with teary, bloodshot eyes. 'If I did what I think I did, I may have hurt someone.'

I sensed what was coming, but thought it best to let her speak.

'That's the point of the doll – to hurt someone. According to Charlie all you need is some blood or skin or something of your victim. That's all you need.'

I closed my eyes, overcome with emotion.

'Do you think my host mother hurt Reiko? Do you believe that?'

I nodded

'Do you believe she was the beast Charlie spoke about?'

I nodded again.

'Then I think I hurt her.'

And then I saw it, an image so clear in my mind that I felt I was actually there.

I saw Mrs Azuma standing in her living room, gathering the dinner plates from the table. I saw Mr Azuma sitting there smoking a cigarette, ignoring her. Then, as she turned to the kitchen, she staggered and the plates began dropping from her hands, hitting the floor with a crash. Mr Azuma looked up with alarm as his wife clutched her hands to her neck and sunk to her knees. But it was not suffering I saw on her face. It was a lifetime of bitterness and loathing struggling against some force of its own making. Some would call it karma. Perhaps in those last moments she thought she didn't deserve to die, that she shouldn't be held accountable for the terrible things she had done, that she had only acted in the interests of her own born. Perhaps as she sunk to the ground and breathed her last anguished breaths, she faced death without remorse for her crimes. I saw Mr Azuma drop his cigarette and rush to her side. And all that time, the incense burned in the ancestral shrine and the dolls in their glass cases looked on with indifference.

'How?' I said.

Sarah leaned over and picked up the doll and held it gingerly in her hands. There was a pencil stabbed straight through it, just below the neck.

'The flesh or blood? How did you do that?'

She pointed to the doll's neck and I noticed there were strands of hair wrapped round it in a knot.

'The brush,' she said, motioning to a hairbrush lying in the middle of the floor. 'She lent me her hairbrush this morning. I still had it in my bag. It still had her hair.'

So that was it. Mrs Azuma had lent Sarah her hairbrush and unwittingly signed her death warrant. As though some invisible force had willed it so. As though, amidst all the evil, there were still benign forces at work in the universe.

'And Reiko?'

'I think I got there just in time. I tried to call to you, but you didn't respond. You just stood there, eyes fixed straight ahead, arms outstretched. I strangled the doll's neck and then you collapsed.'

I drew her towards me again and held her close. I held her as though it were life itself I was embracing. What had I been waiting for in those last moments? What would have happened if Sarah hadn't been there to deliver me?

Relief swept through my tired, broken body and lifted me a few inches off the ground. And overcome with love for the life I'd come close to losing, I began to cry loudly and desperately.

I don't know how long we sat there holding one another. Time seemed to have stopped in the Tower, grown sick of the endless succession of minutes and hours. I held on to Sarah as though letting go meant losing her forever. The wind calmed and the rain eased and the candles blew themselves out one by one, until only one remained, giving off a small halo of light.

It was with an effort that we remembered we were not alone in the building, that our friends had left us and not come back. But the sound of footsteps on the stairs brought reality back into focus.

'Hi.'

Josh came into view through the door and shuffled along the corridor like someone just woken from a long sleep.

'Where have you been?' I asked, as Sarah and I finally relaxed our grip on one another.

Josh appeared a little confused and held a hand to his head.

'I think I passed out. Then I found Etsuko on the stairs. She had the same experience. She's not feeling too good, so I was coming to get her a glass of water.'

'Why did you pass out?' I asked.

'Honestly, I can't remember. When I came to, I was lying on the ground, but my mind's a total blank. It's the weirdest thing.'

Sarah and I joined Josh to bring Etsuko a glass of water. She was sitting on the top stair on the fifth floor, complaining of a headache. She claimed to remember nothing of what had happened the whole evening. The last thing she recalled was walking up the stairs towards my room when she'd arrived with Shinichi.

We found Shinichi lying on the ground in the foyer, either unconscious or asleep, though Etsuko quickly roused him with some cold water on the face. After sitting up and composing himself, he admitted he too had no idea how he'd got there.

The only person we couldn't find was Professor Atami, despite searching the building from top to bottom. Only he seemed to have escaped the building.

As for what had happened, Josh came up with the fanciful theory that the beer had been spiked, that back at the factory they'd slipped some powerful hallucinogen into that particular batch. I was happy to go along with that. Neither Sarah nor I mentioned Reiko or the circumstances that had prevented my death that night.

Josh made his way back up to his bachelor room, vowing to stay off alcohol for a long time. Shinichi and Etsuko walked off into the night, hand-in-hand, vowing to come back when the dorm was a little livelier. As for Sarah and I, we chatted in my room until the first light of dawn.

'Nothing will ever be the same,' she said, as we stood at the window and watched the light spreading over the world. 'After this night, nothing will ever be the same.'

I looked out over the university's campus, over the suburbs of Osaka and the hills in the distance. And I had a sense that something had resolved itself that night, some ancient wrong righted, some balance restored to the world.

'It's a beautiful place, a beautiful country. I'm glad I came.'

Sarah put her arm round me and laughed. 'You've only just arrived. You've still got rose-tinted glasses on. Come back to me in nine months and then tell me what you think.'

We fell asleep soon after, lying on the bed in one another's arms. And the last thing I remember before giving myself up to sleep was opening my eyes to see a dim figure standing by the door, watching us. Perhaps it was a figment of an exhausted imagination, perhaps a symptom of the stress of the night just gone or perhaps it really was the shadow of a dead scholar. But I thought I saw Charlie standing there, watching us from a discreet distance, checking that all was well. And I sensed that I owed my life to him, that he had been with me from the moment I arrived, anxious that I should succeed where he had failed. I sensed that the file, the doll, the brush that Sarah had borrowed were not just fortuitous props in a drama, but that Charlie had somehow placed them in our way. If so, this was a very English ghost. Passive, unthreatening and wanting only to right some terrible wrong.

Professor Atami had been right. Japanese ghosts were different.

EPILOGUE

I never spoke to Professor Atami about it, so I never knew what he saw that night. I think it was better that way. He never asked me to return either the file or the doll, nor whether they'd been useful in any way. But I sensed his relief that I'd succeeded where Charlie hadn't and survived my return from Izumi.

I did, however, change the subject of my thesis and this seemed to please him. It was something unmemorable about Japanese folklore traditions, which involved reading a few dry textbooks and distilling their arguments. I decided to follow Josh's lead – do the bare minimum and get on with having a social life.

Sarah returned to Izumi to find a village pretending to mourn the passing of Mrs Azuma. She told me about it matter-of-factly, as though it were someone we had no connection with. She said she had seen the two sons, Kenji and Osamu, at the wake and neither of them had showed the slightest emotion. A great many people turned up out of duty to pay their respects, but she realized for the first time how much people had disliked her. She had even seen Odagiri-san stopping by to light an incense stick in her memory.

It made me wonder how many people in the village suspected her as much as Odagiri-san, whether others had made the same shocking assumption. But neither Sarah nor I ever raised the question of whether to bring our own conclusions about Mrs Azuma to light. After all, who would we have told and what evidence would we have had to present? Dreams? Visions? A visitation from a dead high school student?

Romance didn't blossom between us, but perhaps that was for the best. What we saw and experienced that night would have been too much to live with. Neither of us said much about it, but we knew we could never have a normal relationship. Sarah packed her bags at the end of her contract in Izumi and headed to Southeast Asia, vowing to keep in touch.

As for me, I made a host of new friends at the university, though I continued to see a lot of Josh, Shinichi and Etsuko. We never spoke about the evening the power failed and the beer was spiked. I had the feeling that each of them had seen things that night they would never be able to talk about. And maybe that was for the best.

I look back and remember everything with the greatest clarity. But there is one thing I remember more clearly than anything else. It is the figure of a high school girl cut down in her prime; the almond-shaped eyes, the high cheekbones, the delicate lips; the three white stripes on her collar; the red ribbon tied around her neck. God knows I wish I could forget. But I can't.

I sincerely hope she no longer wanders the margins of the world looking for redress. And I sincerely hope that she found the peace denied her in life. But sometimes, in dark moments, I find myself wishing that she hadn't left me that stormy night in Osaka. I find myself looking suddenly at my reflection, hoping to catch another glimpse of her unearthly beauty. However perverse it seems, I find myself wishing that she'd taken that final step towards me and that we'd become one.

And I console myself with the knowledge that whatever else I do in life, Reiko will always be with me.

ABOUT THE AUTHOR

James Avonleigh was born in 1970 and lives in the UK with his family.

Printed in Great Britain
by Amazon